TOKYO TIME

Also by Dawn Farnham

Finding Maria
Salvaged from the Fall

The Straits Quartet

The Red Thread
The Shallow Seas
The Hills of Singapore
The English Concubine

TOKYO TIME

DAWN FARNHAM

ISBN-13: 978-1-954841-61-1

Published by
Brash Books, LLC
PO Box 8212
Calabasas, CA 91372
www.brash-books.com

For Sunil

ACKNOWLEDGEMENTS

This project was assisted by the Australian Society of Authors' Award Mentorship Program for Writers and Illustrators, supported by the Copyright Agency Cultural Fund. With grateful thanks to the ASA and especially to writer, editor and broadcaster, Sunil Badami.

Singapore
1942

Syonan
Koki 2602
Showa 17

CHAPTER ONE

Martin Bach lifted his battered panama hat and swept a quiff of hair off his forehead. His paltry supply of Brylcreem had been purloined by a sweaty son of Nippon. He needed a haircut, but his favorite barber's head was stuck next to a dozen others rotting on spikes on Cavenagh Bridge. Alas, poor Yap. Always one foot on the wrong side of the law, he'd been caught looting. He couldn't have known that the new penalty would be so harsh and so swift. None of them could. *Omnia mutantur.* All things change. Certainly. But not usually overnight.

Now, ten weeks after the British surrender, the Japanese were settled in and life under the benevolent rule of the emperor would, as the newspapers never stopped telling them, be glorious. For anyone who didn't think so, punishment would be lethal. Also, they had to stop remembering the British and get on with the job of building the Greater East Asia Co-Prosperity Sphere. He recalled a line from his days of amateur theatricals about a tempest on another isle. "What's past is prologue; what to come, in yours and my discharge." Was it? He doubted it, but fate had penned this bizarre story, and the scene, in any case, was set.

Martin stretched his neck, replaced the hat firmly against the assault of the morning sun, and approached the crime scene. As soon as he saw the woman, the sinews of his body pulled as tight as a cobra's coil. She lay arms outstretched like a novice before the altar of Christ. But this was not church, the gods were Chinese, and her face was buried in the incense burner. Flies crept and slurped. Part-time police photographer Mat Ahmed's camera flashed, stirring a droning multitude of flies into a biblical swarm. Her long red nails stood out like scarlet embers in a shroud of gray dust. Two were broken. No shoes. Why no shoes? And no handbag. Mat took shots of the floor and surrounding area. He fixed his black felt cap at a jaunty angle and grinned, signaling that Martin could approach the body, then joined Martin's two detective constables, Felix Seah and Joseph Santamaria, in the shade of the police van.

It hadn't rained for a week. The city was ashes sculpted into roofs and trees: a landscape of yellow sky and gray dust fueled ceaselessly by the fires of the bombed-out oil depots. Acrid globs and sulfurous fumes clung to the humid air. Ash, soot, and stink among the boats, in the river, the hair, the lungs. A volcanic reminder of what had befallen them and under whose power they now lived.

He shook the sleeves and cuffs of his cricket whites, a wry choice perhaps under the circumstances, but currently the only matching clothes he possessed. The ground around the victim was scuffed as if by the passage of a scurry of anxious squirrels. He bent forward, puffed the swarm with a wave of his hand, and picked up the sweet perfume of incense. A different dust mingled with blood. And on her head an imprint caught within it. He couldn't make out what it was.

"Mat, take a couple of shots of the back of her head."

Her legs sprawled, exposing pale thighs. He ought to wait for the detective chief inspector, but when Mat took the last shots and moved away, he arranged the hem of her dress to cover her nakedness, removed his white cotton neck scarf, and placed it over her head. *"Miserere domine,"* he whispered, then *"daai gat lai si."* He couldn't help it. Old habits. In Singapore, devils hung out on street corners and in the hairy crevices of wayside trees. They could get at you at every turn. Everyone knew that. Death was the doorway and you'd better watch out. When you grew up on an island filled with a mixed bag of ancient beliefs, even if you were a modern British-trained copper, no amount of rationalization ever quite chased them away.

A row of shophouses had been pounded into various states of rubble. The cracked objects and half-shattered signs indicated the myriad of family-run trades they had once housed: a Teochew tea merchant, a Malay barber, a Jewish bookseller, a Kristang dressmaker, an Indian scribe. The body lay in the last shop in the line, a seller of gods, prayers, and incense. Here the blast had been least destructive, and the shop spared the attention of looters. Perhaps they thought messing around with gods was bad joss. If so, he mused, they either had faulty eyesight or a poor sense of irony.

He ran his eyes slowly over the interior. The red wooden shrine stood on a low shelf. It housed the three star gods of Fortune, Prosperity, and Longevity. Longevity lay cracked on its side, Prosperity was on the ground in shards, and Fortune was missing, and that recently, judging by the clear space in the dusty surface. Well, thought Martin, that pretty much sums it all up.

He visualized her last movements. Struck from behind. She could not have been unconscious when the hand forced her face down into the incense, because she fought. Her nails ripped in a spurt of blood. Had she left her mark on her attacker? Her legs scrabbled in the dust. But it was brief, the time of one, perhaps two choking inhalations; thick dust clogged her airways and she ceased to struggle. It was surely over quickly, but the panic and fear of the last moments of this frail girl sat in his mind like a spider. He turned away.

Across the road the work party—all Australian prisoners of war—stood like a spinney of scarecrows, bony chests, grimy vests, and ragged shorts, watching in the shade of the tattered awning of a medicine shop. Two blank-faced Japanese guards slouched on either side. An audience of pigeons lined the roof ledge, cooing in conversation, preening the dust from their feathers and building a ridge of white poop along the edge of the awning.

Martin lit a cigarette, flicked the match, and watched Detective Chief Inspector Kano Hayashi approach. He was mid-fifties, medium height, with a mane of graying hair.

Hayashi stood looking down at the body for a minute of complete contemplation as if fixing this vision in his mind, then sniffed. "Jinko," he said. "But which kind?"

Martin blinked.

"The Rikkoku-gomi of Nanyang. The six countries of the koboku." He sniffed again. "Managa, perhaps. Light and enticing but changing like the mood of a woman with bitter feelings."

Martin gazed at his new boss. He hadn't known what to expect and he was damned right.

"Formed from corruption. A defense mechanism of the tree against the insect burrowing into its heart."

Was he expected to reply? Insect? Corruption? Was it a metaphor? It felt like a metaphor. The deadly infection burrowing into Singapore's heart. Could this Japanese mean that?

Hayashi got down on one knee, raised the cloth, and put his face close to the victim's head. Was he going to sniff her all over? "Smoke, ash, fragrance. A mask and a memory."

Martin opened his mouth then shut it again. Hayashi put his hand to the woman's right hand as if in a caress. When he rose, he held between his fingers one of the victim's ripped nails.

"Ganbatta desho," he muttered. Martin barely caught the words and did not understand them. Hayashi ceased, suddenly, to be in a contemplative olfactory mood. He passed the nail to Martin, who put it carefully into his handkerchief. Hayashi's voice took on a more direct tone. His English was impeccable; his accent was what Martin knew as Received Pronunciation, the acceptable tones of the English public school, which Martin and a host of other Asian boys had caned into them at Raffles. Oddly, for creatures from such alien worlds, they sounded more or less the same. But how could this be so?

"No identification, Inspector Bach?"

"No, sir, not yet. Her shoes and handbag appear to be missing. And she's not wearing jewelry. Possible robbery."

"Her nails, would you say they were well manicured?"

Martin looked at the nail. It had been torn to the quick and was grimy with dried blood but otherwise impeccable. "Yes, sir."

"Her clothes are expensive. Silk. Despite the wound to her head, her hair is clean and styled. Do you think she might recently have attended a beauty salon?"

"Very possible, yes, sir. Might be a good place to start."

"Those things near her hand. What are they?"

Martin moved closer. An assortment of shards lay scattered, among them wooden and glass beads of different sizes. "The shop sold porcelain images and prayer beads."

Hayashi pointed to Martin's shoes. "What are those?"

Martin looked down. "My shoes?"

"Yes."

"Plimsolls."

"Ah. Plimsolls, that's right. You do not have leather shoes?"

"No. Blown up, I'm afraid."

This wasn't true but he didn't mind the detective chief inspector thinking it was. He had a couple of quite decent brogues, but in them his feet felt like concrete. Hayashi was wearing the light rubber-soled cloven-hooved shoes favored by the Japanese soldier, what might once have been a fashionable safari jacket, and a beige pith helmet. Did he think there was big game in Singapore? Also, he was carrying a quite dandyish sort of hairy fly whisk. Sartorially he had nothing to say.

"They are for cricket, are they not?" Hayashi said. "Do you play cricket, Inspector?"

Cricket? Really? They were to talk about cricket? Martin had not thought the Japanese might like cricket, but then he'd never thought of them at all until they'd obliterated his city. "Yes. I played for my school, Raffles."

"Yes. So. Ah. Raffles you say." Hayashi set the whisk moving, sending the buzzing fly cohorts whizzing. He seemed momentarily lost in thought. "Comfortable shoes are important, don't you think?"

The cricket conversation seemed to be over. And it was true that sore feet made you grumpy. The chief inspector seemed to have said something penetrating and Martin opened his mouth to agree, but Hayashi appeared, once again, to be speaking to himself. He turned back to the victim. "Turn her on one side, please."

Martin balked and his stomach heaved. With hindsight, Martin knew his life had been saved when he'd crossed paths with an orangutan in a Japanese officer's field helmet. In shock and surprise, he'd stepped backwards into a ditch seeping with the noxious gruel of decomposing corpses. The orangutan had screeched as a rattle of machine-gun fire had passed over Martin's head and two wounded coconuts had plopped beside him with a syrupy squelch. Martin owed his life to that fortuitous meeting, but the gaseous putrefaction of the ditch—the movement of farting, swollen corpses jostling and bumping around him—was still vivid. He doubted he would ever be able to touch a dead body again.

He signaled to Detective Constable Seah, who despite his youth was apparently unmoved by the job of removing the cloth and rolling the victim onto her right side. Mat shot a couple of photos. Hayashi examined the incense burner.

"Move the koro away. What do you call it in English?"

"Censer."

"Censer. My apologies. My vocabulary is a little rusty. Please place her face on something."

The censer, a large shallow porcelain bowl overflowing with ash, broke, sending a heady cloud of perfume onto the air. DC Seah put a newspaper under the side of the victim's face. A headline trumpeted the fall of Bataan and the surrender of more than seventy-six thousand American and Philippine soldiers. Seah began to drag the broken censer to one side.

"Nose and mouth filled with ash," Martin said. "Suffocated. Semiconscious from the blow perhaps and this finished her off." Hayashi nodded and waggled his whisk. He lifted the hair from the face of the woman gently. This sensitivity seemed out of keeping with the damn vicious nature of these people, but Martin got it: a feeling for the victim perhaps but also the beginning of the chase. This was their first case together. They'd known each other two days, a comic double act—Flotsam and Jetsam—flung together on this shipwrecked island by a typhoon. But they shared the universal instincts of the good detective. Or at least Martin made that assumption. All he really knew about him was that he had been the police chief of Nagasaki. He had no idea where Nagasaki was and cared even less.

Hayashi felt the victim's neck, arms, and hands. "Advanced rigor. What is your opinion, Inspector Bach, about the onset of rigor mortis in this climate?"

Martin was so grateful to be spared this tactile inspection that he responded with alacrity. "Occurs earlier, doesn't last as long. Onset after death is about three hours. Less if she'd put up a fight, which, by the look of her fingernails, she had. I've observed that violent physical activity before death leads to earlier onset in this climate."

Hayashi gave himself a good whisking. "Ah. Honto?"

Martin decided to ignore Japanese interjections on the grounds of incomprehension and moved on. "Reported in at nine thirty. Ten o'clock now. This advanced stage of rigor puts her death, in my view, around five o'clock, just after the end of curfew."

All the time he was talking about hours Martin was doing a curly mental calculation in his head. Time had shifted from the moment the Japanese had taken over. Everyone now lived on Tokyo time, one and a half hours ahead of local time. Ten thirty

7

was now midday. So the official five o'clock in the morning was actually, from nature's indifferent perspective, three thirty, the middle of the night. Anyone out at that hour would be wandering around in the dark with two and a half hours until actual sunrise.

With the lightest of touches, Hayashi raised the victim's skirt, peered underneath, and replaced it. "Underwear intact. No bruising on the legs. I think we may rule out interference for the moment. Light-skinned. Fine features. Possibly Eurasian. Perhaps you recognize her?" Hayashi consulted Martin with a glance.

Martin stared back. "You understand we don't all know each other."

Hayashi ignored this. He looked beyond the dead woman to the shrine. "Attacked from behind. She's fine boned. Wouldn't have taken much to knock her out. Is that a family shrine?"

"Yes. Chinese shop. They'd have lived above it."

"Do you think those gods protected them? Do you think these people survived?"

Martin raised his eyebrows. What did this Japanese policeman want to hear? He didn't feel charitable. "Unlikely, don't you think? Bombs are bombs."

Martin could see that Hayashi had instantly regretted his question. Perhaps he'd discerned the incredulity in Martin's voice. His people had dropped the bombs after all.

"I've had a word with the local watchman. Saw and heard nothing. No surprise there. The Japanese sergeant sent for him when the POWs found the body."

Hayashi examined the dress. It had deep side pockets. "Something here."

He put his hand into the right pocket and pulled out a handkerchief. He handed it to Martin, who opened it. Inside was a ring with five keys. The handkerchief was delicate, more decorative than useful. White organza with an embroidered red rose.

The keys looked similar, standard keys with a metal circle at the top. One was shorter than the others.

"House keys?" Hayashi said.

"Maybe. The short one might be a cupboard of some kind. No marks." Martin wrapped them back in the handkerchief and put them in his pocket.

"About mid-twenties, I would guess," Hayashi said, whisking and looking along the street. "Deserted place. What kind of people live in this neighborhood?"

Martin blew smoke. The Japs needed local knowledge. On their newly captured island, they were out of their depth in almost every aspect of civilian life. With the European civilians locked up, the Japanese needed the engineers, plumbers, electricians, dockworkers, nurses, doctors, teachers, managers, everyone, to start working again. And, apparently, policemen. He had no idea how that was going to work out over the next year under a brutal military regime. But he had reason to be grateful to DCI Kano Hayashi, for he had instantly promoted Martin from detective sergeant to detective inspector, a rank that would have been impossible for him to achieve under the British.

He crushed his cigarette underfoot. "These few streets that back onto the hill are not populated at night. Office buildings mostly, a school, shops. As you see, many damaged or closed down. But all kinds live around about."

Martin ran his hand around the scene. "Take your pick. Indians, Eurasians, Chinese. Malays tend to live in the kampongs. But war has displaced tens of thousands, so could be anyone now."

Hayashi whisked. "One sure thing," he said, looking at Martin. "If we rule out chance, then only someone who knew she would be here at that time could have killed her."

"Yes." Martin nodded. "Isolated, dark, lonely. Suffocation. Her face held down in the ash. The mortal struggle. Doesn't feel like chance. Feels personal. She was here to meet someone, who killed her."

He met Hayashi's eyes. They were in agreement. It was a start.

"Inspector Bach, sir," Seah said, rising to his feet. Martin turned. The constable was holding a chain at the end of which was a silver locket. "I found this in the ash, sir,"

Martin took the locket and showed Hayashi. "Clasp broken." Martin blew a little of the ash away and as delicately as possible opened the locket. Inside were the tiny pictures of two women. One of them was the victim.

Hayashi nodded. "Good. Get one of your constables to take it and start asking at shops and salons in the area. Good-looking woman. Expensive clothes. Someone knew her."

DC Joseph Santamaria stood combing his thick hair and checking his look in the reflection of the only unbroken window of the tea merchant's store.

"Santamaria, for heaven's sake. Get over here."

Martin gave Santamaria the photo and instructions. Seah looked crestfallen. "Well done, Constable, but Santamaria knows the area."

"Yes, sir." Seah's glasses were always in a precarious position on the slope of his nose. He pushed them up.

"You keep looking around. Shoes, handbag, anything else. Particularly the second broken nail."

Constable Seah moved away and began combing the area.

Hayashi glanced at his watch. "Get some more photos and have the body removed to the morgue. Make sure she isn't touched before we get to see her again. I have a meeting with Commissioner Honda." Hayashi reached into his pocket and took out a slip of paper. "This is his number. You can reach me there if you need to."

"Yes, sir."

"I will meet you at the morgue in two hours. I'll tell the guards over there that you need to talk to the prisoners."

Hayashi addressed the Japanese guards, then got into his car—a black Vauxhall 14. It had belonged to the now interned British head of CID. Martin harbored a deep and simmering resentment that his own quite ordinary car—a second-hand 1935 green Baby Austin—had been confiscated in the first days of the occupation and he had no idea where it had gone. The car held the imprint and perfume of Irene. Memory in fragrance. Hayashi was right there.

Martin ambled over to the Australian POWs, not forgetting to bow to the guards, thus avoiding a slap or a rifle butt to the head or worse. Didn't matter that he was older than these sallow youths or even a policeman. First and foremost, he was local, defeated and despised. Detective Chief Inspector Hayashi carried on his armband the insignia of military rank, the stripes and stars of a major in the Imperial Japanese Army, enabling him to order about lesser mortals when required. As a plainclothes detective Martin carried no such thing. He could rely only on his Syonan Keisatsu police armband and his CID card.

"I'm a civilian policeman," he said. "How are things with you men? Where are you?"

"Selarang Barracks. Bad conditions."

Martin had been to Selarang before the war. A British army base intended to house twelve hundred men now imprisoned fifty thousand.

"You're working for the Japs," one said.

Martin let his gaze linger on the men. How bloody dare they think everyone outside was a traitor? It was the British who'd surrendered. His own brother, Michael, a volunteer like him, was missing in action. His tone was harsher than he intended. "So are you."

His regret was instant. They were all so young, even younger than Michael. "Look. We out here are like you in there. Make no mistake. We're all in prison too. The whole island is a prison."

"Yeah, mate," said another. "We know. But we arrived just before the bloody surrender. Didn't fire a shot. It's shit."

"Yes, but that's not the fault of the Singaporean civilians. That's bad joss for you, but we believed it too. The big British lie. I'm involved with civilian crime. Got to try to get some justice done, even here and now."

"Justice. Bit of a joke, isn't it? Whole bloody war's a crime, mate. Starting with bloody Churchill." They laughed mirthlessly.

The guards looked over, annoyed at perceived signs of jollity perhaps. Martin wanted to engage the prisoners as long as possible to allow Seah time to comb the crime scene. He showed the two Japanese guards his packet of cigarettes. "Smoko?

They nodded, their eyes on the State Express 555s. The universal language of tobacco. The men lit up and tension on both sides evaporated.

"Can we get to this crime?" Martin said. "She's dead and should get justice if it can be given, don't you think?"

They all shuffled about, sending puffs of dust flying.

"Who found the body?"

The freckled kid spoke up. He looked about eighteen, gaunt and lanky. "I did."

"What time?"

"Time?"

"Yes."

"No watches, mate," said one.

"I know." The freckled kid. "Just past nine. The Jap sergeant keeps the radio on in the truck and that's when the English-language news comes on. I heard it."

Martin nodded. Observant boy. "Thank you. Can you describe how you found her?"

"We were shifting rubble to load onto trucks. Bloody hot work."

"Okay."

"She was in that shop at the front where the damage wasn't bad. We started at the side and it took us time to get there."

"You all walked near the body?"

They nodded.

"Did you see anything, any kind of footprints or anything that might show you who had attacked her?"

They all shook their heads except the freckled kid. "Marks," he said. "Animal marks."

"What, a dog or a cat? Like that?"

"Yeah, like that. Paw prints."

That was perfectly likely. He'd check her for bites later. He wrote it down.

"The sergeant came up and ordered us away," one chimed in. "Then he had a good look and walked around with his two drongos there."

Well, that was that. The scene was terrifically compromised.

"Did you find a handbag, or shoes?" Martin asked.

"Na. Nothing like that."

"Anything else you can tell me?"

"No. The local bloke arrived. We didn't understand the lingo or what everyone was doing at that point."

"Okay, thanks."

One of the guards, cigarette dangling from his lips, unbuttoned and began peeing against a column of the veranda. This propensity for al fresco urination was more shocking to the locals than almost anything—even slapping. The second guard was staring vacantly at the Chinese medicines in the window of the shop, familiar to him perhaps, thinking of home. Martin had no real idea.

But they were young too. Same age as these poor bloody Australians. Far from home and everything they understood. Cannon fodder. Perhaps the Australians had a better chance. The fate of the two Japanese boys was already sealed. They'd be moved out and within a week or two they'd be lying facedown in the mud of some mosquito-infested jungle. He couldn't hate them.

He slipped his packet of cigarettes and ten Straits dollars, all he had on him, to the freckly Australian kid. It disappeared into his shirt. The men grinned, their dusty faces grimy with sweat. Mat, camera in hand, bounced over. "I'm done. You can move the body."

"All right, thanks, Mat."

Mat grinned and took some shots of the POWs. Mat was the skinny roving photographer for the Japanese weekly propaganda pictorial magazine *Shashin Shuho*. Ragged, pathetic, laboring whites were a hit for the front cover. He always wore his black cap at a jaunty angle, and this seemed to sum him up. His family owned a photographic business and he now doubled up as the CID photographer.

From the corner of his eye, Martin saw the sergeant speak sharply to the two guards. He called to his constable. "Not much time, Seah. Remove the objects on the shrine and the shrine itself. Get the body wrapped and into the van. I'll give you a hand."

"Yes, sir."

When the body had been removed, Martin looked carefully at the place where she had lain. It would be the last time he'd get a chance. No question of keeping the crime scene sacred. Already the Jap sergeant was getting the guards to prod the prisoners into action. There was nothing else Martin could do.

He joined Constable Seah. The van was filled with incense and the faint early odors of death. As they moved away, one of the guards slammed the butt of his rifle into the back of the young, freckled prisoner, sharp, short, painful.

God help them. Any god would do. In Singapore there were plenty to choose from.

Santamaria emerged round a corner and waved. Seah threw on the brakes. Santamaria climbed inside. "Sir, I know who she is. You won't believe it."

CHAPTER TWO

The portly geisha waggling in front of Kano Hayashi must have been fifty at least, a fact that the white-painted face, beesting-red lips, and black wig couldn't disguise. Where Honda had found her didn't bear speculation.

"I must congratulate you, Baron Hayashi, on your elevation to the aristocracy," Honda said.

"Please, it is merely a title that came to me through a lack of a male heir in the direct line."

"Nevertheless. Nevertheless. You mustn't make light of the privilege. It is an exalted lineage."

The two men watched the geisha for a moment. "There's talk of some hot springs at Sembawang." Commissioner Honda gave the geisha a coy wave. He'd had a few cups of sake and was acting like a schoolboy. "It is out in the jungle. I don't care for the mosquitoes. Shocking, perhaps, but I am thinking of a bathhouse here in the garden but with cold water, not hot. But it seems rather experimental."

The commissioner, Hayashi reflected, was not a bad man. He had just become, in his old age, stupendously silly. This posting as head of the civilian police force, his renewed position in the Japanese hierarchy dragged from bored oblivion, had inflated his sense of his own importance. He occupied a mansion of imperial British space and splendor. It was clear he had never in his life seen a house of such elegance, such furniture, such grounds, such magnificence, such deference, so many servants, so much power. He was bedazzled.

"It's certainly a change of stance," Hayashi said. "Hot to cold. You are, sir, leading the community in such important progressions."

Hayashi knew Honda well. They were related distantly through their mothers, both daughters in different lines and generations of the Shimazu Clan, ancient lords of Satsuma. In his old age, flattery had become honey; the thicker the smear, the happier the man. Clearly pleased at the thought of being ahead of his time, he inclined his head to Hayashi.

"The new mayor, Ogata, is a favorite of His Majesty the emperor. I met him yesterday. Charming fellow. He was very pleased to meet me. Took me into his confidence. The urgent work of the civilian administration is to keep the peace, he told me. Give the military a peaceful backyard as they prosecute the war to the south and west. Win the hearts and minds of the people to our vision for Asia. The Greater East Asia Co-Prosperity Sphere. Think of it. What glory to His Majesty? His great southern empire. Burma is collapsing, Australia will not stand for long, and soon we shall have India too. The police and justice departments have their part to play. Mayor Ogata was most complimentary. He made it clear he's counting on me. That's our job. You see."

"I see." Honda had made his little speech. Speeches filled Hayashi with more dread than villains. He'd heard too many. For the past ten years Japan had been drowning in speeches by reckless, heartless, and ambitious men.

In the distance a telephone rang.

"So, this case you've got. The young woman."

"Yes."

"The mayor is watching. He's hoping for a juicy case which will make headlines in the newspaper. Beautiful young woman. Vicious murder. Crack police investigation. Justice done. That sort of thing."

"I see."

"A gift for the emperor's birthday, eh? What do you think?"

"Well …"

Honda's young clerk entered and bowed to Honda, who signaled him to approach. A low conversation took place masked by the sounds of the shamisen. The shamisen player, Kano noted, was as old as the geisha. How had they ended up here? But then how had they all?

"Hayashi-san," Honda said. "Telephone call for you. Your office."

Hayashi rose and bowed to Honda. "Thank you, sir." He picked up the telephone and listened for several minutes. "Certain? All right. Thank you."

The geisha looked tired, the sweat trickling through the white paint of her makeup. Hayashi felt sorry for her. Waggling was hot business in the tropics.

"Some news, Commissioner. We know the identity of the victim. I think Mayor Ogata will have his wish. This will make the headlines in all the newspapers."

CHAPTER THREE

"This is a damn bloody nuisance, Martin," Harry drawled. He placed two coffees on the table.

They were on the veranda of the Alibaba Café, overlooking the deep slow waters of the Rochor River. The café was run by a fat Hainanese nicknamed Toenails. Toenails' wife, pointy nose and pointier chin, was called simply Ting. She handled the money at the counter while Ting's younger sister waited on the ten plastic-covered tables. They were all KMT supporters but, so far, somehow, that fact had escaped the attention of the Japs.

Martin looked around. It wasn't stylish but it served some of the best *kaya* toast and coffee currently in Singapore. It stood some way away from the gates of the Kandang Kerbau Hospital, and its watery, peaceful location and tasty food made it popular with nurses and doctors.

At this hour it was empty, few vehicles of any kind traveled along the road on the other bank of the river, and birds lent their songs to the trees. Martin sipped the coffee. Unadulterated Javanese. Delicious. He savored the moment, watching the light reflected through the leaves of the branches overhanging the water on the far side of the canal.

Of course Harry was annoyed, but it was his fault. The Iyers, with their wealth and Indian connections, could have gotten out, but they'd stayed, their faith in the British unshakable to the last. With the Japanese trusting no Chinese doctor, Harry had been pressed, rapidly and reluctantly, into the position of medical examiner. Naturally there was no question of refusal.

"There's a war on, Harry," Martin said. "We all have to do our bit."

"Do we have to do our bit for Japan?"

"For the people of Singapore. Think of it like that."

"Don't talk such rot. And why are you wearing your cricket whites?"

"Nothing else, old man. Unless you think I'm being ironic." Harry's lips flicked into a smile. He put a cigarette in his ivory holder and lit it. "Will we ever play cricket again, old chum?"

Martin grinned and shook his head. "And is there honey still for tea? Get used to it, Harry. Your men with splendid hearts aren't in Grantchester. They're in Changi."

"My uncle Dev says it's a damnable disgrace and we're all bloody collaborators."

"Is it honestly any different to working for the British? What about that moron who was your chief surgical whatever? We've never worked for ourselves, have we? And do we have a choice?"

Harry shrugged. "Patterson. He wasn't just a moron, he was a drunk."

"Right. See."

Harry produced a card from his pocket. "I've joined the Indian Independence League. Everyone's joining. We can't get rations unless it's stamped by them."

Martin smiled. "Do you mean you don't care about Indian independence?"

"What? No. Well, I don't know." Harry sighed and sipped his coffee. "Singapore's going to the dogs."

"Tut-tut, Harry," Martin said. "Singapore has vaporized. We are Syonan-to." He gave a quick cold smile. "I could have you arrested for sedition and bolstering the cause of the enemy by utterance."

"Don't be so beastly. It's just hard to get used to. KK's name is now Chuo Boyin or something, which apparently means Central Hospital. I have been urged to go to Japanese lessons."

Martin lit a cigarette. So had he. "Back to school. It's like being reborn, isn't it?"

Harry laughed. "All right for you. You can read the squiggles and speak bloody Chinese."

"I can't read any of the bloody squiggles and I only speak Cantonese, which is nothing like Japanese."

Of course, Harry knew all this. He was just being provocative. They'd been at school together. Harry went on to medical school and Martin had, a few years later, joined the police force.

"You still out in Katong with that brother of yours?"

"Yes." Harry didn't know the half of it, but Martin didn't care to discuss it.

Two brilliant black-and-yellow orioles swept down to the river to drink and were gone. A couple of Japanese soldiers ambled by on the road opposite, rifles in hand.

"How's your new boss?" Harry asked, keeping an eye on the soldiers. "No Jap doctors at KK."

"Chuo Byoin, " Martin said and they both grinned. "I don't know yet. Early days. Bit odd but seems solid and honest."

A frail old Chinese man on a tricycle piled with baskets pulled into the street from an alleyway. He hadn't noticed the soldiers. He pedaled with the slow and careful concentration of age and infirmity, grew level with the soldiers, then inched past them, oblivious of his requirement to stop and bow, oblivious of them altogether. Martin had seen it time and again even after weeks of occupation. The Chinese man, stubborn perhaps, or simply distracted, hadn't yet learned to appreciate that a Japanese command was sacrosanct and that tardy compliance was not a mere peccadillo but an affront to the emperor himself.

Harry tensed and Martin's shoulders stiffened. In an instant one of the soldiers hauled the old man off his bike, sending baskets flying. He slapped the man twice, so hard the sound came to them as an echo. Blood danced off the gash to his jaw. The second soldier kicked him to his knees and thrust the rifle butt into his back. The man sprawled and lay stunned.

The soldiers screamed abuse. The old man got to his feet with difficulty, murmuring something, probably some kind of apology. He bowed from the waist, legs trembling, barely able to stand, blood dripping from his face, his bony hands clenched into fists stuck to his sides. The first soldier raised his rifle and aimed it at the old man's head.

Harry began to rise. Martin grabbed his arm and pulled him down.

"No," he hissed. "Stop it, Harry."

The soldiers exchanged words. The rifle was lowered. Apparently satisfied with this display of physical harm and humiliation meted out to a helpless old man, they decided to move on. A young Indian woman rushed out of a nearby house, warily eyeing the backs of the soldiers. She went to the old man, gathered up his baskets, and moved him and his tricycle away as fast as she could.

Harry's face flushed with anger. "They're animals. Don't talk to me of solid and honest."

"*Vae victis*," Martin said. "Woe to the vanquished."

"For God's sake, Martin, just because you can say some bloody thing in Latin you think it's filled with wisdom."

"Not wisdom, Harry, reality."

Harry rose, shoving his chair back with a heavy scrape on the wooden floor. "I've got to go."

Martin nodded. "All right, Harry. See you at the mortuary."

Martin watched Harry's stiff back and bowed head disappear along the edge of the canal. Harry, Martin knew, was angry at what he perceived as callousness on Martin's part. He got it. But what would either of them have been able to do if the soldiers had shot that old man? A shouted insult, a reprisal, a rush to help, would have meant forty dead, not one. This is what they did. The tiniest sign of pride or rebellion brought a neighborhood bloodbath. Knowing it didn't alter the worms of shame that burrowed into everyone at these sights, but it did mean you could rationalize inaction not as cowardice but as sense and try to live without being consumed by guilt. Some managed it better than others.

He ordered another coffee. "Toenails," he said as the man put the cup on the table, "pull up a chair."

He put a dollar note on the table and Toenails picked it up and turned it over. "A banana note. No one wants to pay me in Straits dollars."

"They have deemed it the equivalent. I've got no say."

In fact, Martin, like he supposed most people, always spent the new Japanese currency with the banana tree on it and hoarded the Straits dollars. They might deem it equivalent, but one day it would certainly be worthless. It would all be over by next Christmas. That's what everyone whispered. With the Americans in the war, how long could it last? Martin wasn't at all sure of that but was hedging his bets. "The rooms over this joint," he said. "They empty?"

The upstairs rooms of the Alibaba Café had been used before the war as a place for casual prostitution, KMT meetings, noisy mah-jongg parties, and New Year banquets.

"Nah. We live in them. A bomb landed not far from our house. Took out the back wall. Now seven of us are crammed up there."

Martin sighed. Opposite, hawkers had begun setting out their wheeled carts and stools along the roadside to sell chili noodles and fried vegetables to the rickshaw pullers who gathered at the gates of the hospital. He took a card from his pocket and put it on the table. "Ration card. It's a fake. And a bad one."

Toenails got up from his chair. "Yeah?"

"Japs cut off heads for it." Martin left the fake ration card on the table. Before the war Toenails had had an uncle with a printing press somewhere on Lavender Street. "There's an investigation." Toenails nodded.

Martin crossed the bridge and pulled up a stool at a hawker stall. It smelled good, of hot fat and spice, and the hawkers chatted convivially among themselves and their growing crowd of customers. He ate the steaming, oily noodles, watching the glossy black myna birds scavenging among the stalls. They were the survivors of the avian world, the best adapted to life among their aggressive human companions. They just got on with it.

He turned towards the hospital.

CHAPTER FOUR

"Please uncover the body, Dr. Iyer," Hayashi said. "Inspector Bach, tell us what you know about the victim."

Martin, Hayashi, Constable Santamaria, and Mat Ahmed were with Harry in a makeshift mortuary in an outbuilding of the KK. Before the war the central mortuary was in Singapore General Hospital, but the Japs had taken that over exclusively for themselves. Even the dead couldn't mingle; perhaps especially, the dead couldn't mingle. Martin was beginning to learn that Japanese military culture was a death culture. The dead and the living—who after all were merely the walking dead—must be pure in the service of their own living god. It paid never to forget this about them, and he wished Harry would get it inside his head. But maybe that was easier for a detective than a doctor.

"Sir, this is the body of Eva Abraham, the widow of Sir Solomon Abraham, one of the richest men in Asia. He died of natural causes in early February. She was identified by the owner of a beauty salon where she was a regular customer. Eva Abraham last attended the salon two days ago."

Hayashi approached the body. To Martin's surprise, with the flourish of an old-fashioned conjuror, he produced a large, ornate magnifying glass from his pocket and proceeded to examine the back of her head and the wound. He and Harry exchanged a glance.

"There appears to be one jagged wound to the back of the head. Please look, Doctor."

Harry took the magnifying glass. "Yes, I concur."

"Inspector?"

The glass was passed. "Yes, I see," Martin said. "Also there is an imprint in the ash and blood. I can't make out what it is."

Hayashi took the glass and moved in closely. "A heel, a plain unmarked print of part of a shoe heel, I believe." For a moment, the image of a foot on the back of this frail creature sat heavily in the room. "Speaks of hate, I'd say, or at least anger and power." Martin nodded. Hayashi examined her clothes. "Here," he said. "Those appear to be marks, in the dust on the edge of her dress."

Again, Martin took the glass. The marks of paws were smudged but not enough to disguise them. "One of the POWs said he saw paw marks. An animal had a good sniff round." Martin took her right hand. "Not only are her nails ripped, but it seems like there is a bite on her hand."

Hayashi looked. "Deep gash on the fleshy part of the thumb. Torn skin. Yes, perhaps you are right. A photograph, if you please."

Mat's camera flashed. "Feral animals live on the hill, Chief Inspector," he said.

"Ah. I see. Turn the body over, please. Take pictures of the face. Constable Santamaria, remove all the ash you can and preserve it."

Santamaria's face clenched, but he took a small brush and pan and began to sweep the ash from the face and hands into an old Huntley & Palmers biscuit tin. When he finished, Hayashi signaled Harry to remove the clothes. The body was stiff and Harry was obliged to cut the dress and underclothes to remove them. Santamaria took the items, folded them, placed them neatly onto that day's edition of the *Syonan Times*, wrapped them for removal, and retreated, brushing ash from his clothes.

Hayashi moved forward. "Doctor, please do a preliminary examination of the body."

Harry arched an eyebrow. "You understand, Chief Inspector, that I am not a trained pathologist. Nor a chemist or forensic scientist. I am a gynecologist."

"Yes, yes. I understand." Hayashi sounded tetchy. An indiscreet reminder that those specialists were languishing in prison perhaps.

"Very well, I shall do my best." Harry moved around the table as he spoke. "The woman is young, approximately twenty to twenty-five years of age, I'd say. She has been struck a blow to the back of the head and suffered apparent animal bite marks."

Harry stopped and bent more closely over the victim's head. He examined her nose and mouth. "Neither of those things killed her. I believe death was caused by suffocation. The passages are stuffed with incense. I will need a closer examination, however, to be sure."

Hayashi nodded. "Proceed, Doctor."

"The body is in advanced rigor mortis. I'd say she's been dead for around six or seven hours. The lividity in areas at the front of the body indicates she died where she was found. Not moved after death, I mean. It is clearly advanced. Maximum livor mortis occurs twelve hours after death. I am not an expert in this area, sir."

Martin nodded. "I'd confirm that livor mortis looks like she's been dead between six and seven hours."

Harry threw Martin a grateful glance. "She appears from this cursory examination to have been in good physical condition. Other than some foot problems. As you can see, she has quite a prominent bunion on the left foot."

Harry touched the bunion and all eyes swiveled to the foot. "Her hair is dyed with henna, probably, by the outgrowth, about a week ago. This and the color of the pubic hair show that she is naturally a brunette." Eyes moved to the groin. Martin felt Hayashi tense.

"All right, Doctor. Cover her."

Harry replaced the sheet, leaving the arms visible. He picked up her left hand. "Tan lines indicate that a ring, possibly a wedding band, and a watch, have been removed. Her ears are pierced.

Two of the nails on her right hand are broken, one, the middle finger, is torn off down to the quick."

Harry turned to Hayashi. "May I borrow your magnifying glass, Chief Inspector?"

"Certainly. Do you not have one yourself?"

"No. All the hospitals were looted." Harry indicated the biscuit tin. "Or we would not be using that as a surgical receptacle." To his credit Harry managed to keep the sarcasm out of his voice. Hayashi seemed to take this in for a moment, then handed the glass to Harry.

Harry examined the fingers. "The area around the thumb is torn and the fingernails bled profusely. The entire finger and hand are caked in dried blood. The other nails contain dust and possible debris. She might have scratched her attacker."

Harry looked at Hayashi. "Chief Inspector, that's the best I can do until I've been able examine the body more fully. I am not an expert on cadavers, but I have consulted a book I managed to locate in the pathology department. I have based my opinions on that."

Hayashi waggled his whisk. "All right."

"Time of death, then, probably around five o'clock," Martin said. "That is Tokyo time."

Martin turned to Harry. "What about the blow to the head? What can you tell?"

"From the angle of the blow I'd say she was struck from above. On her knees perhaps or bending down in some way, and the attacker had room for a big swing." Harry raised his arms above his head and made a two-handed chopping motion.

Martin thought of the chain and the locket. Was she searching for it when the blow was struck? "A rock, do you think? Bit of rubble."

Harry surveyed the wound with the magnifying glass. "Yes, jagged indentations." He passed the glass back to Hayashi. "Sir, we could do with some of these and some microscopes."

Hayashi gazed at the antique Victorian magnifying glass. "My father gave me this. He was an ardent follower of Sherlock Holmes."

Martin turned away, rapidly converting his barely controlled pop of laughter into a cough. Harry didn't appear to find it amusing. "It is very fine, Chief Inspector. I always preferred Raffles, the gentleman thief."

Martin coughed again. Hayashi gave him a piercing look.

"Chief Inspector, what is it you wish me to do with the body?" Harry asked.

"Establish cause of death absolutely. And anything else. Send us your findings. Then preserve the body."

Harry threw an anguished glance at Martin. "Sir, currently there is no way we can preserve the body. No refrigeration."

"Embalming, Chief Inspector," Martin said. "That would preserve her until we can find out more about her."

Harry scowled. Hayashi bobbed his head up and down. "Yes. Good. Do that. For preservation only. On no account wash the body or in any other way prepare her for burial. You understand?"

The chief inspector gazed at the dead woman a few moments longer as if he was looking at someone else. Perhaps he was, Martin thought. Perhaps in their job, they were always looking at someone else. Hayashi turned and left the room. Santamaria took up the dead woman's clothes and, alongside Mat, followed him.

"Raffles, the gentleman thief. Really?" Martin smirked.

"Shut up. And thank you very bloody much," Harry said with a grimace. "Embalming? Really? Is there even any embalming fluid on the whole bloody island?"

"Ask Old Zhao. He'll know. But first I want you to take some of her blood. I don't know if we have the technicians or equipment capable of carrying out forensic bloodwork, but until I know I'd like some of her blood. Can you do that?"

"No."

"Yes, you can. This is basic stuff, Harry. And this is a hospital. Know anyone who can?"

Harry sighed and his eyes sought to display his displeasure. Martin ignored the dramatics. "Good. Get it done. Perhaps DCI Hayashi will lend you his magnifying glass again."

CHAPTER FIVE

Martin disgorged the contents of his pocket onto the evidence table. Constable Seah had carefully sifted through the bag of dust and dirt and the objects he had found were laid out. "That's it, sir," Martin said as Hayashi joined him. "One painted nail, by the look of it from the ripped middle finger. Handkerchief with a rose, five keys, a locket with a broken chain containing the photographs of two women, one of them the victim. We don't know the identity of the second woman."

He ran his fingers above the other objects. "An assortment of broken porcelain and a quantity of what look like prayer beads of differing sizes and materials."

Seah was joined by Santamaria and Sergeant Adnan Ibrahim. Martin addressed the room. "This is what we know about Eva Abraham from the statement of the owner of the beauty salon which Eva frequented. She was the fourth wife of Sir Solomon Abraham, the patriarch of an old Baghdadi Jewish family from Calcutta who came to Singapore at the turn of the century and made a fortune. He died of natural causes in February this year. Sir Solomon was famous throughout Asia, received a knighthood from the king, and was friends with powerful men in China, Japan, and India. He had one child, a daughter, Miriam, by his second wife. Miriam Abraham lives in Meyer Mansions." Martin turned to Santamaria. "What else do you know, Santamaria?"

Santamaria consulted his notebook. "The women at the salon said she was always dressed expensively and had loads of jewels. They remember pearl earrings, a gold necklace with a drop pearl in a setting of diamonds. Also, she wore a watch. They remember that because it wasn't as expensive. A Rolex Princess, gold-plated."

"All right. Anything else?"

"Her feet. She had bunions."

"Well, yes. I mean—"

"This is a high-profile case," Hayashi intervened with a sudden whisk. "The mayor wants it solved as quickly as possible. It would establish our reputation here in CID and ensure continued financing, extra staff, and support. These are important considerations, as I'm sure you all understand. Our first duty is to the victim, of course, but we have to consider public perception and interest."

Martin got it instantly. Hayashi had been leaned on. The Japanese wanted the gossipy death of the young, beautiful, and murdered wife of the richest man in Asia to occupy the minds of the locals and get them off the war. "Right, sir, a splash in the newspapers but of course no actual details of the crime to leave this room."

Hayashi nodded stiffly, but Martin thought he detected relief fly across his boss's face. This was no strange occurrence. His English bosses had been the same. The case and the public perception of the case were two different things.

"Right." Martin continued. "What we say in here stays in here. The rest is up to the commissioner. So, the crime scene area was deserted. A chance crime seems unlikely. We think that she went there to meet someone, who murdered her and possibly removed a watch, earrings, wedding ring, handbag, and shoes. A question we have to ask ourselves is why leave the expensive clothes? Good clothing, expensive underwear, these are hot commodities. Why not strip her and dump her? Was the perpetrator disturbed? Or hadn't intended to kill her? Or had but took what was quick and got out?"

"What's the situation with stolen goods?" Hayashi said.

"Black market. Before the war we had informants, but now … And we can't be sure of the jewelry, can we? That she was wearing any, I mean."

Hayashi turned to Sergeant Ibrahim. "Thoughts, please, Sergeant."

Ibrahim, if he was surprised, hardly showed it. His face was always the same. Pockmarked and impassive. Martin approved. No British officer would have asked his opinion. The natives couldn't be trusted to do any thinking. Or maybe the detective chief inspector knew how much he needed help. Either way it was a departure from the standard British procedure of haughty disdain.

Ibrahim's hand went to his pocket, withdrew his prayer beads, and held them absent-mindedly. "If there's jewelry it is likely that it is being sold to a Formosan fence. They're the go-betweens. Almost certainly the only people with any money to buy jewelry or luxury items currently are the Formosans and the Japanese."

Seah's and Santamaria's eyes swiveled warily to DCI Hayashi. Could you say that?

Hayashi looked at each of them. "Please be at ease. We can be honest. What happens here stays in here. We'll get nothing done without trust. Do we know who these Formosans are?"

The sergeant put the beads back in his pocket and shook his head. "We should."

"All right. Your job, Sergeant. Use any contacts to make a list of potential fences and informers."

Hayashi flicked his whisk, apparently, Martin thought, for effect, since the room contained no intolerable or pesky insects. "Let's be clear, though. Anything involving high-ranking officers of the military will be off-limits. That I can guarantee. We are all here under sufferance of the military administration."

"Yes, sir," said Ibrahim. "Special Branch papers. Are they available?"

"Special Branch?" Hayashi looked at Martin.

"British intelligence. Counterespionage. Kept tabs on spies, subversives, communists. It's your Tokko."

"Oh yes. Special Branch. Yes, I see."

"If any Special Branch papers were left undestroyed, they might be in the hands of the Tokko."

"I'll check, but they won't be cooperative. Right, Sergeant," Hayashi said, turning back to Ibrahim. "You were with this Special Branch?"

"Yes, sir. In my experience an informant for the British is just as likely to spy for the Japanese."

"Start putting down names, Sergeant. I shall organize a fund for payment to informants. What about getting some younger boys involved? Street boys who can keep their eyes and ears open. Like the Baker Street Irregulars."

Hayashi smiled widely. Ibrahim's face did not change. "Yes, sir," he said.

"We shall think of a name for them, eh, Inspector? Something pithy."

Martin nodded. It was vaguely amusing and almost touchingly naïve. "Certainly. I'll give it some thought."

"Thank you. You know, the Tokko will use intimidation to get information. Their way is brutality. We shall use the rice bowl instead. Money will speak better and more truthfully. Do you agree, Sergeant?"

"Self-interest usually works more swiftly than fear in getting genuine factual information."

Hayashi faced the men. "If, at any time, Japanese names come up in the investigations we will be conducting, no matter who or how high, military or civilian, I want you to come to the inspector right away. He will discuss them with me and I will be the judge of how far we can pursue the matter. There can be no perfect justice in these troubled times, but we must try. All right?"

"Yes, sir," they said in unison.

Hayashi returned to his office and shut the door.

"Street kids?" Martin looked at Ibrahim and smiled.

"Not so far-fetched. There used to be those three-dot kids who ran around for the triads. They are still out there somewhere." Ibrahim said. Martin knew that the triads had many sub-groups and names in Chinese. Three Dots was one of them. Usually, but not always, its members had a tattoo of three dots somewhere inconspicuous on their body. "The gang bosses have gone underground, spread to the winds, dead, who knows. But the street kids are still there. They had a leader. Charlie Chan."

Martin laughed. The whole of this little speech was unexpected. But Ibrahim had been Special Branch and they watched the Chinese secret societies, so he must know.

"Charlie Chan? You're kidding."

"No. Tough as nails. Orphan child. Brought himself up on Charlie Chan films. What his real name is nobody knows. He may be still alive."

"Well, Sergeant. It would make the chief inspector very happy I've no doubt to find a Charlie Chan. Think of a pithy name while you're at it."

Martin laughed, tickled by a thought. "Weren't the Charlie Chan books written by Earl Biggers? Think I might have read one or two. Could call the chief inspector's irregulars Biggers' Brigade. What do you think?"

Ibrahim's face remained expressionless. It occurred to Martin that the sergeant might not realize that the Charlie Chan films came from books. "Or not. Cheer up, Sergeant."

Martin picked up his hat. "Seah, go over the victim's clothes carefully." He saw Grace Tobin and Mary Tan, the office secretaries, in the doorway. Mary was giving the eye to Joseph Santamaria, who didn't seem to mind. Martin minded. Santamaria was married and he didn't want any hanky-panky in the office. He picked up the locket and removed the two photographs. "Mary, get Mat to photograph and blow up these photos. We need to identify the second woman. And hurry him on the crime scene photos." He frowned at her and she flushed. "Santamaria, get over to the hospital and get the doctor's written autopsy report. Grace, make an inventory of the evidence."

"Does he mean all that," Constable Seah said, adjusting his glasses, "about the Japanese?" The others looked at Martin.

"Yes, I think he does." He didn't add that, when it got down to the wire, Kano Hayashi would surely have his moments of doubt as well and wonder how to balance this lofty sense of justice with his own natural loyalties and inclinations.

CHAPTER SIX

M artin stepped into the cool dark hall of Ah Loy's pawnshop and dinged the bell.

Whatever this new city was or whatever its new masters decreed, it wasn't dead to its past. How could it be? That was its only tangible reality, filled with shadows holding a grip on the present. This place was the gateway and Ah Loy was the perfect gatekeeper, the personification of pragmatism, a man who could work with any side without the remotest qualms.

Before the war Martin had kept Ah Loy out of jail for receiving stolen goods. And Ah Loy had been grateful. Whether he was still was something Martin needed to find out.

Ah Loy emerged, wiping his mouth. Martin switched the mode of communication to Cantonese, the Chinese he'd learned at his amah's knee. "Morning."

"Detective Inspector Martin Bach. Congratulations on your elevation, eh. Our new masters recognize quality when they see it."

"Cringing flattery, Ah Loy. Nice. Thanks."

"Sure. What can I do for you?"

"You get any ladies' jewelry recently? Earrings, watch, wedding ring maybe. Stones of some kind."

"Yeah."

"Show me."

Ah Loy produced his docket book and a tray of brassy rings, two women's watches, and some cheap earrings. "Nothing of value. But I've got competitors these days. Plenty on the black market, eh. Legit man like me can't make much money."

"Okay, sure." Martin took up the watches. They had no inscriptions, cheap, pathetic indicators of desperation. "Who brought them in?"

Ah Loy ran his finger down the docket reading out the Chinese names. They meant nothing and Martin knew she hadn't worn anything like this.

"You telling me the truth? There's a murder case."

"Inspector, I've always been a good friend to the police, eh? I run a legitimate business."

"There are no legitimate businesses anymore."

Ah Loy shrugged. "Bad times. Bad times. I got a bit of a shock, I can tell you."

"Nice understatement. Very British."

Ah Loy smiled, displaying his silver-capped front teeth, a self-inflicted source of some pride. Martin pressed on. "I'm not interested in the black market. That's a different lot. Meaner than me."

"Ah. Ah. Murder. What does that actually mean these days? You looked around?"

"I don't make the rules of war. This is a civil matter. She was a young woman. Classy. Found bashed in a condemned building. Robbed. Wedding ring, possibly earrings, wristwatch. Keep an eye."

He waited while Ah Loy wrote this down. Every transaction or possible transaction Ah Loy did he wrote down in spidery calligraphy in his record book. Martin thought he might record his bowel movements there as well.

Martin put the locket on the counter.

Ah Loy took up his loop. "What do you want to know?"

"Tell me about this."

Ah Loy put the loop to his eye. "Silver, but not expensive." He turned it over. "Engraved. Looks like *E. R.* Initials or symbols of some kind."

Ah Loy placed the loop on the counter. "Monetarily I mean. It might have meant a lot to E.R., eh."

He handed the locket back to Martin. "Anything else?"

"If I wanted to buy something against a rainy day, what would you say?"

Ah Loy eyed him. Martin could almost see the wheels of his brain whirling. What to say? A police inspector asking about the black market. Was it a trap?

"Not a trick question, Ah Loy," Martin said. "Times have, as you may have noticed, changed, and it's not my department so I don't care."

Ah Loy hesitated, then seemed to make up his mind. In this uncertain world you had to trust someone. Martin saw that Ah Loy had decided to trust him and, in that moment, also decided to trust Ah Loy.

"Good time to buy luxury goods," Ah Loy said. "Porcelain, silk dresses, diamond rings. Maybe you got a sweetheart?"

"No."

Ah Loy laughed. Again the silver teeth. "The rainy day's right here, right now, but it'll get rainier. Best buy for you are Rolex watches. Market's flooded with them. And gold and diamond rings. You got money?"

"Some. How does this work?"

Ah Loy sucked his teeth. "Okay. It's like this. Singapore has miles of wharves and thousands of godowns. The British stocked them with goods to last Singapore for more than three years, certain of its standing as a fortress. That's a lot, eh?"

Martin nodded. He had not ever given any of this a thought.

"Also they were holding supplies intended for Hong Kong, Siam, Indochina, and Malaya. Despite some war damage, most of this vast treasure is intact. Add to that the goods belonging to enemy commercial firms, all confiscated and now under Japanese control. What is Singapore but a vast storehouse? Those things will not be available for civilian consumption."

"Aladdin's cave," Martin said.

"Aladdin's cave: equipment, food, medicines, machinery. All under Jap control. Except of course that there was looting. Slowly, too, pilfering from the godowns has begun. A steady stream of stuff trickling onto the market."

Martin's attention began to fade. It all blended into one vast, incomprehensible calculation of exploitation.

"What does it mean for me?" he said. Ah Loy's grasp of the manipulation of this disaster for current and future profit was beyond the scope of his understanding. And he saw too that Ah Loy knew it.

"Means some things are plentiful and some not. Plentiful things are cheap. Like watches."

"Okay. How much is a watch?"

"Before the war two hundred fifty dollars. Now twenty dollars. You buy now, hold on to it, in three months it will be two hundred fifty dollars again."

Martin sighed. "Why will it be two hundred fifty dollars?"

Ah Loy looked at him as if he was simple. Perhaps he was. "No new watches in town. New Japanese arriving all the time. They're like kiddies in the sweet shop. They want stuff. You see. Like watches. And they have the money."

"So why don't you just stock up on them, then? Why sell them to me?"

"I need cash too. I don't need a thousand Rolex watches. I keep the best and sell the rest, eh. You see?"

Dispiritingly, Martin did see. His life was being counted out in Rolex watches. He didn't have that kind of money. "What else will have no new stocks? Cheaper than a Rolex and which the Japanese love."

"Booze." Ah Loy smiled. "French champagne, Scottish whisky."

Martin perked up. "Oh yeah?"

"You're a smart fellow. Can't lose with booze, as we Cantonese say."

Martin eyed Ah Loy. He'd never heard such an expression.

"Right now, it's cheap because it's coming out of the warehouses through the hands of the Jap guards themselves."

Ah Loy spread his hands. "Why not? They only have a short time here before they'll be moved on to fight in some jungle. They want quick money to spend on their pleasures. The brass haven't figured it out yet, but they will. Then they'll crack down, maybe shoot a few soldiers, and in three or four months it will start to be expensive."

"No new stocks. Right. How much?"

"Two dollars a bottle. Great deal. Cheap because none of the brain-dead sentries and few of their dumb-assed officers know anything about champagne and whisky, but that won't last long. You got a storage place?"

"No. Hardly got a bloody bed."

"Never mind. I'll store it for you."

Martin mulled this over. It made sense. He could see that the Japs would pay plenty for that kind of stuff when stocks ran dry. Jesus, he was already thinking like a profiteer. And he did know Ah Loy. His particular villainy was familiar in an unfamiliar world. He was almost reassuring in his sameness.

And the Japs were already corrupt. Two months and the kanji was on the wall. All the high-minded talk about a new vision for Asia was bullshit.

"You know, Inspector, as a policeman people will want to— let us say—give you things."

"Eh?"

"Your position, you know, will be an incentive to offer you certain priorities."

"Priorities? Is that a euphemism for a bribe?"

"Well, I didn't say that." Ah Loy examined his fingertips. "But you have a power to control the lives of others. To see or turn a blind eye."

"I'm not on the beat, Ah Loy. I don't have any power over imports or food regulations or even money. I solve murders."

"Yes, but some murderers may be rich or have influential relatives. Or a Japanese friend. When money is short and food is short, the temptation … well."

"I will make every effort to not shock you, Ah Loy, and resist temptation," Martin said, feeling slightly queasy at this turn in the conversation.

Ah Loy shrugged. "I wouldn't blame you. Way of the world."

"How generous of you. And philosophical. But there were corrupt coppers when the British were running things."

"Except we now live by the law of the jungle and in a year or so we will all be starving. And the jackals will circle."

Martin gazed at Ah Loy. "Yes, we must be vigilant. Will you be vigilant, Ah Loy?"

Ah Loy smiled. "I will take care."

"Good," Martin said. "There will be an end to this one day and even possibly a reckoning for the jackals. We must try to think of that."

"Right. So, the booze. I'll get it?"

Martin heard the sarcasm in Ah Loy's voice. "Let's get one thing straight. I know we will all be swilling around in the black market. But I will only deal with stuff that doesn't oppress the population. No medicine. No food. Nothing like that. Understood?"

Ah Loy sucked his silver teeth. "Sure."

"This will all be over by Christmas in any case."

Ah Loy smiled. "That's what the Chinese said about the Mongol hordes."

Martin shot a quizzical look at Ah Loy. "What?"

"Nothing. You'll hear from me."

Martin left the shop and set his feet towards the crime scene. What was that all about? The Chinese had an irritating habit of seeming to have secret wisdoms no one else knew. But they knew bugger all. Except hunger. They knew that. When it got down to starvation, what would he do? What would any of them do? He shook these thoughts away. It wouldn't come to that. It would all be over by Christmas.

CHAPTER SEVEN

Martin headed to Meyer Mansions and Miriam Abraham. It was a five-minute walk from the crime scene. The modern apartment block on South Bridge Road occupied a large square of land opposite St. Andrew's Cathedral and diagonally across the road from the Adelphi Hotel, now renamed the Nanto, the very place, the newspaper announced, where General Yamashita would be meeting his fan club. They must be certain of themselves to announce it. He was easily the most important target in Singapore. But who would dare? Beheadings, screenings, the constant harassment, the daily viciousness of the soldiery, ensured a docile and obedient population, at least on the surface. He'd heard that there were reds in the jungles of the mainland, anti-Jap forces, but there was no certainty of it and he saw no sign of anything resembling a resistance in Singapore.

The side tradesman's entrance of Meyer Mansions on Coleman Lane led to the large square inner courtyard. It was blocked by a Japanese army truck. A dozen soldiers were unloading what looked like boxes of ammunition and mortars to the shelter of a long internal veranda. The buildings next to the Mansions had become the home of a garrison of soldiers, perhaps to offer protection to the general and other officers living in the Nanto. Martin skirted them and went into the front entrance.

The residence certificate attached to the notice board in the lobby was issued by the Kempeitai, the police arm of the Japanese army. This was one of its invasive but more mundane duties. Others were more secret and deadly, including dealing with anyone suspected of anti-Japanese activities. The certificates recorded every citizen of every household in Syonan. He found the names of Eva and Miriam Abraham on the second floor, apartment 27. He didn't bother to wake the snoring concierge. He took the stairs. The building was well constructed and elegant. It appeared to have suffered little bomb damage.

He examined the door. Inevitably one of the keys fitted this door and he was sorry he didn't have them. Until they found a way to inspect for fingerprints, they were untouchable. He could have picked the lock. He always had his lockpicks on him.

He knocked and waited. The door opened a crack and on a stout chain. A short, young woman peeped round, a richly patterned veil covering her hair and the lower half of her face.

Martin showed her his police card. "Don't be alarmed. I'm a civilian policeman. Are you Miriam Abraham?"

"I'm Miriam Weber."

"Oh. I see. You're married?"

"Well. I ... We are betrothed."

"So you are not married."

Her eyelids flickered, mothlike, as if she was fluttering around a flame searching for some sort of answer he would understand and she could accept. "It is a matter of custom. We are betrothed as husband and wife but we do not yet live together. We are waiting to complete the marriage as Jewish custom demands."

"I see." Martin didn't see at all. He was unfamiliar with Jewish tradition in this respect, but he didn't care enough to pursue the matter. His business was the law, which currently, despite the Japanese takeover, was British. "Well, perhaps I should address you as Miss Abraham. Since, despite your customary laws, your legal status under British law is unmarried."

She gave this a moment of thought, then nodded. "Well, all right."

"Thank you. I'm sorry to say that we have found the body of a woman we believe to be your father's wife, Eva."

"Oh." Her eyes opened wide.

"Perhaps I might come inside to discuss it."

"Oh. Well. I don't know. My husband is not here."

"Your betrothed, you mean."

"Oh yes. All right. Gosh."

"However, I still have to ask you some questions. Perhaps you'd prefer to come with me to the police department."

There was a moment of hesitation. He got it. An orthodox Jewish woman, she was hesitant to see a man alone. The indecision lasted a moment or two. She could hardly refuse and she must have seen that. But perhaps to go to the police station filled with the dreaded Japanese was a greater fear.

"No. No. All right. Wait a moment, then." She shut the door. The wait stretched. He began to grow impatient and was about to knock again when he heard some muffled conversation, then a fussing with the chain. When it opened fully, it was to the sight of a wrinkled but wiry Chinese woman who had the distinctive bun and loose white-and-black *samfu* of the *majie*, the Cantonese maid. She reminded him of his old amah and he smiled at her. She didn't smile back.

Miriam was standing, leaning heavily on a thick cane, next to the maid. Martin looked round the hall. A mirror, a hat rack, an elaborate porcelain stand crammed with walking sticks and umbrellas. A pile of elegant silk shawls and scarves lay scattered on the hall console, on top of which perched a large, rather ugly doll with rose cheeks and yellow ringlets. The maid eyed him as if he was going to rob the place.

"This is my amah, Ching," Miriam said.

"She is not on the residence certificate."

"She was not permitted by the Japanese to stay with me. They were horrible. It wasn't fair. I need help."

Obviously, the Japs wouldn't have cared about any of that, Martin thought. Racial divisions were simplistic for them, as black-and-white as the *majie*'s uniform. She looked Chinese, the

Japs didn't like the Chinese, so they wanted them all lumped together, not dispersed uncontrollably throughout the town.

Martin turned to Ching and addressed her in Cantonese. "What is your full name, please?"

"Yip Ching Sam."

"Miss Yip, where are you living?" Martin knew she was a miss; the Cantonese *majie* swore a life of celibacy and married into domestic service.

Ching was living in a tenement with other *majie* on Victoria Street. Martin noted the address. "Have you always been employed by the Abraham family?"

"No. But for twenty years."

"What are you saying? I don't understand." Miriam pouted and stamped her cane.

"I'm asking about her relationship to you."

"She is my amah," Miriam said. "She has always worked for us."

Ching nodded. She obviously understood English well. Martin switched. "What hours do you come here?"

Ching looked at Miriam. Perhaps she didn't speak it so well.

"She comes from eight thirty in the morning until ten at night," Miriam said. "That's Tokyo time, of course, which is actually seven, already barbaric enough, don't you think? I can't abide early mornings, so Ching doesn't need to be here. I'd be happy for her to come later, but she insists on coming at that time. Don't you, Ching?"

The *majie* nodded.

"She knows someone with chickens, so she brings eggs on her way in. Don't you, Ching?"

Another nod.

"A lovely omelet with some fried spinach. She's a good cook, aren't you, Ching? I don't know what I'd do without her. Really, I'd be terribly lost. Wouldn't I, Ching?"

Martin had had enough.

"Thank you, Ching," he said. "You can go."

Miriam stared at Martin as if she'd been struck. "How dare you tell my maid what to do? Do you know who I am? Do you know who my father was, you… you…?"

Ching took a step backwards and stared at Martin. He smiled at her. "Thank you, Ching. For the moment, please leave us." Ching didn't move.

"Miss Abraham, I know who you are. I am not here to annoy you. I am a police inspector and I need to speak to you about the murder of your father's wife."

She pulled the veil up and turned to Ching. "Yes. Well. You may go, Ching."

Ching pointed to the shawls and the doll and turned down her mouth in disapproval. "This. So messy. I take."

Miriam gave a curt nod.

Leaning heavily on the cane, Miriam limped into the living room of the apartment. Spacious and solidly, if inelegantly, furnished. He could see the grounds of St. Andrew's Cathedral with its white iron railings and large shady trees. He felt a little green pang of envy at all this space in such a place. She sat, laying the cane alongside her leg, which projected stiffly away from the chair.

"You are injured, Miss Abraham?"

"Polio," she said, "contracted when I was a young child."

Martin's gaze went to the boot on her right leg and the metal and leather contraption surrounding it. He had seen many of these on the children with polio. The brace peeped out from under her long cotton dress. A silver chain jingled on her left ankle. She saw his gaze and arranged her dress to cover her feet. "I'm sorry," he said.

"Oh, that's all right. Just my one leg, you know. Not my breathing or anything else. Really, I'm quite lucky."

Martin took in Miriam Abraham. From her modest dress she appeared to be a traditional orthodox Jewish woman. The headscarf, however, was surprisingly attractive, Indian cotton arranged in intricate folds and plaits with small tassels that framed a pretty face. It served to cover her hair and her modesty at his ingress into her private sphere. To this she had added a veil. It was made of elegant patterned Indian silk.

"Miss Abraham, the body of your stepmother has been found in a condemned building. We estimate she had been dead for around four to five hours."

Miriam's eyes fell to the floor. "Is that true? Are you sure?" Her voice was quiet, small. "Oh, that's horrible. What happened?"

"She was suffocated."

"Oh no. Oh no." Miriam's eyes grew wide and her hands began to tremble.

"Your identification will be needed."

"Identification? Oh, I don't want to see a dead body. I can't do that." Miriam gripped her veil.

"Perhaps not, but it will be necessary to have a positive identification."

"David will do it. I want David to do it. Can he do it?"

"David?"

"Weber, my ... betrothed."

"We prefer a relative. Did Eva have any family other than you?"

"No. She wasn't my family. She was my father's wife."

"Perhaps you would explain that to me."

"My father was a widower. Eva became his secretary. Then she married him. It was all quite sudden."

"I see. What did you think about that?"

"I was in India with my mother's family. They were shocked but I thought it was fine, really. Someone to take care of Daddy."

"So, you liked her?"

"Oh yes. I liked her. Oh, it's so terrible. All this death going on around us. The Japanese slapping and hurting people. We know what's been going on in Germany. That's a crime, isn't it, but where is justice for them?"

"I can see how you would think that. This is war. Injustices and crimes will pile up like sand drifts and there will be nothing I can do about it. Crimes of war are dealt with after the event. I don't like this situation any more than you do. No one does."

With a small movement through the material of her dress she unlocked the brace and drew her knee up. It was deft, strong fingered, and spoke of years of practice. She crossed her good leg over the weak one and a silver anklet jingled. She had a quiet dignity and ease in this affliction that he respected.

"But civil crime," Martin went on, "must be dealt with if only so that people can see there is order, some kind of justice and decency at least. And have some hope that in the course of their daily lives they can get a measure of fairness. For the moment, the Japanese have decided to retain British civil and criminal law and I have to investigate a murder."

Miriam gave a short, bitter laugh. "Don't speak to me about law. The Japs have taken over my father's house on Mount Sophia. Some unspeakable puffed-up colonel is living in it and riding around in my father's car."

These were unwary words. If he reported them, she would certainly be interrogated.

"I would not advise speaking of that in public, Miss Abraham, but perhaps you will tell me what happened."

Miriam shrugged, but he saw she had understood. "What's to tell? An officer turned up and said the house had been confiscated. He gave us an hour to get out."

"You and your ... Mrs. Abraham?"

"Yes. You see, my father was very ill. We couldn't leave Singapore like many did. They got out to India right away."

"You could have. You had family to go to."

"Yes, but my father was too ill to travel. I couldn't leave him. And then I'd met David, so ... "

"I see. No one else was living with you at the time."

"No. Well, most of the servants had left, except Ching. He had a heart attack. We went to the hospital and he never came out."

"We?"

"Yes. Eva and David Weber, my betrothed."

Martin wrote this in his notebook.

"We barely had time to bury him," Miriam said. "It was ghastly. By then there was the surrender, and we were stuck."

"And you came to live here."

"My father owned several apartments in this building. The tenants of many of them had fled. So we moved here."

"You and Eva."

"Yes. Thank goodness for Eva and Ching. I don't know how I'd have managed without them. Of course, it was meant to be temporary. Until things settled down and David and I could marry. Then almost immediately Ching was told she had to leave. She didn't like it a bit. Terribly upset. Anyway, I was so glad Eva was here. Oh, poor Eva." Miriam put the veil to her eyes. "I can't believe it."

"Miriam, do you have a photograph of Eva?"

"No."

"I mean a wedding photograph, perhaps."

"No. I don't pack things, you know. You'll have to ask David. He was wonderful. Really wonderful. I don't know what we'd have done without him."

Martin took the locket from his pocket. "Is this Eva's necklace?"

She glanced at it and turned away. "Yes, I think it is."

"What about Mrs. Abraham's family? Did she have anyone? A sister, perhaps?"

"She never talked about any family."

"When was the last time you saw Eva?"

"On Sunday morning. We had a bit of a row and she left."

"A row? What about? Where did she go?"

"I don't know. We rowed. Living all together here in this little flat, you know. Tempers a bit short."

"She left and did not return," Martin said, "is that what you're saying?"

Eva's body had been found Monday morning. Miriam nodded.

"At what time?"

"Late morning."

Martin allowed a certain time to pass. Where had Eva been during Sunday? He drew a crab and two prawns in his notebook while she stewed for a minute or two. He was hungry. "Can you think of anyone who would want her dead?"

"No," Miriam shouted. Through nervous energy or just stewing, Martin couldn't tell. "Why are you asking me these questions? Who do you think you are? Don't you know who ... ? My father ... ? I want David. He should be here. Eva must have been robbed. I don't know why ... The city isn't safe for anyone." She began to cry.

Martin waited. When she found a composure he asked gently, "What time did you wake up this morning?"

"I don't know. Around eleven o'clock Singapore time. I get so confused I have to keep two clocks by my bedside table."

Martin nodded. Everyone got confused. "Miss Abraham, where were you all day Sunday and Sunday night?"

"I was with David. He's a lawyer."

"Is he?

"Yes. We were together all that afternoon and evening. We went to Orchard Road and saw a film at the Pavilion. *The Great Lie.* I liked it and it was lovely to be doing something normal. And David said it would do us good."

This was possible. Oddly, American films were still being shown. "You were together all night?"

It was a very direct question. Whatever her customary law dictated, they were not married. She was religious. How could they alibi each other throughout the entire night of Sunday and the early hours of Monday, the period when Eva had met her death?

"I was so nervous. The whole business gets on my nerves," she said, biting her lower lip.

Martin took "the whole business" to be the war and the occupation. It was one way of looking at it.

"I look out of the window and see nothing but Japs. It's horrible. So sometimes David stays here."

Martin arched an eyebrow. She flushed and the veil came back across her face. "He slept in Ching's room. It isn't orthodox. But times are not orthodox. And we are betrothed. We shall be married as soon as we are permitted, and everything will be all right."

Martin turned the page of seafood over and handed Miriam his notebook. "His address, please, and telephone number."

"He lives in this building on the first floor. It was David who knew of the empty apartments and helped us move here."

"Can you write his full name, apartment number, and telephone?" She wrote it in a light, childish hand and returned the notebook.

"What is David's background?"

"German Jewish. They lived in Rangoon. That's all I know."

"I want you and David to go to the morgue at the Kandang Kerbau Hospital and identify Eva positively and then come to the CID office this afternoon. Do you understand? I need you both to make statements."

She avoided his eyes but nodded.

"How is it that you weren't interned, Miss Abraham?"

"Eva, well, she is, was, Eurasian, so when she told them I was her stepdaughter, they just let me go. David thinks they didn't understand the concept of a stepdaughter, so ... "

"So Mrs. Abraham saved you from internment?"

"Yes, she did. It was good of her. But when we moved here, she suddenly became terribly bossy and difficult. She didn't like David. She wanted to stop me marrying. She had no right. No right. You understand. She wasn't my mother. Anyway, we didn't row about David. We rowed about the other thing."

"The other thing?"

"Yes. When she took up with the Japanese man."

Blast, thought Martin and felt his case sliding like snowdrifts down the slopes of Mount Fuji. He sighed and took up his notebook. "Which Japanese man?"

CHAPTER EIGHT

Hayashi gazed out from his office on the third floor of the Municipal Building across the grassy acres of the Padang, the spreading canopies of the rain trees on the water's edge and, beyond, to the silver glints of the distant sea. The sky was filled with the streaky orange of the dawn and the air with the strident, lusty call of cuckoos. The heat was already steamily oppressive. A night of monsoonal rains had washed the city clean, but a long smear of oily black smoke from the still-burning oil dumps was bent by the wind to the far horizon.

Little by little, the grass became a creeping tide of red and white flags as thousands of children gathered for a rehearsal of the celebrations for the emperor's birthday. More flags billowed from a hundred poles and festooned the elegant façade of the cricket club. It was as subtle as a mortar attack. But then the Padang was being readied to welcome its martial hero, General Yamashita, the man they were all now to call "the Tiger of Malaya."

Despite all his doubts about the road Japan was now traveling, the prospect of meeting Yamashita held a certain thrill. He'd smashed the fortress in seven days. What a triumph against the greatest empire in the world! Kano felt, unbidden, a great swell of pride for the brilliance, courage, and daring of his fellows, but then, just as quickly, mopped his brow and turned away, ashamed.

That achievement was tarnished. By the spikes of severed heads blackened and festering on every bridge across the river. By the murders of countless thousands of Chinese men, whose bodies, he'd learned, washed up on the beaches. By the random beatings and slaps administered to ordinary men and women on the streets. By deeds suspected, hidden and foul. The heat suddenly became crushing, and he felt sick.

He cranked up the fan and waited for the nausea to pass, staring at the dark wood paneling on the wall. What was it about paneling, he wondered, that the British found suitable for a tropical climate? On the corner of one of the panels there were some scratchings into the surface. He leaned closer.

It was the figure of a face with a long nose hanging over a wall, and underneath the words: *WOT, no planes? WOT, no ships? WOT, no idea! Mr. Chad.*

He read it again. He had no idea what it meant nor who was this Mr. Chad. Was he the man who had previously occupied this office? Was it sarcastic? He had learned that this was the kind of humor which the English liked. But he could not quite grasp its meaning. And why had someone defaced this wood paneling? It was barely visible. What was its purpose?

Perhaps Inspector Bach might know. He looked through the open door to where Martin was seated at his desk. He had little time to sum the man up, but he understood that the British despised men like Martin because of the issue of his bloodline. Hayashi knew about that sort of thinking and did not care for it. One of his professors in London had been Eurasian, a man he admired very much. Martin seemed a worthy working partner, especially in a place he did not understand. That was his opinion. But they hadn't yet found an easy relationship.

This issue of the Japanese man in this Abraham case gave him the opportunity to show that he did not say things he did not mean. He went into Martin's office. "Inspector Bach. May I call you Martin?"

Martin smiled. "Yes, certainly. And how may I call you?"

"Just Hayashi when we are alone. I know it is not natural for foreigners to use the honorific '-san.' I am used to that from my time in England and actually quite like it. As a race we have too many layers of formality in my view. I very much like the films of John Wayne. I cannot imagine calling him Wayne, John-san, can you?" Hayashi chortled, evidently pleased with himself. Martin frowned.

"In company call me Detective Chief Inspector. In Japanese the term is Keibu. Strictly correct usage when talking about me or addressing me would be Keibu-san."

"I understand. Thank you. Your English is excellent."

"My father was a student of French and English. He encouraged a broad outlook. I studied with an English tutor from a young age, then at an English school in Tokyo and at University College in London."

Martin found nothing to say. After the cricket stuff anything might be expected. A London university? Why not dining with the king? Flying the Atlantic? Meeting Dr. Livingstone in Africa? It occurred to Martin suddenly that Kano Hayashi might be a fantasist.

"The mayor of Syonan is in a difficult position."

Martin waited, straight-faced, but felt a bile-load of withering scorn in his gut. Difficult position. Was he? Poor fellow.

"He is a civil administrator. We are all to a certain extent answerable to the military government in the form of Colonel Watanabe. The mayor was a vice minister in the Ministry of the Interior in Tokyo and Commissioner Honda was head of the Tokyo Police Bureau and chief adviser to the minister of public security. They do not take kindly to answering to jumped-up military types."

Hayashi swung round and walked to his office. He returned with two cartons of State Express 555, a bottle of Hennessy brandy, and two glasses.

He put the cigarettes on Martin's desk. "My allocation. I don't smoke. These may come in handy."

"Thank you."

Hayashi opened the bottle of brandy. "Also part of my allocation. Will you join me?"

Martin nodded. Hayashi poured two small glasses and handed one to Martin. The aroma was heady. Like a genie from a bottle, it transported him to another time and another place. A small hotel by a beach.

"Thank you, sir."

"Did you like working for the British, Martin?"

"A dangerous question. But I will answer it. I liked being a policeman. They trained me well though they tended to think the natives were generally hopeless."

"So."

"They never socialized with anyone but themselves. We were all utterly beneath them. But then we believed it ourselves, didn't we?" Martin shrugged. "I suppose some were less offensive than others."

"Much, I imagine, as you will find us."

"Doubtless."

Hayashi smiled. "If we are to work together, we must understand each other. Do you agree?"

Martin looked at Hayashi. "Certainly."

Kano polished off his glass and poured another. Martin sipped his and waited. "Of course, what we say inside these walls should stay here."

Martin put his fingers to his lips. "*Labia signati*, Keibu-san."

Kano wiped his brow. "Mattaku! It's so damn hot. Look, I just want you to know that there is a line. We are not here simply to do the military's bidding. I'd like you to remember that."

"I shall."

Hayashi smiled. "Have you read Gibbon's *Decline and Fall of the Roman Empire*?"

To Martin's relief a knock came at the door. He shot up and opened it.

"Good morning, sir," Santamaria said, bowing to Hayashi.

"Good morning, Constable."

"A message for you, sir."

Hayashi took it. As he read, a barely perceptible change came over his face. Then it was gone.

"Something wrong, sir?"

"This is a message from Colonel Masuda. He is the head of the Tokko. He is vetting the personnel of this unit."

Hayashi fell silent and Martin knew there was something not being said here. When Hayashi spoke again it was if he was chewing glass.

"It is a question of fussy interference. Apparently, your file did not include your birth certificate. Colonel Masuda has asked for it. I'm sorry to raise the issue with you but I'm sure that it's not a problem."

Martin frowned. Fussy interference. Was this an example of Japanese understatement? He was absolutely certain that the man in charge of the Tokko didn't do fussy interference. His birth certificate? Had he ever seen it? Did he even have one? Surely, he must have? He smiled and inclined his head to Hayashi. "No problem, sir."

"Excellent. Thank you. Now, in regard to this Japanese man, what is his name?"

CHAPTER NINE

Tante Helga's wrinkles wobbled. She sat intently over the cards, placing and replacing them in an elaborate game of solitaire, creating some meaningless order out of chaos.

She'd lost weight and now resembled a loose-fleshed pug. Whether she had once been good-looking, Martin did not know. He hardly knew her at all. She'd arrived one afternoon just after the war began and moved like an armored tank into her dead brother's house in Katong, then occupied by Michael. She'd had no children of her own, lost a husband somewhere along the way, and never remarried.

At the ceasefire, Martin had ditched the volunteer's armband, kept his rifle, and set out east towards Katong. Police quarters had been bombed weeks before. He'd lived in the volunteers' dormitories since then or in abandoned houses with his unit. He had nowhere else to go. He knew the war had been fought from north and west. The east, he hoped, had been spared.

He'd joined the streams of Chinese and Indian civilians with the same idea. Heading east away from the burning town, heading anywhere away from the Japanese, hoping for survival in the village kampongs. A grandmother pulled the shafts of a squeaky rickshaw piled high with sacks of rice, a man bent double grunted under the mattress he carried on his back, children clinked and clanked with pots and pans dangling from their necks. Heat blanketed them. Rain was a momentary relief washing away the stench of sweat and blood, before the sun blazed again.

Those newsreels of the French fleeing the Germans had turned into them. They trudged and trudged silently, sweating, exhausted, stepping over, round, through, the rotting corpses littering the drains and roadsides, grotesque shapes of exploded men, vehicles, bullocks, children, trees, dogs, arms, heads, legs, willy-nilly, a patchwork of death in the abominable heat of a kingdom of flies.

Those not fleeing were looting on a monumental scale; entire department stores swept clean, government offices stripped of desks, papers, typewriters, even windows and doors. Any house, bombed or abandoned, was devoured as if by white ants.

When he arrived, Michael hadn't returned, and he discovered he was to share the house with his aunt—and, worse, his elder brother, Walter. Walter's large house, his car, and all his possessions had been requisitioned by the Japanese military the day after the surrender, and he, Joan, his wife, and their two children had been flung out.

If any situation could be said to be almost worse than the war, it was to find himself under the same roof as Walter. Seven years older than Martin, he had always been a distant and harsh sibling. When they did see him, he would alternately torment or ignore both Martin and Michael. At nineteen Walter had left for Hong Kong, returning only ten years later. He had married a woman Martin barely knew. They had always lived separate lives. Now they were flung together, and Martin deeply resented having lost his independence, the noisy clamoring of his two silly nieces, and the lonely grief as each day passed and Michael didn't return.

Brutish men smelling of sweat and battle stalked the streets in their split-toed shoes like grim-faced Visigoths terrifying the citizens of Rome. They burst into houses screeching and sending men flying against the walls. Children howled and crouched in fear as the soldiers grabbed radios and food, sweeping plates, cups, pots, and pans crashing to the floor, trampling photos, ornaments, family mementoes, underfoot. They rushed from room to room, seeking booty. "Girru, girru," they screamed, pointing rifles at heads. When they found girls, they dragged them screaming from the houses and herded them into trucks. As the word spread, females of every age were hidden in woodsheds, cellars, attics, smuggled from houses to villages, disguised as boys.

Joan and the girls never left the house. Every bang at the door sent them whimpering into the hot darkness of the half-collapsed bomb shelter at the bottom of the garden. Walter smoked, silent and grim as a tomb. Martin queued for water at the stand, glad to get out of the prison of the house, joining the lines that coiled under the boiling sun. Dogs loped by, unheeded, jaws clamped round a human arm, half a leg, a foot.

Gossip, fed by fear, passed from mouth to mouth. Chinese men had gone missing. Maybe thousands. Everyone knew, in that long, hot, and thirsty line, of a Chinese family that had lost a son, brother, father, uncle. The word was that the Japs didn't punish the Indians or the Malays. They hated Eurasians. But they killed the Chinese. Eyes flitted, suddenly wary of neighbors they'd known for twenty years. In what seemed like a moment the Japs had done a first-class job of divide and conquer.

"Haven't the British played us a dirty trick," said a woman in the queue. Base desertion rankled in the minds of them all. Rage sizzled and spat, like hot fat, as Martin evaluated his life under the British. He, like them, had believed it all. The stories told in school. The flag. The anthem. The king. Believed that swagger and arrogance represented wisdom and superiority; that their armies were invincible; that their snobbish clubs and condescending sneers were justified in the name of intellectual and moral superiority.

He felt like a stupid, ignorant child. Deception. Lies. Calumny. Betrayal. He wrote those words again and again. How many times had he been looked down on by men more stupid than him, passed over in rank by bumbling idiots just off the boat? For the sanity of his bewildered and beleaguered house, he contained his fury, but it was the confinement of the pressure cooker. Bursts of steam flew out of him at unlikely moments. He wanted to punch the walls, scream, and curse. He swallowed the urges and hid himself away. Though he hated the Visigoths, he was hysterically glad that the pathetic armies of the empire had been trounced in seven days by soldiers they regarded as short-sighted, bucktoothed monkeys.

Now its dominions were dirt, its flag ground into dust. And for this filthy stain of empire, his brother had given his life. He fumed at night, raging into the pillow. For a moment he teetered, he knew it, on the edge of a nervous breakdown.

Then he found, read, and read again one book: *The Count of Monte Cristo.* It was like a bible, filled with a consolation of truth. *Captivity has brought my mental faculties to a focus.* A hundred times he read that line. It seemed to speak directly to him. *From the collision of clouds electricity is produced, from electricity, lightning, from lightning, illumination.* He found calm. And from the calm and illumination he knew one thing.

God would never be white again. Nothing of that world could be left. Singapore was a prison as isolated and grim as the Château d'If. They were all alone and alone they must find the way to see it through.

For weeks they were like insects stuck in glue. They buzzed and beat their wings, then lay still and waited. Then the Japs had spread the word, flinging leaflets off the backs of trucks. Anyone caught with loot would be beheaded. A man with four fridges was dragged out of his straw hut, his screams cut short in a gur-gle and a gush of blood. Fires fed with pianos and sofas blazed into the night.

The newspaper appeared. The island had been renamed Syonan, Light of the South, the year was 2602, noon was half past one, and everyone, it shrieked, had to get registered and get back to work. So, they did.

Tante Helga eyed the bottle of Hennessy brandy in his hand. She liked liquor. That much he knew about her. He kept a grip on it and headed upstairs. His aunt had moved her brother's old suits and hats into Walter's old room like a ghoulish, tobacco-stained shrine to his memory. He went to the room his mother, when she was present, had occupied. His two nieces now slept there, but he knew there was an old suitcase under one of the beds.

He took out the small silk scarf he had given her for a birthday and put it to his face. Memory in fragrance. Her perfume had been French. In all things she loved to be French. Matou. She called him Matou. What had happened? There had been an autopsy, but he had never discovered the result. The subject never came up. Even had he dared ask, Walter's attitude forbade it, and until war had driven them into one sheep pen, they'd had nothing to say to each other.

He took from the suitcase two photograph albums. Ancient photographs of people, old-fashioned clothes, smiling faces, serious faces, events attended unknown now except by the dead. They were mostly of the Bachs and he discovered what he thought might have been his aunt in her youth. She'd always been plain. He felt a pleasurable pang of satisfaction.

He put that one aside and picked up the next. This one began with his parents' wedding day. There followed pictures of the couple with her Indochinese mother's family and his French grandfather at some church event, possibly Easter. A few group photographs around dinner tables in hotels. The usual pictures, the sort taken randomly by a photographer at dances and parties. Maman. Lovely, vivacious, so utterly her own person. French and Indochinese, that wonderful mix. He turned the photographs over. In her small, sloping hand, she had written the names of her companions. He traced the lines where her hand had moved, then put them back in the album and closed it, shoving it back into the suitcase.

There were no certificates. Most urgently, not the one he sought. He took the Bach family album and went downstairs. Joan was in the kitchen boiling water and buffalo milk. The water hadn't yet been restored to their house and she didn't trust it anyway. The milk was delivered by the buffalo man, who had a herd in a field somewhere. No electricity, no water, buffaloes next door. Stamford Raffles would have been right at home.

"Where are the girls?" he asked Joan.

"Out, messing about with some urchins in the neighborhood. With no school, they've run wild. I can't be bothered attempting to stop them. If they see Jap soldiers, they soon run home. And the paper says that St. Hilda's in Ceylon Road will reopen again soon. I shall have to get a job too."

Martin nodded. "Good idea. Get you out of the house."

"We need the extra rations."

"We'll be rolling in it. More than we know how to eat."

Joan laughed. A rippling chuckle.

"What's on the menu?"

"Spam, *kangkong*, and rice," Joan said with a wink. In their enforced life together, he had discovered Joan. She was a calm and cheerful foil to Walter's misery and a brave face for her two girls. If war had anything to recommend it, it was to discover the true heart of people you hardly knew. She mothered her husband and children. She tolerated and administered to Tante Helga. With Martin, she had simply become a friend.

"But I have a pineapple and some rambutans," she said with a grin.

"Can I ask you a question?"

"Certainly."

"Do you have any idea where I might find my birth certificate? Is it in the family papers Walter has?"

"Aren't you supposed to be the policeman?"

"I'm being the policeman. I'm interviewing a witness."

She smiled. "Well, all you can do is ask Walter when he gets home. He'll probably know. He knows things."

Martin fell silent and Joan glanced at him. "Or I can ask."

"Yes, please. I'm surprised he decided to go back to the bank and work for the dwarves."

"He adored being asked, of course. I'm just grateful. He was so bored it was impossible."

Walter had been personal private secretary to the head of the Overseas Chinese Banking Corporation, a man with sufficient wealth and clout to grab his family and set sail in January as the bombs began blowing Singapore to bits. Walter had sworn blind he would never have anything to do with these brutish bloody dwarves and sat all day brooding, reading books, and smoking. Now, in a remarkable about-turn, he had decided he had a duty to preserve the empire from this momentary and ridiculous aberration and keep the island and its institutions intact until the day it would be handed, unsullied, back to his English masters.

Frankly, Martin didn't care. He opened the photograph album and Joan tucked in next to him.

"Gosh, all the old Bachs. I don't think I've ever seen them. Walter doesn't have anything but the portrait of your Germanic grandparents on their wedding day."

They turned them page by page, laughing at some old-fashioned hairstyle or costume until Tante Helga came into the kitchen, sat down, and began to tell them at length who every Bach was back a half a century.

Dinner was, as usual, a silent affair. Walter did not encourage chatter at table, and Martin had little to say in any case. He would rather have eaten alone in the kitchen. It was purely out of respect for Joan that he ate with them. What did Joan find attractive in this man? His daughters sat glumly shoving in food, then asked to be excused. They ran off like rabbits and Joan cleared the table. Martin rose to help as he always did. As always, Walter looked disapproving. Walter's ideas about familial roles were stuck in the nineteenth century. Martin did not agree and saw no reason why Joan should wait on him hand and foot as she did Walter. On this occasion, however, he did not pick up plates but brought the bottle of Hennessy and placed it on the table. Walter was partial to brandy and on this evening Martin required something from his brother.

When Joan returned, Martin poured three glasses. Joan broached the subject.

"Martin's birth certificate?" Walter said in his monotone way. "He must have one, I suppose."

"Well, yes," Joan said. "Dear, do you think you could find it? It's quite important. For the Japanese authorities."

Walter, without a glance at Martin, left the room. He returned with the steel box that contained all the family papers.

"What about some coffee with the brandy?" Joan said brightly. "I'll serve in the living room."

Walter went through each paper meticulously, laying them out. The deeds of this house. The deeds of his own, now requisitioned, house, the deed to the apartment in Tiong Bahru. Martin picked it up.

"What happened to the apartment?"

Walter did not look up. "No idea."

"You rented it out, didn't you?"

Walter didn't reply.

"Was it bombed?"

"I don't know."

Walter's voice warned him not to pursue the matter further. He should have just pressed on, but Walter made him feel like a noisy nuisance child. Always had. He tossed back the brandy.

Certificates emerged: birth certificates of Walter and Michael, of Joan, of his children, his marriage certificate, their parents' marriage and death certificates. There they lay, the British Empire's bureaucratic validations from cradle to grave.

It was the stuff Walter loved. But no certificates of any kind emerged for Martin.

"This is all I have." Walter's eyes met Martin's in a cold stare.

"Coffee in the living room," Joan called, and the men rose. Martin brought the bottle of brandy. He felt like getting drunk. Being with Walter always made him feel like getting drunk.

Tante Helga joined them clutching the photograph album. The girls were upstairs. The night was silent. The house felt safe and familiar. The Japanese with all their brutality and bureaucracy ensured a generally peaceful neighborhood in the lowest sense. It was the peace of repression and fear, of course, but for this moment Martin was grateful.

The faint strains of a Strauss waltz on the radio in the kitchen came to an end. "Kimigayo," the national anthem, played twice, and Radio Syonan fell silent. A breeze ran through from the inner courtyard and the pit-pat of rain began on the tiles. Joan, a basket of sewing on her lap, looked over at Tante Helga.

"Auntie," she said, "any idea why we can't find Martin's birth record?"

Tante Helga turned the pages in the album, occasionally resting a finger on a photograph. The brandy had dulled her. Martin could see by the sagging folds of her face in repose that she was half-drunk.

"Probably because he's a bastard," she said, and smiled at an old memory and an ancient, long-dead face.

CHAPTER TEN

Hayashi entered the offices of the Custodian of Enemy Property in the Supreme Court Building. The man he sought was Deputy Custodian Lieutenant Shigeo Nomura, a small, bony man with thick glasses somewhere in his early thirties. Nomura bowed deeply. Sweat beaded his upper lip. "Keibu-san, how can I help you?"

Hayashi motioned him to sit and put the picture of the dead woman on the desk. Nomura looked at it and shifted in his seat. "What happened?"

"Do you know this woman?"

"Yes. It looks like Eva Abraham. Oh. Terrible. What happened?"

"Never mind that just now. You saw active duty?"

"Yes, sir. Signals Unit with the Twenty-Fifth Army. I was given this post after the victory."

Despite his eyesight, Hayashi realized, Nomura had been on the front line of what must have been a series of incredibly fast-moving and bloody battles. Despite his unprepossessing appearance, he could think on his feet.

"Tell me about Eva Abraham."

"Oh, sir. I haven't done anything."

"That remains to be seen. Just start at the beginning."

Nomura took a large white handkerchief and wiped his upper lip and brow. He might have been nervous or just bloody hot. It was bloody hot. Kano moved his chair under the ceiling fan. "I met her because I had some paperwork for her to sign."

"Explain."

"Yes, sir. The job of this office is to register and record all the enemy property seized by the government. All owners of seized property are to be found if possible and sign their property over to the bureau for the duration of the war. In return we make an inventory of their furniture, furnishings, cars, and so on. We are meticulous. In the course of this duty, I had to find Mrs. Abraham and summon her to this office."

"She came? She signed."

"Yes, sir. None of them really like doing it, but since officers have already moved in, most of them are happy that something official is registered at least. We are scrupulous."

"What if you can't find their owners?"

"In that case we simply record all the details. We keep all the deeds we find here and all cash and jewelry, gold, and so on."

"And what are you going to do with them?"

"Guard them, manage them. Until the end of hostilities. The houses, the furniture, are rented out to the military or civil personnel. A large part of the assets in Syonan are industrial or agricultural." Nomura sat back, steepling his hands. "The factories, mines, and the rubber and pineapple plantations, for example, are currently being regularized. We are very busy."

Kano contemplated this. What a strange thing was war. Men and women were expendable, but property was sacrosanct. The houses, cars, and bank accounts of dead or fled civilians were guarded in some bizarre governmental game. Those that weren't plundered, of course. It all seemed quite futile.

"Can anyone come to you to register their properties?"

"It is obligatory. They must bring deeds or proof of ownership and pay any debts."

Nomura looked far too relaxed. Kano decided to stiffen him up again. "Tell me about you and Eva Abraham."

Nomura flushed, spots appearing on his cheekbones. He moved to the edge of his seat and mopped his brow. "I invited her to dinner several times. She was happy to get some nice food and show me some of the city. She liked to ride in my car and I liked having her on my arm."

He shot a quick glance at Hayashi. "I am not a handsome man, Keibu-san. And she was very beautiful. It was nice for other men to be envious."

Hayashi leaned back, the better to feel the effects of the fan. He understood. A beautiful, exotic woman on his arm. A perk of victory. "What else did you do?"

"We went to the cinema. We went to the swimming club. I wanted to see her in a bathing suit. Is that very bad?"

Hayashi shrugged. "Take any pictures? In a bathing suit or out?"

Nomura flushed bright red and looked at his hands. "No, Keibu-san. She wasn't like that."

"Nothing sexual?"

Nomura mopped his face. "No. Nothing like that. I believe she liked me and felt safe with me. And I liked her. And she was so beautiful, you know. Like a lovely picture."

Nomura looked down, a movement of sadness creasing his face. This news had shaken him and it felt genuine. Hayashi ran the matter through his mind. Nomura probably afforded Eva Abraham a few good dinners and amusements. An ogle at her in a bathing suit to show her off. In a way she had been playing a dangerous game and Nomura was every kind of fool. Any officer higher than Nomura could have filched her in an instant and neither she nor he would have had any say. It was so naïve he was inclined to believe him.

"Tell me about you, Lieutenant."

Nomura blinked and sat back in his chair. "I was recruited out of the Foreign Language Institute in Tokyo. I was studying English." He glanced at Hayashi, who was staring at the whirring blades of the fan slicing the humid air. "It was in 1937. I was sent here to work in the Echigoya Department Store. You know I had this rustic idea of the south. I was surprised to see how modern the city was. My job was to make maps, take photographs, you see. Roam around on my bicycle. I enjoyed it."

"When did you leave?"

"June 1940. Things became very dangerous in Singapore. There was a lot of ill feeling about China. The Echigoya Department Store closed down. There was a boycott of Japanese goods. So I went back and had to go into the army. Signals Unit."

"Right. Are you married?"

"No, sir."

"Have you any idea who might have killed Eva Abraham?"

Nomura wiped his brow and dabbed his chin. "I don't. But there was a strange thing."

Hayashi stopped staring at the fan and looked at Nomura. "What?"

"Well, when we'd been seeing each other a couple of weeks she told me a story."

"Go on."

"She said that from the back of her house she could look down into the garden of a big mansion on Adis Road called Eu Villa. Mr. Eu had moved to Hong Kong, so the place was empty but very well guarded. One afternoon, she said she saw a couple of the guards carrying chests into the garden."

Nomura looked at Hayashi as if he had said something pithy. Hayashi waited. "She thought no more of it. Her husband was very sick. He died sometime in February. Anyway, she didn't see exactly where they took the chests, but she thought they might have been buried in the bomb shelter at the bottom of the garden."

"All right. Why did she tell you this?"

"She was a bit drunk and I think it was just a good story. But then, suddenly, she said she wanted me to go and get it."

"Did she?"

"Yes. I mean dig it up and share it."

"Good idea. Did you?"

Nomura's eyebrows shot up. "No, of course not. I'm an honest man. Even had I contemplated such a thing, Eu Villa is occupied by Lieutenant General Kawamura, the head of the Syonan Garrison, and his officers. When I told her that, she burst into tears. It was very sad. It felt like she was desperate."

"When did you last see her?"

"Then. That time. I never saw her after that."

Hayashi examined Nomura. He seemed plausible but who knew what darkness was lurking inside this unprepossessing exterior? "So you say. Were you anxious for her? Jealous perhaps? Did you try to find her?"

"No. No, sir."

Hayashi asked about the places he took Eva, then rose. "Lieutenant, I shall make a check on what you have told me. She may have been consorting with anti-Japanese elements. Perhaps they killed her. It would mean your head."

Nomura blanched and swallowed hard. Hayashi left with a small smile of satisfaction.

Back in the office, Hayashi related this information to his deputy.

"Desperate?" Martin said. "She had an apartment and jewelry. Nothing lasts, but why was she desperate just then?"

"I don't know. You'd better speak to the daughter again."

"I will."

Martin looked over at Hayashi, who was now gazing at the Padang. Tante Helga's words still rang in his ears. A bastard! Walter had said nothing, and it was Joan who had demanded to know what she meant, but his aunt's eyes had retreated like frightened kittens into the folds of her skin and she'd rushed to her room hugging the photograph album.

Walter had left the room promptly, and after a period spent staring at each other, Joan and Martin had agreed to speak about it the next day. Martin tried to put it to the back of his mind and concentrate on the matter in hand. "Have you ruled Lieutenant Nomura out, Chief Inspector?"

"No. He was a big man when she was on his arm. He probably felt a fool when she dropped him. I will ask about him. He gave me the names of the restaurants Mrs. Abraham took him to and spoke of one where there was a woman Mrs. Abraham knew. It is a contact." He turned to Martin. "It is a Chinese restaurant over the river. Perhaps you would like to have dinner together tonight."

A knock and Santamaria entered. "Report from Dr. Iyer," he said and handed it to Martin.

Martin ran his eyes down the page. "Well, well," he said. "She definitely died of suffocation. And Dr. Iyer tells us that the widow was pregnant."

"Pregnant?"

"Fourteen to sixteen weeks. Autopsy confirmed it. She was pregnant. But who by?"

"Almost four months pregnant," Hayashi said. "Conceived in January. Not Nomura. Can't be a Japanese."

"No. Dr. Iyer says he can't preserve the body. No embalming fluid. What do you want him to do?"

"Keep her as cool as possible and get a coffin." With a whisk, Hayashi dismissed Martin.

Martin went to the main office and put the autopsy notice on the incident board. Grace Tobin approached, smoothing down her skirt, and stared at the paper. "She was pregnant?"

"Yes."

"Sir, may I tell you something?"

"Yes."

"My brother Colin is a messenger for the Tokko. He has a bicycle and a stamped pass. He can go almost anywhere, and he knows how to get things."

"Does he indeed?"

"Yes. Together we've been able to get some evidence bags, some surgical gloves, baby powder, vinegar, hydrogen peroxide, a set of sable Chinese calligraphy brushes, and a large box of Scotch tape."

Martin frowned. "Have you? All right."

"So, you see, sir, with these things I can take fingerprints on many surfaces. I would like your permission to take prints from the keys found on Mrs. Abraham's body."

"What?"

"Your permission to—"

"Yes, I heard you. What do you mean?"

"Well, we have no forensic experts, but my cousin Francis worked for years as an assistant in the police laboratory. He showed me how to do all kinds of things and he had many books on the subject, which I possess."

"Heavens. Where's Francis?"

"He was killed in the bombing of Singapore Hospital."

Martin paused a moment. "I'm sorry. My brother is missing."

"Yes, sir. What do you think?"

"I'll run it by the detective chief inspector, but I'm pretty sure he'll be okay with it. You're sure you know what you're doing?"

"Yes. And, sir, if Colin can get some microscopes, will you be able to pay for them?"

Martin laughed. "Yes. Why not?"

Hayashi asked no questions. If someone could do forensic work, he didn't care who did it so long as it was reliable. If someone could get microscopes, he would find the funds. Within half an hour, Grace released the keys to Martin with a small smile of triumph.

"Inspector, I understand that the body of Mrs. Abraham cannot be preserved. I would like Constable Santamaria to drive me to the morgue. I think I should take Mrs. Abraham's fingerprints and any other forensic information I can obtain from her body as soon as possible."

"Yes. Good. Also tell Dr. Iyer to get her into a coffin. I think we shall have to proceed to burial after your examination. You up to this, Grace?"

"Oh yes, sir. We're a typical large Irish family. I've dealt often with the lavage and laying out of dead relatives. I enjoy it."

Martin cocked an eyebrow and gazed at Grace. Sweet-faced, nice-looking, slim and neatly presented, yet clearly she had a dark side. Everyone did, of course. Martin called Santamaria and gave instructions, then grabbed the keys and headed out.

At Meyer Mansions, Martin questioned the concierge, awake this time, a middle-aged Indian man with a lazy eye and a harelip. She was out, he said, and, obviously wary, disappeared.

Martin headed to Miriam Abraham's apartment. He knocked. No reply. The third key turned, and he went inside and closed the door behind him. He tried a few doors until he came to one that was locked and tried the keys again. The fourth key turned and the door swung open. He'd pocketed a reel of thread found by Grace for the purpose and now he took one strand and tied it to the front-door key. He then marked the bedroom door key with two threads and entered.

Eva Abraham's bedroom was neat and tidy, the bed made. The wardrobe showed her clothes, elegant and expensive and impeccably organized. Shoes and handbags lined up neatly below each dress. He recalled the dress she had been wearing. It was a pale green and white bamboo silk print with puffed sleeves. Tight fitting with a large skirt and deep pockets. A pair of new green high heels sat under another pale green outfit and an empty hanger next to these seemed to indicate the space where the dress might have been and below it a place for the shoes, which were missing. A green bag that might have matched both these dresses was on the bedside table. There seemed an identity between these ensembles and Eva seemed a woman of fashion. He emptied the contents of the bag onto her bed. A mirrored compact, a lipstick of the color she seemed to have worn on the day of her death, a comb, a purse with something like fifty Straits dollars and change, a pair of sunglasses. That was it.

There were no photographs of any kind in the room. No pictures of Eva with her husband, at her wedding, or with Miriam. No outings by the coast, picnics on the lawn, convivial dinners at Raffles. Nothing. Had she left them behind when they were all evicted? Miriam had told him she had no pictures of Eva either.

He opened a jewelry box on the dressing table that contained a quantity of necklaces, earrings, and bracelets. At the back of one of the bedroom drawers, he found a small address book. He scooped up the stuff on the bed, put it and the address book in the green handbag, took up the jewelry box, locked the bedroom door, and retreated.

When he got downstairs, there was a sudden and violent commotion outside the opaque glass double doors of the lobby. With a resounding thud, a body slammed into them. Behind the glass, like the puppets of a shadow play, he could make out the shapes of soldiers with guns and hear loud Japanese voices. A shot rang out and one of the glass doors shattered in a shower of green glass. The soldiers, shadows no more, grabbed the man by the arms and hauled him away.

Martin peered through the smashed door. The street was deserted. Fear had cleared the area. He stepped outside and looked down at his shoes sitting in blood. A trail of blood led towards the man being thrown into the back of a truck. The Kempeitai headquarters in this area was close by at the YMCA building on Stamford Road, and rumors of what went on inside were rife.

He cursed and moved away, leaving bloody footprints in his wake, wanting, angrily, to leave these marks of shame on the pavements. Thunder rolled in the distance and the wind whipped up. Soon the rain fell hard and furious, the streets were awash, and the blood disappeared.

CHAPTER ELEVEN

The one thing Martin had to say about Kano Hayashi was that he wasn't a man to be hurried. "Sir," he ventured as Hayashi pulled the Vauxhall slowly round a bullock cart and a gaggle of rickshaws and, following Martin's pointing finger, finally crept into Keong Saik Road.

"Yes."

"Did you have a car in Nagasaki?"

"No. It was not necessary."

"Did you drive a police car?"

"I had a driver."

All became clear. "Would you like me to drive you, sir?"

Hayashi shot Martin a look of surprise. "No. I like driving."

Hayashi pulled round three Indian women yakking in the road and skirted a food stall and a bunch of kids.

Martin lit a cigarette and blew bursts of smoke out the window. "Any chance of getting another car?"

"What for?"

"For me."

"What about the police van?"

"It's for bodies and villains. Surely there is a little car somewhere that nobody wants?"

"There may well be a car somewhere, but even if there were, it is most likely that there is no petrol to put in it. We have an allocation."

Martin gave up for the moment.

The Japanese flag fluttering on the bonnet of the car seemed to make little difference to the busy inhabitants of Chinatown. It was the law of humanity that it constantly adjusted to whatever came its way. Once the English had bustled around bothering them; now it was the Japanese. A tragedy of Shakespearean proportions had fallen on the people of Singapore, but what mattered was simply getting through each day.

Patiently, and without once resorting to his horn, crawling round handcarts and hawkers, Hayashi pootled along the road and drew to a halt outside a hot pot restaurant Martin knew as the Marco Polo. Now it was the Kublai Khan and sported its new name in Japanese katakana writing.

Japanese language books had been distributed to the police offices and it was suggested everyone should learn it. Language schools had sprung up and there were ration rewards for earning certificates. The assiduousness with which the Japanese promoted their culture and the speed with which every single street and shop sign in English had been replaced was worthy of their lightning attack down the Malay Peninsula.

The owner of the Marco Polo had been Khoo, a friendly source of information before the war. Martin wondered if he was still here. Leaving Hayashi to park the car with all the speed of a wounded tortoise, he went through to the kitchen.

Khoo grinned as he saw Martin. "Good grief, is that you?"

Martin slapped Khoo on the arm. His wispy beard appeared just a little barer and the eyes wearier, but otherwise he seemed just the same. "How are you?"

Khoo grinned. "Everything's a bit shit, but all things considered not bad."

"How's this working for you?" Martin waved his arm around the kitchen. It was well stocked: a tank of live fish to one side and produce in abundant supply.

"I have a partner. Can't do a thing if you ain't got that."

"Formosan?"

"You guessed it. Mr. Grand he calls himself." Khoo raised an eyebrow and they both smiled.

"Strange times."

Khoo nodded and yelped smartly at one of the staff, a scruffy-looking teenager missing his left ear. "You, boy, wash your hands. Oi, Cookie, get him sorted out."

The boy put his pinky finger up to Khoo when he turned away and Martin smiled.

"Does Mr. Grand do the cooking?"

"Only of the books."

They both laughed.

"Mr. Grand changed the name. Seems that Mongols ruled China for a hundred years."

Ah Loy's quip came to Martin's mind. The dismayed Chinese had thought that the Mongol invasion would be over by Christmas. Smart aleck.

"Makes the Japanese happy," Khoo said, "so they love to eat here. He procures and makes sure we are left alone and well patronized. For this he takes only fifty percent of the profit and I do all the work. I believe Mr. Grand has many restaurants and businesses. I'm not his only lover."

Martin smiled. Khoo was always upbeat. "Your family?"

Khoo shrugged. "All right. We made it through the bombing at my cousin's farm in Bedok. I couldn't believe the surrender. I watched those lines of British soldiers going by and, you know, oddly, I felt, well, you know."

"Maybe just the devil you know. So mixed clientele."

"Fridays, Saturdays, Sundays, Japanese only. Closed on Monday for cleaning in the morning and Japanese lessons in the afternoon. The Japs are sticklers for cleanliness. We're all supposed to go to the lessons. Some go, some don't. The teacher's a Chinese guy who barely speaks it better than us and couldn't care less." Khoo shrugged. "Rest of the week general population, mostly Formosans, Korean, some Chinese if they're doing business with those guys. You still with CID?"

"Yep. Got a Japanese boss name of Hayashi. We're eating here tonight."

Martin took a photo of the dead Eva from his pocket. Khoo looked at it and winced. "Not nice."

"No. Recognize her?"

Khoo took a closer look. "Yeah, maybe."

"Did you ever see her with a Jap?"

"No. But I spend all my time in the kitchen these days. Have to watch pilfering. Food theft is a big thing. Can't wander round and socialize like I used to. Don't really want to anyway."

"No. Who might?"

"I'll send May to your table."

May. The woman who knew Eva Abraham. The woman they'd come to speak to. "Yes, good."

When he emerged from the kitchen, he caught sight of Hayashi through the haze of cigarette smoke and joined him at a table set away from the main dining area. A large party of Formosans were noisily consuming beer, but it was early and many tables were still awaiting patrons.

May came over. She walked with a slight limp, somewhat plain in looks but slim with clear brown skin and dark, glossy hair pulled back into a tight plait that ran down her back. Her blouse was short-sleeved. Her right arm was bandaged from elbow to wrist. She bowed to Hayashi and greeted him in what sounded to Martin like pretty good Japanese.

Hayashi smiled, evidently pleased, and put a photo of Nomura on the table. "You are May Desker? You know Eva Abraham, I think, and possibly this man?"

May nodded. "Yes. That is Nomura-san. He comes with Eva."

"How did you know Eva Abraham?" Martin asked.

She hesitated. "Is she in trouble?"

Martin glanced at Hayashi, who nodded. "I'm sorry to say that Mrs. Abraham was killed a few nights ago."

May's eyes shot open and her hand went to her mouth. Tears sprang and she rapidly wiped them away, trying to bring herself under control.

Hayashi rose. "It is a shock. I'm sorry. Please go and compose yourself."

May bowed and rushed away. Hayashi's gaze lingered on her as she left. "Poor woman."

She returned a few minutes later, composed.

"Would you sit down for a moment, please, miss?" Hayashi asked.

"Arigato," she said and sat, putting her hands in her lap.

"What happened to your arm, May?" Martin said.

"Fat. Hot fat. I was in the kitchen and brushed the pan. Splashed me."

Easy enough to check up on. "I see. May, what did you do before the war?"

"I was working in the main post office at Fullerton. My boss was Mr. Anderson."

Her eyes slid to Hayashi and away as if she had forgotten to shut up about the English. Everyone knew the Japs got furious if you talked about the English.

Hayashi, however, nodded and smiled at her and she relaxed. "But now you are a waitress," he asked. "You did not return to the post office?"

"No. I needed work. The government offices were not yet open, so I came here."

"Perhaps you would consider returning to the civil service?" Kano said.

This seemed wildly off subject. Martin frowned.

"I would like that. Perhaps when my Japanese improves."

"Let's talk about Mrs. Abraham," Martin said.

May bit her lip but remained calm. "Yes, of course." Her voice thickened and she looked as though she might again begin to cry.

Hayashi put up his hand. "Let's leave this for now. We shall eat first."

She bowed to both men and left. Martin let it go but thought it peculiar. It was always best to strike while the witness was off-balance. Still, he had no authority to say, and he was immediately distracted by the arrival of food.

A bowl of hot charcoals was placed in the middle of the table and the hot pot filled with boiling spiced water set above it. A large platter of thinly sliced beef and pork, shrimp, fish, and vegetables was set down along with a bowl of egg noodles and dishes of pickles, sesame paste, and sambal. It was a feast. Both men picked up their chopsticks.

When they'd gotten through half the food, they paused and ordered beer. This time May smiled at them and seemed calmer. But by now she was very busy. Martin could honestly say that this was the most normal life had felt for a long time. The tables had filled up and the Formosans had burst into raucous song.

Martin lit a cigarette. "Thank you for this wonderful meal."

"You're welcome. The municipality is paying." Hayashi sat back. "Are you married, Martin?"

"No."

"I am a widower. My wife died almost five years ago." Hayashi took out his wallet and put a small photograph on the table. "That is my wife, Yukiko, my daughter, and two sons. My eldest boy is nineteen and the younger seventeen." Hayashi's finger rested on the face of the girl. "Yoko was my first child. She gave us two grandsons."

Martin heard the change in his voice. Yoko was not alive: that was obvious. But Hayashi did not elaborate. Sorrow. Martin's thoughts flew to Michael and a lonely death in a dark jungle. Suddenly the orangutan appeared out of nowhere: the ape in the officer's helmet he'd bumped into on the jungle track that had spooked him so much he'd fallen into the ditch. Had the animal survived? That bizarre encounter had saved his life and Martin desperately hoped it had.

Another photo. Martin saw two little grandsons surrounded by numerous relatives. "You have a large family."

"Yes. My mother is still alive. She lives with her two sisters and their children. Since I was ordered here, my sister and her husband take care of my children. My grandchildren live with their father's family in Hiroshima. I am fortunate in many ways. How about you?"

The question suddenly made him nervous. He didn't want to talk about his family and particularly not about Michael. "Two brothers. One married, two nieces."

Hayashi put away the photographs and drank his beer. "Do you believe there is life after death, Martin?"

Martin paused. Now what? What did the man want to hear? Was this the same as the bombed-out buildings? It was impossible to say, but what other choice but to answer honestly? "No. This is it. This is our only chance to find happiness, to do some good. I suppose that's what I think."

"Yes. I too believe that. My wife and her family are Presbyterians. Most of the men in my family follow Zen practice." He laughed. "Though not very assiduously."

Martin smiled. Most of his mother's Indochinese family were Buddhists, though Maman's mother had converted on marriage to Christianity and as far as he knew his mother had become Protestant when she'd married.

"My elder boy will be twenty in eight months," Hayashi continued. "He will then have to join up. He wants to be in the navy like his uncle. He is anxious to go to war."

"Because he doesn't know what it means."

Hayashi looked at Martin. "He does not know what it means. And nothing I can say matters. He wants to die for Japan."

"*Dulce et decorum est pro patria mori.*"

"That is Latin, is it not? I studied classical European art. There was some Latin but I don't really understand it."

Classical European art? Really? Well, why not? He was an Asian lad who learned Latin. Anything was possible.

"It means how sweet and right it is to die for your country. It's by Horace, a Roman poet. But it is also the title of a poem I learned at school about the Great War in Europe."

"Tell me this poem, if you please."

"Good grief. It's been a while. It's by a young man who was a soldier in the trenches of France during a terrible gas attack."

"I've read about this war but I don't know this poem."

"I can't recall the beginning at all, just the end. Because it struck me as very powerful and ends with that Latin phrase. So I remembered it. Let's see."

Martin saw himself again behind a school desk in short pants nervously reciting the poem to Mr. Stevens, the sensitive, poetic English master. Most of their teachers had been grumpy, super-cilious types desperate to beat some proper Englishness into mixed-blood boys, but Mr. Stevens had been kind and instilled in him a love of English literature and amateur dramatics.

"If you could hear, at every jolt, the blood come gurgling from corrupted lungs, obscene as cancer, bitter as—mmm—of vile sores on innocent tongues, my friend, you would not tell with such high zest, to children ardent for some desperate glory, the old lie; dulce et decorum est pro patria mori."

Martin felt a quick pride in having dredged the damn thing up and took a long drink of beer. He watched Hayashi contem-plate this, apparently chewing it over in his mind.

"The old lie. So, he saw war and knew. My boy is that child ardent for desperate glory, but I cannot change anything nor would he believe it a lie. Japan is full of old lies."

"The world is full of lies, old and new. The British lied to us. Governments lie to the people."

Hayashi nodded. "Yes. Truth is the mortal enemy of the lie. And so, truth is the enemy of the state. We cannot change those lies, can we?" He gazed at Martin. "Though we know what they are. But some lies we can change. I know the mayor wants to solve this case. But I want to solve it too. I sometimes think that if I can solve every case, give justice to every victim, then perhaps I can gain merit and save my children." Hayashi's voice thickened. "And my grandchildren."

Merit. A Buddhist concept. Good deeds, honorable thoughts, these were among the actions that accrued merit like credit in a bank account. The detective chief inspector wanted to pass those credits spiritually to his sons as a sort of protection. It wasn't any more outlandish than believing in prophets or men rising from the dead. He too wanted to solve this crime, not for a son but for his poor beleaguered city. And maybe for Irene. And his mother. He wanted justice for those he loved. So did Kano Hayashi.

"Then, sir, we shall." Martin smiled and picked up his chopsticks. "After dinner."

The restaurant slowly emptied, as did the hot pot. Martin finished the beer, his stomach full of food and his mind of purpose. "Perhaps I should speak to the waitress alone? Do you think?"

Hayashi looked at his watch. It wasn't a Rolex but a Seiko. Martin looked at his own timepiece, not a wristwatch but a silver J. W. Benson fob watch. His wristwatch had been removed by marauding Japanese foot soldiers within a few days of the surrender. He had found the forgotten fob watch among his things. An heirloom or something, he recalled, given to him by his mother, but unappreciated then for its lack of fashion. He had chucked it into a drawer and forgotten it.

Only later, when he needed a timepiece, had he appreciated not only that it would be safe from theft by its concealment in his pocket but also that it was very fine. On the back it was engraved with the words "for my son," and those words had oddly touched his heart. He was not the son it was destined for, but it spoke of a bond, which he liked. He hadn't been able to ask his mother where it had come from. All that came too late.

It was ten p.m. Tokyo time. The evening curfew had just been extended to midnight, which, after all, was really only ten thirty Singapore time. The Japanese had recently reopened the entertainment centers and advertised for workers and patrons. Restrictions had eased and the authorities encouraged the locals to get out and about and spend their money. Opium was available for sale at their outlets and gambling dens licensed. A certain bizarre commerciality in this, the great emporium of the East, had descended on the city.

"Yes. I will see you tomorrow," Hayashi said.

"Thank you again, sir."

Martin went to the kitchen. Khoo was locking food away in cupboards and the cooks and waitresses were cleaning up and sharing the leftovers. The kid with one ear stared at him, then went back to his mopping. Martin indicated May, who was finishing her meal. "The arm. What happened?"

"Burn. We can get rushed in here. An accident. She knocked the pan."

"Bad?"

"Fat splashes. They hurt. I didn't see it, but she was pretty quick. She knows how to deal with things. Clever girl, good worker."

He joined May as she finished her meal. "Speak to me."

"What happened to Eva?"

"She was found bashed in an abandoned building. Robbed."

"Oh. Oh. Bashed? Was it because…?"

"Because what?"

"Well, she came here quite a lot with Nomura-san. Nothing out of the ordinary. Then one night… Well, she knew I lived in Chinatown. She asked if I knew anyone who could be of service to her. Course I don't really know anyone like that, but there is this woman, Neo, who's the girlfriend of this one guy, Hong. We live in the same building."

"She wanted to hire this Hong?"

"Yes, I think so. To do what, I don't know. Oh, do you think that's what got her killed?"

"It could be."

"Oh. I'm so sorry."

"Not your fault, May. When do you get off?"

"Fifteen minutes."

"All right. I'll walk back with you and you can point this Neo out to me."

Martin produced two packets of 555s. She frowned. "No. I want to help. That's all."

She turned away. Martin passed the cigarettes to Khoo. A gesture of goodwill that he wouldn't forget. She'd surprised him and he liked her for it. He returned to the restaurant and made some notes.

When May joined him, they set off deeper into the tenement streets of Chinatown. Before the war, this had been the territory of the ruthless Tong triads. Now it was knee-deep in patrolling Japanese sentries and the gangs had disappeared. Here two hundred people could occupy one shophouse, the cubicles of whole families, hutches no bigger than a cupboard, with only one tap and one squat toilet for them all. It was dirt-poor and filled with disease and misery, rich pickings before the war for criminal recruitment. Currently it was a mass of bombed-out buildings and here and there amid the rubble squatters' fires blazed. The smell of the drains was agricultural. It was dark and only the light of the moon guided them. But May was surefooted and knew her way.

They entered a grimy tenement on Temple Street. The atmosphere was gagging. Cooking fat and excrement. He followed

May through the long, dark, narrow corridor between the two rows of cubicles, lined up like rabbit hutches, and covered from the passage by a ragged curtain. The only light was that which occasionally seeped, like sewage, from beneath these curtains.

They climbed to the next floor, picking over filth, eyes swiveling to him from the wakeful and wary inhabitants of the cubicles. It was every bit as smelly, crowded, airless, and depressing as the one below. May unlocked the door to her room at the front of the building. She turned at the door. Behind her he could see clothes hung from hooks on the wall, her small toiletries, soap, and towel, on a chair. It was neat, tidy, and clean. A mosquito net draped the small bed. The faint odor of incense hung in the room, covering the outside smell the best it was able.

"I'm lucky," she said as she saw the look on Martin's face. "I'm single and this is all mine. I have a window. I can breathe the air from the street, catch a breeze. I have a door I can lock. It costs more but I don't care. I don't get rats."

"I'm sorry."

"Don't be. I got this room because of someone else's misfortune. Her husband went to the Chinese registration and never came back. Did you know about that? What the Chinese call the Sook Ching?"

Martin frowned. "What do you mean?"

"The purge. The roundup, whatever you call it. They murdered thousands of Chinese. She told me about it. Three days of hell, right after the surrender. She was interrogated. The Japanese let her leave with her children, but her husband and her brother were taken away in trucks."

"I don't know about this."

May shook her head. "No. Neither did I. She had four children and no money, so she had to move out even of this tiny stink hole. God knows where. I can't think about it. Nobody can care for anyone but themselves."

She gave a quick, bitter smile. "And that Khoo is all right. He pays and I get food. I'm studying Japanese. When I speak to Japanese officers, they're so thrilled they leave me a huge tip. I give a quarter to the cooks. The rest is mine. With good Japanese, I can eventually get a job in the government offices."

She pointed back down the hall. "Last cubicle on the left. You didn't hear it from me." She shut the door.

Martin gazed around him. He couldn't in his wildest dreams imagine Eva Abraham entering such a place. The last cubicle on the left was dark. Most people were sleeping, though in some cubicles a wavering light shone. Just enough for him to see his way. Did he want to disturb this woman in her slumbers? God, it was bad enough having to live here. He felt hot and claustrophobic and toyed with just coming back tomorrow, when he heard the sound of snoring. Deep snoring, coming from the cubicle. He pulled back the curtain expecting to see a woman and by the dim light he saw a much larger shape.

Was there a mistake? Had he gotten the wrong cubicle? He was sure it was the one May had indicated, the last one on the left. It was in that moment of indecision that shouting began from somewhere in the building. A man and woman screaming at each other. The cries of children added to the noise and the snoring in the cubicle stopped. A man stepped out and lit a cigarette. He spewed out a loud volley of invective in Hokkien to the hall in general, then noticed Martin. More words, screamed at full force. Martin vaguely recognized them as something like "What the fuck do you want?" or it might have been "Fuck off, you dickhead." That was pretty standard.

"Are you Hong?" he said in Cantonese.

The man moved so fast Martin had no time to react. He flung himself headlong down the stairs. By the time Martin had followed and gotten to the street, he was gone.

He called it a night. He was never going to get back to Katong before curfew, so he walked back to the office, fed up, wishing he had a car and a flat, bowed to the sentry, showed his pass, unlocked the office, used the bathroom, turned on the fan, drank a glass of Hayashi's brandy, lay down on the battered old leather sofa in the incident room, and went to sleep.

CHAPTER TWELVE

The Malay waiter poured the champagne into the glasses, settled the bottle back into the ice bucket, and bowed. The fans ruffled the palms. On the far side of the courtyard of the hotel a small orchestra of Hungarian musicians played a polka. Hayashi disliked polkas— what was there to like?—but most of the other patrons of the courtyard were tapping their feet.

"Dom Pérignon 1932," Shinzo said. "I heard that the British governor ordered all the booze in town smashed just before the surrender. Glad some of it escaped, aren't you?" Shinzo smiled at Hayashi and raised his glass. "To the emperor and to General Yamashita, the Tiger of Malaya."

The day had been long. The rally on the Padang in the searing heat. Thousands of children waving flags and singing "Aikoku Koshin Kyoku," a fatuous and tuneless patriotic march composed in the thirties, which would have been damn difficult to memorize for the native kids. He certainly couldn't do it. Yamashita had tears in his eyes at the sight and even more on hearing the massed voices of these southern children sing "Kimigayo."

At the hotel afterwards, Yamashita had greeted them all in a potbellied strutting manner and made a little speech that he hardly listened to. He'd caught sight of Shinzo Asanari, a senior Domei News Agency correspondent who'd been transferred as the editor of the *Syonan Times*. They'd been at college together in Tokyo and kept up with each other through the changing times. They chatted about the past, avoiding in every way the current lives they were leading. It had been a joy to be with an old friend, and Hayashi had a swelling feeling of hope that it might be possible to have thinking and cultured friends here, even to enjoy it.

"Old friend," Shinzo said, "did you imagine we would ever be drinking French champagne in a luxury hotel in Singapore? A Singapore which is now Japanese? Four months ago, I was freezing my arse off in North China."

Hayashi contemplated Shinzo. "I'd rather it had cost less blood."

Shinzo's smile disappeared. "I can assure you this is bloodless compared with what is going on in China."

"Can you bear it, Shinzo? Can we get through this with our souls intact?"

Shinzo contemplated the bubbles in his glass. "We've argued about this before. There was no choice. What did we learn from the crushing of China, Kano, except that weakness gets you annihilated, humiliated by Western imperial powers, forced to sign disgraceful treaties? We learned that to be strong, to not be crushed, you had to act like the imperialists, you had to be a great power."

Shinzo drained his glass then refilled it, the foam spilling over. "And we learned it fast. We grew our military and learned their game. How they loved us when we helped the Allied powers pick off Germany's Asian colonies in their European war." Shinzo leaned forward. "Eh? What did we do that was any different to England and France then? Until it didn't suit them anymore. The West taught us to play poker; then, when we won all the chips, they declared the game immoral."

Hayashi shrugged.

Shinzo threw open his hands. "It doesn't matter now. We're on this road and idealism is not in demand, Kano. Patriotism is. Japan needs resources. That is the reality. Look, old friend, I don't want to argue."

"No." Hayashi smiled.

Shinzo gave a bark of laughter. "Do you think the British are all sitting in Changi wondering what happened?"

"I should think so. I don't know what happened. Do you?"

"Course I do. They underestimated us. It's as simple as that. Arrogance, stupidity, and a collective denial of what lay before their eyes. Rome and the barbarians. China and the Western imperialist powers. It's no different. They thought that what had always been would always be. To think that way was their doom and the consequence of their own making." Shinzo lit a cigarette and blew smoke. "Personally, I intend to spend my time writing whatever my masters decree for the newspaper and some shatteringly beautiful poetry, read books, and try not to think about consequences."

Hayashi smiled. "I, too, will read books."

"And you will right wrongs, Kano. That is what you like to do best. Fix all the broken things."

"I can't right all the wrongs."

"No, but you will try, my friend. You believe in natural justice. For a policeman, I always thought you had less respect for the law than you probably should. I think you know what I mean."

"Laws are made by men. They are subject to change. Justice is not always found in the law."

"Yes. A higher law exists. For me it is the law of survival. I have the absolute right to survive and will do what it takes to do so. I'm a selfish man. But you aren't. You believe in justice before survival, I think."

"I have the same instincts for survival as you do."

"Though not quite so finely honed. You're prepared to take risks for the sake of justice." Shinzo shot a sharp glance at Kano. "The death of your son-in-law, for example. Do you have anything to say on that subject?"

"An accident."

"Ah yes, an accident. His death gave you a sort of peace. I remember it well."

"It is late, and you are a little drunk."

"I was there, Kano. I was reporting in Nagasaki. His death was high-profile. The nephew of Iwasaki Koyata, the owner of Mitsubishi, of course it was high-profile. And dodgy. Very dodgy. If you did it, I don't blame you. This is between you and me."

"You should stick to poetry, Shinzo. Your imagination is your greatest asset. I will say good night."

Shinzo plucked the bottle from the ice bucket. "Have it your own way. But wait a moment. I have to speak to you about this murder case of yours. The woman."

"What about it?"

"The mayor has asked me to report on it. It's also a very high-profile case. And, by the way, it is not just the mayor. The Marquis Fujimoto, our newly appointed civil governor of Malai and, as you may or may not know, the brother-in-law of the emperor also takes a personal interest. Solomon Abraham was an old friend of his. A friend of Nippon and the richest man in Asia. And his wife was beautiful and young. So long as there is no Japanese involvement it will be front-page news. Show the population that justice is being done. And the punters love a juicy murder with a femme fatale. Helps them forget the war. There is no Japanese involvement, I presume?"

"Not as far as I know."

"Good, then keep me informed. The mayor needs this to impress Tokyo and please the emperor. Solve it and you'll make the mayor and the marquis happy." Shinzo refilled his glass and plopped the bottle into the icy slush. He gazed at Hayashi. "And justice may be done. Or at least seem to be done, eh?"

In his room, Hayashi took out the photograph of his dead wife, Yukiko, and Yoko, his dead daughter. Yukiko had been related to a distant branch of the Iwasaki family and Yoko had been sought in marriage by a nephew of the head of Mitsubishi, an engineering officer working in the research division of the navy's Kure shipyard at Hiroshima. It had seemed the right decision. The young man came recommended by his illustrious family. Yoko wanted to marry.

But that marriage had become the biggest regret and the greatest disaster of his entire life. He let the tears flow down his cheeks, but no quantity of tears could wash him clean.

The first sight of Yoko after a year had sent shock waves through him and Yukiko. There was no one to appeal to, though he had written to the husband many times in desperation. Polite, quiet letters filled with honorifics. He felt a scream leap into his throat and threw his hands across his mouth. He was ignored. Once married, Yoko belonged to her husband and his family. She had slipped out of his grasp and turned into a dead-eyed wraith.

One morning, the husband had simply bashed Yoko to death. For what reason, no one would ever know. There was no inquiry, nor even outrage. A wife chastised. An accident. That was all. A husband's right. Kano had been to the morgue and seen her broken face, her jaw punched up into her nose, her teeth knocked out, her eye sockets fractured. His firstborn child. His little girl.

He sobbed with all his body, hardly able to draw breath in the agony of it. He had done this. He had abandoned her to this fate. He could not save her and he should have saved her and he knew he would never have been able to save her and it ate his insides like acid. She had been raised to be polite and placid, obedient and loving, a perfect wife, a perfect daughter. They had made her that way. They never spoke of it, but he knew Yukiko felt that way too. She gave up eating and died within a year.

Yoko had not even put up a hand to defend herself. He had searched her body like a frenzied thing. No defensive wounds on her hands or arms, no broken nails. Just the testimony of dozens of bruises old and new and her jaw punched into her nose.

He rested his face in water in the sink.

The law of karma says that no one can escape the consequences of their actions. The husband, all alone in the hush of the small, locked, top secret division of the Kure shipyard, had been proudly inspecting the construction of Japan's first midget submarine when it slipped from its scaffold, crushing his legs. His death, solitary, slow, and painful, the newspapers reported, lasted all the hours of the long night.

Hayashi put the photograph away and went to bed.

CHAPTER THIRTEEN

Martin jolted awake, escaping the recurring dream of his youth, arms held out to his mother as she sank below the waves. It wasn't always the sea; sometimes it was the earth swallowing her up or a descent into cavernous darkness. Whatever it was, he could never get to her. In this dream she seemed even more nebulous and ghostly, as if she might disappear entirely.

The morning was soft and hushed. The office was empty. He looked at his watch. Six o'clock. He lay back and tried to make sense of what Joan had revealed to him in her telephone call yesterday afternoon.

She had cornered Tante Helga and made her tell what she knew. There had been another man. Their mother had been unfaithful to their father and Martin was the child of an entirely different man. Tante Helga did not know this man. She just knew of the business because Ernst had written to her after Maman had left him, asking her, his sister, to come to Singapore to help with his household. She had refused. He had married an entirely unsuitable half-blood woman well out of his social bracket and had to live with the consequences. She heard no more. Then she had discovered through a mutual acquaintance that her brother was planning a divorce because Marie was pregnant by another man. She had written to Ernst, consumed by the horror and shame that had devolved onto her. The family had become the subject of gossip. He had never replied.

About Michael, Tante Helga was certain. He was Ernst's son. The divorce had not happened. The next time Ernst had written to her was to tell her that Marie had come back, he had accepted her shame and repentance with the grace of God, and Marie was pregnant. Joan had confided to Martin that she thought there might have been much harsher words between sister and brother that his aunt did not wish to reveal.

That hardly mattered. What mattered, they both agreed, was that Martin was the little middle bastard. Whether he was shocked or disgusted, Walter refused to speak of it. Joan simply said it made no difference, but those were words of kindness merely. Of course it made a difference. It had to. He felt the earth shake. He no longer had any idea who he was.

No matter how much this bothered him, Martin knew he couldn't dwell on it right now. The immediate issue was not who this unknown father might be, but the fact that he desperately needed proof of his birth to Ernst and Marie Bach for the Tokko. Without it he was doomed. The Japs were obsessed with identity and regularly killed anyone who misled them.

He rose from the sofa, went into his office, and rang Ah Loy. "Hello, Inspector."

"Ah Loy, I need a birth certificate." Despite being alone in the room, Martin instinctively looked round and lowered his voice. "I'll come to your place at seven tonight. You going to be there?"

"Yes. Singapore time or Tokyo time?"

"Wristwatch time, for Christ's sake."

Everybody in Singapore as far as he knew kept wristwatch time on Tokyo time and house clock time on Singapore time.

Martin hung up, thoroughly irritated.

CHAPTER FOURTEEN

Martin made a coffee and waited for the others to trickle in. As soon as Ibrahim arrived, he sent him to Meyer Mansions. "Bring in Miriam Abraham and David Weber. I asked them to come in on Monday and they haven't. I don't mind a bit of a heavy hand."

He wrote the address in Chinatown on a slip of paper and handed it to Seah. "Get over there and find a Neo something who lives in one of the last cubicles on the first floor and has a low-life boyfriend called Hong. He scarpered like a guilty rat when I tried to speak to him last night. Mrs. Abraham may have contacted this Hong for purposes of digging up buried treasure. Or something else. Find them. And search her cubicle."

Martin approached Grace. "Where's Santamaria?"

"DCI Hayashi asked him to get some things for him," she said.

"What?"

"I don't know."

"All right. Grace, did you get evidence from the victim's body?"

"Yes, sir. You said she might have scratched her attacker. I cleaned her nails and cut them. Each of them is in a different packet. I have put the torn nail in a separate packet. I would like to take these things to the hospital and see if we can find any blood. The blood laboratory is up and running and the technician there is very good."

"Yes. Good." Martin went to the jewelry box and the handbag on the evidence table. "Also, that box is Mrs. Abraham's jewelry box. I want a list of everything in it. And that is her bag. Inside it is her address book. Do some fingerprints right away, please. I want to have a look at the book."

Grace smiled. "Sir, I need to take everyone's fingerprints in the office for exclusion purposes. Can you speak to the detective chief inspector?"

"Yes."

Hayashi came in fifteen minutes later. Martin got the go-ahead for the fingerprints, then filled him in about Hong.

"You think this Hong killed her?"

"Not out of the question. Sounds like he's a tough customer. I've sent Constable Seah to find him and Sergeant Ibrahim to bring in Miss Abraham and the fiancé."

"All right. I have some news from the mayor." Hayashi sat at his desk and took out a notebook. "First of all, the new civil governor of Malai, Marquis Fujimoto, has thrown his authority behind finances for this case. Apparently, he was a close friend of Sir Solomon Abraham. Money to find forensic equipment and microscopes."

Hayashi looked at Martin and whisked. "This will be a big case. A showcase for the people. Justice being done. The mayor wants to show Tokyo how valuable the civilian authorities are and how the local population is happy to cooperate with us. He wants to please the emperor and make the authorities in Tokyo pay attention."

"I see his point. But does he want anyone or the real one?

"I imagine he doesn't care. But I want the real one."

Martin nodded.

"The commissioner will be giving an interview with the press later today. It would be good if we could find this man Hong."

"You know, sir, things would be a lot smoother if I had a car."

Hayashi smiled. "Unfortunately, petrol is currently more valuable than justice. The oil fields in the southern territories have not been restored."

This sentence had been delivered in the most conversational manner. He might have been talking about delayed mail deliveries or a shortage of paper. But it was oil. Oil fields. Petroleum. Did Hayashi understand what these words meant? It was April and since the surrender in February, the *Syonan Times* had reported nothing but relentless victories for Japan as they overran the Dutch East Indies and landed in New Guinea, knocking on Australia's northern shores. But now came this tiny sliver of news that the Allies had destroyed the oil fields or at least the refineries of the Indies that supplied Japan's war machine to such an extent that they were not operational. He wasn't sure what that meant, but he was pretty sure he wasn't meant to know it.

A shrill scream came from the outer room and Martin left Hayashi and went to the reception area. Seah had hold of a Chinese woman.

"This is Neo Kho, sir," Seah said, his glasses sliding down his nose. "And look what else I found." He held up a pair of green leather high heels, old but expensive. The shoes were distorted with bunion marks.

Martin approached Neo. She smelled of musty filth, as if mushrooms were growing in her armpits; hollow-chested, rheumy-eyed, with pockmarked skin and skeletal hands. Martin was certain she was diseased, possible with syphilis or similar. Her life had clearly been one of absolute poverty, living on the margins. That she had been a prostitute was written on her with all the marks that that filthy work left on a woman. That she was an opium addict was no surprise. She'd been half-unconscious when Seah found her.

"And these, Inspector," Seah said with a small air of triumph.

From his pocket he took a pair of jade earrings set in a silver mount. Neo fell into a listless slump.

"How did these earrings and those shoes get into your cubicle, Miss Kho?" Martin said.

"I dunno."

"Perhaps you got them from your mother," Seah said. "An heirloom."

"Shut up."

"Constable, take Miss Kho to the interview room and ask Mary to get some coffee for her."

In the interview room, Martin pointed to a chair and she sat. He offered her a cigarette. She puffed deeply and darted her eyes at him, then around the room. "Nice here, ain't it. How the other half lives."

It was hardly nice. A storeroom, a half window high in the wall through which escape was impossible. That's why it had been chosen for the interview room. A table and two chairs. But it was spotlessly clean. Perhaps that was nice enough in Neo's world.

"Miss Kho," Martin said. "You have nothing to fear. I just want to get to the bottom of this matter. How did the shoes and earrings of Mrs. Abraham, a murdered woman, come into your possession?"

"I didn't do anything."

"I don't think you did. I think your boyfriend did. I think he killed a woman and robbed her and put these things in your cubicle to hide them. Is that right?"

She shook her head, but he wasn't sure whether it was a denial or a flick of despair.

"What is your boyfriend's full name?"

Mary entered and handed Neo a coffee. She drank it, gulping. Martin signaled Mary to stay.

"Just Hong," Neo muttered. "That's what everyone calls him. Ain't seen him for days."

"What do you know about his dealings with Mrs. Abraham? We have a witness who knows that Mrs. Abraham wanted Hong to do something for her."

Neo eyed him through the smoke of her cigarette. Her shoulders sagged.

"Get me some food and I'll tell you."

Martin nodded at Mary, who departed.

"She wanted to meet him," Neo said. "She knew where we could get our hands on some money. She didn't know what she was dealing with. Some bloody toff from up the hill. She's no idea what goes on in our world."

"No. I should imagine not. But she insisted."

"Yeah. Gave me five dollars so course I was happy to help."

She smiled, pleased with herself, revealing stumps of blackened teeth. How old was she? Forty perhaps. She looked seventy.

"I told her to meet him in a coffee shop on South Bridge Road by the Indian temple."

Mary placed a bowl of noodles on the table. Neo fell on it, ravenous, slurping and shoveling. Seah poked his head around the door.

"Sergeant's back. Got the party you asked for and the fiancé with him. Where do you want them?"

"Seah, you stay here. Mary, tell Grace to get their fingerprints. Elimination purposes tell them. Then put them in my office."

He turned his attention back to Neo. "Did Mrs. Abraham meet you in the coffee shop?"

"Yes. Some story about treasure buried on Mount Sophia in a big house up there. She knew where it was. She'd go half share with us but he had to get it."

"The hill's covered in Japanese officers."

"Course it is. But they have servants, don't they? So, they can be bribed or threatened. That didn't worry Hong. Nothing worries Hong if money's involved."

"Did you believe her?"

"Eh. Yeah. Loads of rich people up there burying their money when the bombing began."

"So, what happened?"

"So, Hong said he would do the job."

She shoveled the last of the noodles, burped, and went back to her cigarette.

"Miss Kho. What happened then?"

She shrugged and crossed her skinny legs. Martin began to grow impatient. "What happened?"

She threw him a sour look. "He went to meet her in some place by the hill. She said she'd tell him the name and location of the house, draw a map or something."

"When did they arrange to meet?"

"A few days ago."

"Monday?"

"Yeah. But I ain't seen him since." She laughed. It wasn't pretty. "Maybe she didn't go. Just as well. Stupid rich bitch. He'd have done the job and she'd never've seen him again. Neither would I. If he got his hands on stuff, he wouldn't share with her. That's how stupid the whole thing was. Just didn't know who she was dealing with."

"When did you last see him?"

"I dunno. Friday maybe."

"He was in your cubicle on Wednesday night. He was sleeping."

She looked up and he saw surprise. She was incapable of hiding her reactions.

"Nah. I ain't seen him, I tell you."

"Let me tell you what I think. I think Hong met Mrs. Abraham on Monday morning and having obtained the information about the hidden money, he murdered her and stole her shoes and those earrings at the very least. I believe you are an accessory to murder."

She rose unsteadily from her seat and stared at him.

"I never did. I never did. And he'd never take shoes. Shoes bring bad luck. Why'd he take shoes?"

"Because he's a thief. A rough, murderous man and a greedy woman. You planned it together, didn't you?"

Her face had turned a pale shade of green.

"No. No."

"Then where is he? Give him up or you'll see a very different sort of justice, I can tell you. The Japanese will cut off your head."

She squealed and leapt away from the chair, retreating to a corner.

"Where is he?"

"I don't know. I swear, I don't know."

She collapsed into a heap.

"Constable, take this prisoner to the cells."

Seah threw Martin a startled look. There were no cells in the Municipal Building. The only cells were next door, holding cells for prisoners on trial in the Supreme Court. The courts hadn't yet resumed. They'd be empty, but God knew where the keys might be. Fortunately, it didn't come to that. She gave in.

"He stays with his brother. I ain't seen him for days, I tell you."

"Where?"

She gave them an address in Chinatown, Nanking Street, another street filled with cheap hawker stalls, opium dens, and tenements.

"But she didn't have no jewelry," Neo said, as Seah brought her to her feet and sat her on the chair.

"She never wore no jewelry. Not when I saw her. Except a watch, nothing else. What kind of fool comes to Chinatown in jewels?"

"What was she dressed in the day you met her?"

"Plain dress. Blue maybe. Nothing fancy. She wasn't wearing no bloody jewels."

"What about shoes and a bag?"

"Shoes. Dunno. The bag was blue too. I remember that because she gave me money from it. Crocodile. Nice."

Martin turned to Seah. "Get the sergeant and get around to Nanking Street and find me this Hong."

"Miss Kho," he said. "You have a cigarette. Later you can have some dinner if you're good."

Santamaria came in. Martin left Neo in his charge. Grace stopped him as he crossed the evidence room.

"Inspector, I've got Miriam Abraham's and David Weber's prints. They were cooperative. Also, I've taken prints from the address book and made a list of the names separately on this sheet of paper."

"Thanks. Good work. The Keibu-san approves of taking the fingerprints in the office. He's getting some microscopes."

"Yes, sir. What about the shoes and the earrings?"

"Log them, see what you can find on them. Then, as soon as possible get them to me. I want Miriam Abraham to identify them. And, Grace, get Miss Koh's fingerprints."

Martin examined the names on the paper. There were twenty or so. He ignored various shops and salons, which left around ten. One was marked D. Weber. That left nine. Grace returned with the shoes and jade earrings. She smiled.

"All done. Also finished with Mrs. Abraham. I'm typing up a report for you. There are fingerprints on the shoes and the ear-rings but without microscopes I can't do any kind of analysis or tell you whose they are."

"All right. I understand. Thank you, Grace."

"Do you want me to record the interview, Inspector? I was a court reporter before the war and I have my stenograph machine and paper. I kept them safe at home during the war."

Martin gave a short nod of assent, which belied the surprise and gratitude at the immensity of her disinterested and civic sensibility in the face of chaos. An immensity that she seemed to simply take for granted. She hadn't been sure of the outcome of the war and once released from her duties had simply kept the accoutrements of her employ. Was it natural? Perhaps, but it was in some strange way also a small miracle of life's desire for order and continuity. Of course he wanted a record of the interview. What could be more useful? Grace was suddenly absolutely invaluable.

He put the shoes and earrings into a paper bag, folded the paper with the names, put it in his pocket, and entered his office.

CHAPTER FIFTEEN

The most obvious thing, the thing his eyes went to instantly, was the long scratch on Weber's face and the gash on his right hand.

"Miss Abraham and Mr. Weber. I asked you to come two days ago. Why didn't you?"

"Apologies, Inspector," Weber said. "That was my fault. I couldn't believe what Miriam told me. She was very upset and I needed to offer her comfort. Naturally, I should have come in as you requested. It is entirely my fault."

His presence was considerable. He was about thirty, tall, well-built, and good-looking, with a trimmed beard and a head of wavy black hair. He was confident, educated, and in control. Miriam had chosen a similar dress with white gloves but a different head covering. Less attractive, plainer, less elaborately arranged; a simple snood-like arrangement covering all her hair but without adornment and minus the glamorous veil. She arranged her walking stick, a different one, plain wood, and sat, eyes down, her hands in her lap. Martin addressed Weber. "I asked that you identify the victim, but you did not."

"No, sorry, Inspector. As I said, I couldn't believe any of this. And I wasn't certain where the morgue was. Perhaps I can do that today. Naturally Miriam is reluctant."

Martin put a picture of Eva Abraham on the table. "You can do it now. Is this Eva Abraham? You, too, Miss Abraham."

Miriam flicked her eyes to the photo and looked away. She nodded. Weber also nodded but did not look away. He stared at the photograph in what seemed genuine consternation. "Oh dear. That is Eva. What happened, Inspector?"

Martin put the photo away and pointed to Weber's hand. "We are pursuing inquiries. You have some injuries. How did they happen?"

Weber looked at his hand. "Helping a friend repair his roof. A couple of artillery shells landed on it."

"And your face."

"Same thing. I'm not very handy, really. Fell off a ladder."

"I see. Who is this friend?"

Weber frowned. "Well, I can give you his name, if you'd like."

"I would. And his address, please. When did this happen?"

"Is this important, Inspector?"

"It is routine."

"Monday afternoon."

Martin slid his notepad towards Weber with a pencil. Weber scribbled and shoved it back.

"Thank you. You know of course that courts will soon reopen for civil matters. You were practicing before the war?"

Up to now the Japanese had established barely functioning military courts issuing summary justice for looting and theft. Martin had seen the MAD decree in the *Syonan Times* ordering local lawyers, magistrates, and judges to return to work. That the Military Administration Department had decided, out of ignorance or arrogance, on the acronym of MAD for all their published demands was the cause of local ridicule and quiet satisfaction.

"Yes," Weber said. "I practiced as part of my late father's law firm. Lawyers registered before the occupation may apply to reregister. For the mere sum of five hundred dollars."

He gave Martin a knowing look. Martin did a quick calculation. On the currently reduced wages the Japanese were paying, that would be more than four months of his salary. It was extortion on the part of the municipality to raise funds. And it was a very large sum.

"Do you have five hundred dollars, Mr. Weber?"

"Fortunately, Miriam has advanced me part of that sum. The rest I have from some money which I had the sense to withdraw from the banks in a timely manner."

"That was prescient."

"Just common sense. Anyone could see what would ensue once the Japanese had taken Kuala Lumpur." He said this with a slight arrogant turn of his lip.

"Not everyone," Martin said. "Including the British high command."

"No. Well."

Martin, in sympathy with his opinion of the British, offered Weber a cigarette. Miriam Abraham had yet to say a word.

"You are going to be married," Martin said and smiled. He'd established that Weber was a clever and shrewd man with a lawyer's mind. He was also in charge of this little ménage. He decided to change tack.

Miriam Abraham's face became animated. "Yes," she said. "But there are no rabbis to marry us, they've been interned, and the synagogues closed. Even the civil registry is not open."

"We are waiting for the Japanese to regularize these matters," Weber said. "We have asked for the release of several of the rabbis, those without any European antecedents, which, frankly, is most of them. We wait."

"Ah yes. That is difficult. You are Jewish, Mr. Weber, and German?"

"Yes."

"Can you tell me something about that?"

"My father opened a successful law practice here. In my parents' homeland, we would almost certainly be dead. The Japanese don't much care about religion and thus here I am entirely acceptable as the son of an allied nation. On such things do our fortunes turn."

He gave a small smile. Martin understood that David Weber saw life from behind a veil of educated irony as if it was a series of inevitable setbacks and opportunities and he was ready for whatever turned up. It wasn't a bad attitude to have and he recognized many of those qualities in himself.

"How did you meet?"

Miriam Abraham spoke up. "David was doing some work for my father. We met when I got back from visiting my aunt and uncle in India." She gave Weber a tender glance.

Martin looked at Weber. "What work were you doing?"

"Lawyer business. Somewhat complicated. My late father was Solomon Abraham's lawyer. I took over his affairs."

"We fell in love instantly," Miriam gushed.

Martin thought a fleeting shadow of irritation moved across Weber's face but he might have imagined it. Perhaps he just didn't want his personal life bandied about. Martin understood. He didn't either.

Weber looked at Miriam and smiled. "Miriam is a generous and loving person. I only wish to protect her in these dangerous times. I'm sure you can understand that, Inspector. Perhaps you have a wife, a family you wish to protect. Marriage will do that, and I only wish this ridiculous waiting could end."

Martin let that sit in the air for a moment, while Miriam turned her eyes onto her fiancé. They were a somewhat incongruous pair. He all good looks, confidence, and suavity; she pretty but dull with a bit of the hausfrau about her.

"And Eva Abraham, Mr. Weber. She was a Christian woman. Yet Solomon Abraham married her. What did you think about that? Did you know her?"

"Of course I knew her. Solomon was an elderly man, and I went to his house for all our business together. So, I knew her but she was often out when I went there. As for the marriage, as

I said, he was an old man. It is not hard to understand. A man, at death's door, he did what he wanted, I suppose, took what pleased him."

Miriam sat up, her voice hard. "Eva hardly knew David but she didn't want me to marry him."

"I see. So that's what the arguments with her were about?"

"Not always. But she wasn't my mother and had no right to tell me what to do."

"Why didn't Mrs. Abraham like you, Mr. Weber?"

He shrugged. "Who can say? We rarely spoke. Not me, perhaps, just the thought of me. Not good enough. An employee."

"Mr. Weber, when did you last see Mrs. Abraham?"

"About a week ago. We passed each other in the lobby of Meyer Mansions. She ignored me."

"Be more precise, please. You are a lawyer."

"Yes, of course. Well, let's see. It was the eve of the Sabbath. The twenty-fourth. I came to Miriam so we could light candles and share the evening meal together. It's difficult to keep to ritual in these times, but we try."

"Is that right, Miss Abraham?"

"Yes."

"I see. So, between Friday evening on the twenty-fourth and her death in the early hours of Monday morning, the twenty-seventh, you did not see her again?"

"No. Miriam told me she had left the apartment on Sunday morning and not returned."

"You were not concerned for her safety."

"Well, I'm not sure she was in danger. I understood that she had taken up with a Japanese man."

"Why do you think she had done that? Taken up with a Japanese man?"

"Doubtless it procured certain privileges."

"Did you despise her for doing so?"

David crushed his cigarette into the ashtray on the desk and blew smoke. "Frankly, Inspector, I rarely gave Mrs. Abraham a thought. I knew about her only what Solomon told me."

"And you and Miss Abraham were together all of the evening of Sunday and the morning of Monday, the day Mrs. Abraham died?"

"Yes."

"You said it was difficult living together with your stepmother, Miss Abraham, under these circumstances?"

"Well, only when she got so bossy and nasty about David. And we were so cramped in that small apartment, so … "

"Even though she'd kept you out of Changi?"

It was Weber who answered. "Gratitude can only go so far, Inspector. Miriam was, is, grateful for that, but it didn't change Eva's fundamental objections to our marriage and her attitude to me. That was at the heart of all the disagreements."

"You were angry, Miss Abraham? Angry enough to wish ill to your stepmother?"

Weber rose. "You've no right to make unfounded accusations. Miriam is an innocent young woman. Eva could not stop us getting married. We are both above the age of consent. There was nothing she could do, so she didn't matter. It was simply a matter of time. If the war hadn't intervened, we'd be married by now. We were together during the time you say Eva was killed. We have nothing to do with any of this."

"Sit down, Mr. Weber. This is a police interview. I can't see you practicing law if you don't cooperate with the authorities."

Weber sat, his face fixed in stony affront. Martin let them stew for several moments. Weber made a good point, like the lawyer he was. Without the surrender and ensuing mess, they'd be married by now. Nothing Eva Abraham could have done would have stopped that. He put the paper bag on the table and removed the shoes and earrings.

Miriam Abraham clasped her hands and stared.

"You recognize these things?"

She nodded and looked down. "Yes. Oh goodness. How awful. They are Eva's."

"The shoes and the earrings?"

"Yes. The jade earrings are part of a set my father gave her the year I came back. He had them made especially."

Martin replaced them in the paper bag and removed it from sight. "Miss Abraham, I think that the body of Mrs. Abraham will be available for burial in the not-too-distant future. Have you made arrangements?"

"I'll deal with that, Inspector," Weber said.

"How long before I can unlock Eva's room?" Miriam said.

"Is it important to unlock Eva's room?"

"Well, there are some items. She had a lot of jewelry."

The sight of the jade earrings had reminded her perhaps of Eva's jewelry. Well, too bad.

"I see. Not just yet. Perhaps you can both help me with something else."

He took the paper from his pocket and put it in front of them on the table.

"Please look at the names here and tell me if you know any of them."

She picked it up. "Most of them are my father's friends. Most of them left." She passed the paper to Weber. He tapped his own name and then another. "This one, Rose Shultz. Shultz was Eva's maiden name."

Martin felt his chest tighten. Why hadn't he asked about her maiden name? It was the mistake of a rank amateur. A man who didn't know what he was doing. His mind became swamped with Helga's voice. He was a bastard. A worthless, stupid bastard.

"Inspector, are you all right?" Weber said.

"Yes, yes, thank you. A little hot today." Martin rose and went to a sideboard on which stood a jug of water and three glasses. He poured a glass and drank it down, then turned. "Water?" he said.

They shook their heads and by the time Martin regained his seat, his composure had returned.

"Shultz is Mrs. Abraham's maiden name. So Rose Shultz could be a relative."

"I suppose so. But she told Miriam that she didn't have any family. She said she had no one. I don't know any more than that."

"So you didn't know she was pregnant?"

Miriam Abraham let out a small cry and put her hand to her mouth. Weber frowned. Was he surprised or just concerned for Miriam? It was hard to tell.

"Who could possibly be the father?" Martin asked.

"The Japanese man," Miriam said after a moment. The shock of the news had evaporated and in its place she'd found disgust.

Eva Abraham was by Harry's estimate around fourteen to sixteen weeks pregnant. That put conception sometime in early January of 1942. Well before the Japanese occupation. He didn't share this information. Time to come back to it when he knew more about Eva's activities before the war.

Martin let them go. Grace retained them for the time it took to type up and sign their statements. He gave the address of Weber's friend to Santamaria to check the story of the ladder.

Rose Shultz had an address in Chinatown. That was where he needed to go.

CHAPTER SIXTEEN

The boardinghouse on Neil Road was at the better end of Chinatown. The woman who greeted him was some forty years of age. Her name was Lina Goh and she lived with her mother, Tatiana.

Martin was surprised not to know of her. She looked like a gypsy, straggling brown hair tied in a scarf, large hoop earrings. How had he missed such a character on the streets of Chinatown?

"Miss Goh, I'm Detective Inspector Bach and this is Detective Constable Seah."

He showed his card, which she eyed suspiciously, but she stood back, allowing them to enter a parlor with old furniture covered in colorful cushions and shawls.

"Do you own this house, Miss Goh?"

"My mother does. I take care of her and manage the place."

"I haven't seen you in Singapore before. You are hard to miss."

She lit a cigarette, didn't offer him one, and sat back, eyeing him. "You've had some sadness in your life. A woman. Give me your hand."

Martin frowned. "No. What are you talking about?"

"I read fortunes."

"I see. Not today. How long have you been in Singapore?"

She shrugged. "Four months or so. I got out of Hong Kong as soon as the war was declared. And straight into this. Still, I'm better off here with my mother and I have a roof, which is a consolation."

"You didn't foresee the Japanese takeover of Singapore?"

She arched an eyebrow.

"Who else lives here?"

"My mother, my grandparents, and two aunts."

"Your father was Chinese?"

"Obviously, yes. My mother is Russian. What they call a White Russian."

"This is still a boardinghouse?"

"Yes, we have some tenants and some family. Housing's very short. My grandparents' house was bombed, so they all came here. We are fortunate in having enough rooms for everyone."

"I see. Do you know of anyone called Rose Shultz?"

"No."

"What about your mother?"

"I don't know."

"May I speak to your mother?"

"What's this about?"

"Just please fetch your mother."

Lina left and Martin looked around the room. A heavy Chinese sideboard was covered in photographs. Two stood out. An icon-like image of the last tsar of Russia, Nicholas, and his wife, Alexandra. Next to this was the wedding photograph of a youngish blond-haired Tatiana and her short, much older Chinese husband. A White Russian. They were people who had fled Russia during or after the revolution. Many went to Harbin and Shanghai, but the war in China meant many sought safer havens. Hong Kong, Singapore. They were found everywhere more or less over the East.

When Tatiana came into the room with Lina, he was surprised at how lovely she still was. She must have been sixty or so, with pure white hair, but retained an air of great grace and austere beauty. She sat.

"How do you do, Mrs. Goh?"

"Thank you. What is the matter?"

Her English was accented but correct.

"Do you know a woman called Rose Shultz?"

"Yes. Is she in trouble?"

"No. At least not that I know of. What can you tell me about her?"

"She lived here for many years with her sister, Eva. They were orphans. So young, just sixteen and eleven. Their father died in a car accident. Their mother was a friend of mine. She died of typhus."

"You took them in."

"Of course. I knew what it was to be an orphan. I took pity on them just as dear Mr. Goh took pity on me. Rose was a companion to an old English lady and took typing and shorthand lessons."

The old woman smiled, remembering. "Such good girls. After the old lady passed on, Rose got a job with the civil service. She took very great care of Eva. Always kept her in school and paid for her typing lessons too."

"Typing lessons. Where did she go to learn typing?"

"They both went to Mrs. Warshowski's Secretarial School on New Bridge Road. Not sure whether it got bombed or not. I liked having those girls in the house. Eva got married and Rose left not long after."

"When did she leave?"

"Before the war. Just before. October maybe. I forget."

Tatiana pointed to the sideboard. "There's a photo over there of them both. Eva got married to a rich Jewish man."

Lina brought the photograph and gave it to Martin. It was a picture of the dead woman, who had instantly come alive. Eva was in her white satin wedding dress standing arm in arm with her sister. Rose was wearing a salmon-pink lace dress and was as beautiful as Eva. They were smiling at each other. The photographer had caught a moment of pure happiness and love. Eva was wearing pearl earrings and a drop pearl necklace in a diamond setting. He turned the picture over. The photographer was Claude Laval, South Bridge Road.

"They were close?"

"Oh yes. They would do anything for each other. Anything."

"Do you know where Rose Shultz went?"

"Oh goodness. She must have told me her address but I can't remember. That's very bad of me. I would like to see her again. The war, you know. Everything is so terrible. When you think life can't get worse, it does."

Her eyes gazed into space. He waited until she looked back at him. "Mrs. Goh, may I please borrow this photograph? I will give it back to you when I find Rose."

"Yes. Yes. Please tell her to come and see me. Those girls were a joy."

Martin paused. It would be a shock, but he had to tell her. "Mrs. Goh, I'm very sorry to tell you that Mrs. Abraham, Eva, was killed a short time ago. That is the reason for my visit. We are investigating her death."

The serenity of her face deserted her. She began to tremble and tears filled her eyes.

"I'm sorry. It is bad news in a town filled with bad news."

She held a handkerchief to her eyes and began to sob. Lina went to her mother. She threw a filthy glance at Martin.

"I'm sorry," he said. Lina ignored him. He left and once outside gave the photo to Seah. "That's them. Rose and Eva Shultz on Eva's wedding day in March '41. Rose is five years older than her sister. That makes her around twenty-eight or so. She left here in October of 1941. She must have had friends around here. Someone must know where she went. Anything about Eva and Rose you can find out will be useful. And check out Warshowski's Secretarial School in New Bridge Road."

Martin left Seah and walked up Neil Road onto South Bridge Road. Number 92 was a bomb-damaged building and if Claude Laval had survived, he could be anywhere.

He stopped in a quiet alleyway at a street vendor for some food. The man at the wok clattered and chattered, but Martin wasn't listening. He had the unpleasant job of finding Rose Shultz and telling her that her beautiful and beloved sister was dead. Of course, he had no idea if Rose was even alive. He almost wished she wasn't.

He looked at his watch. He needed to get this back to Hayashi. Everyone in Singapore had to carry an ID card. If she was eating, she'd need a ration card; if she had a bicycle, a radio, or a fishing rod, she'd need to register it.

At the office, Martin reported to Hayashi.

"The registration of the population was carried out by the Kempeitai," Hayashi said. "I don't want to alert them to anything."

"Can I make a suggestion?"

"Yes, of course."

"Radio registration or a bicycle. That's just bureaucracy."

Hayashi picked up the phone.

Martin went to the interview room. Neo was curled up in the corner fast asleep.

Ibrahim joined him. He had returned from Chinatown empty-handed. The certificate on the building stated the Hong brothers lived there but the local watchman hadn't seen them for several days. The small cubicle they both occupied contained clothes and their neighbors had agreed it belonged to them. A search had revealed nothing incriminating.

"If they've moved on," Ibrahim said, "theoretically they'd have to report to the local station. The residency certificate would have to be changed and a new ration card issued. Hong and his brother are hedged around by Japanese red tape. Of course if they have accomplices and food they could lie low, but for how long?"

"Correct," Martin said. "What did you tell the watchman over there?"

"To arrest him on sight. I know a couple of informants. If he goes back, they'll get him. Asked about Charlie Chan too."

Martin rolled his eyes. "Don't be ridiculous, Sergeant."

"Found a man who knows the kid."

"You did not."

Ibrahim shrugged. "You can believe what you want, Inspector. But someone knows where Charlie is. I'll track him down."

"Do let me know when that vital information becomes available. In the meantime, what do you think I should do with this one?" He pointed to Neo.

"I can get a watch on her too. Plenty of the older rickshaw pullers are sick or need opium money. It's not a problem."

"All right. Take her back and set all that up. Don't harass her unless she's seen with Hong. Tell her there's some money if she gives him up. Not sure she will, but we can try."

Ibrahim shook Neo awake and led her away. Martin returned to his office.

"I've located Mrs. Abraham's sister, Rose Shultz," Hayashi said. "A radio registered to her in Petain Road. Do you know where that is?"

"Yes," Martin said, somewhat amazed and frankly terrified at how quickly the Japanese administration could work. "Will you come?"

"No, you go ahead. I've a meeting with the commissioner. The Finance Department have released more money for the CID. Pressure from the marquis doubtless. We need informants. Sergeant Ibrahim has given me a list and we're up to forty already. He says he is trying to locate a street boy named Charlie Chan. Do you know this?"

"Yes," Martin said. Was Ibrahim simply serving the chief inspector's vanity? Irregulars. Sherlock Holmes. Charlie Chan. Was Kano Hayashi that naïve?

"So, I'll go and interview Rose Shultz, then. Might need a car."

Hayashi smiled and put his hand in his pocket. He dropped the keys on Martin's desk. "Enjoy yourself, Inspector."

CHAPTER SEVENTEEN

It was liberating to be behind the wheel of a car. He'd decided both to drive alone for the sheer pleasure of it but also to interview Rose Shultz in a low-key way considering the kind of news he was bringing.

To avoid nosy neighbors and interest by the Japanese soldiery, he parked the car two streets away from the address on Petain Road and walked past some of the old meatpacking factories and gang-run bars and brothels in this part of town. Before the war, it had been a dangerous place to be at night even for the police.

No gangs now. The Japanese terror kept them all in line. He crossed the street to avoid drawing attention to himself as he approached an old soy sauce factory, now a billet for locally stationed Japanese soldiers, all noisily eating and drinking. The radio inside blared, the sentry was inattentive, and he was glad to leave the group behind.

Whatever else might be going on around it, Petain Road stood out as one of the most beautiful series of houses in Singapore. The style was known as Chinese baroque for its exquisite floral adornments, fluted columns, and Grecian plinths. He stopped at number 24 and looked up to the first floor. The shutters were closed, but that was often the case against the afternoon sun. He stepped under the veranda and knocked on the door. Not a sound came from inside the house. There was no one on the street and the houses on either side looked equally quiet. He tested the door, but it was locked, and without knowing what was inside he decided against using one of the keys.

He walked around the long line of houses to the back alley. The heavy courtyard door to number 24 was ajar and, as he went in, a flock of pigeons took flight. The sunlight slanted into the courtyard, but it cast a melancholy light. The door to the house was hanging from its hinges. Dusty, unkempt, smelling of old decaying things, broken dishes in the kitchen, a cracked stove, food store empty, almost no furniture that wasn't broken. Everything covered in a layer of dust. Evidence of multiple occupants was clear by a number of broken beds. No mattresses in evidence. On the first floor at the front was the largest bedroom. A finely carved Javanese bed was in pieces, a radio smashed. He touched it. It was this that had led him here. He saw, crushed and broken, lying on the floor by the bed, a picture frame and picked it up. It was the same picture of Eva and Rose on that wedding day.

Something terrible had happened here. He began a detailed inspection of the room, opening drawers and the wardrobe. They were all empty except for a lone shoe. Everything pointed to a removal in a hurry and a subsequent looting.

He retraced his steps downstairs. At the front door he tried one of the three remaining keys. The second key turned. Eva had a key to this house, but where was her sister?

He returned to the back of the house and shot across the bolt of the courtyard door, then exited from the front, locked the door and looped three pieces of cotton around this key. Two more keys remained. He had a feeling that when he had identified these, he would know exactly how Eva Abraham had been killed, why, and by whom.

He knocked on the neighboring door. An Indian man looked out of the side window, presumably realized he wasn't Japanese, opened it, and stuck his head out. "What do you want?"

Martin showed his ID card, and the man, corpulent and sweaty, dressed in a vest and a loose pair of cotton shorts, withdrew in a hurry. The door opened.

"Sorry, I didn't realize it was the police."

"You are?"

"I am Pillai."

Pillai had a wad of betel in his mouth and a dribble of red juice ran down his chin. He wiped it away with his hand. Drops scattered on the veranda. Martin took a step backwards, fearful for his white plimsolls. It was hard enough keeping them clean without betel stains on them. Pillai told Martin he was the main tenant of the house. He'd been left in charge of it when the Chinese owner had been ordered out of town.

"Gone to Malaya. The Highlands. Japanese didn't let anyone from Malaya stay. I was his driver."

"And you're in charge?"

"Well, I live here and make sure it isn't looted."

"Who else lives here?"

"I have my family and rent three rooms to some other families."

Martin gave him the once-over. This might be true or not. He might have murdered his boss and taken over this house. Or he might be thoroughly decent fellow doing exactly what he said. He didn't have time to bother with this.

"The house next door. Tell me about that."

Pillai's left eye twitched and he spat the wad of betel into a spittoon by the door.

"I'm not military police," Martin said. "I'm trying to solve a crime. You can speak frankly."

"A lady, name of Miss Shultz," Pillai said. "Very nice lady. During the war, she took in refugees, you know, tried to help people. I saw that when I was working for my boss. A good woman. But a month or so ago something changed. Maybe some of those people were, well, I don't know if it's true, but might have been anti-Japanese."

"What makes you think that?"

"Because the Japanese soldiers came and took them all away. Her too."

Martin took out the photo of Rose and Eva and held it out. "Is that Miss Shultz?"

The man peered. He nodded. "Yes. And that other lady. She came here a few days after the arrests. She was asking for Miss Shultz. Said she was her sister."

"What did you say?"

"Same. She was taken away by those Kempei soldiers."

Martin let this sink in. Rose was in the hands of the military, might already be dead. Had she been involved in activities with others that the Japanese had reason to believe were against their interests? He couldn't know.

"The place was looted. That you?"

"No. No." Pillai mopped his brow with a hand towel. "At night, people come. What can we do? They have knives. We stay inside."

Martin nodded. The man seemed genuine. "You and the others in here. Are you all right? Japanese treating you all right?"

The man smiled, his red teeth gleaming. "Oh yes, sir. Thank you. We have all signed up for the Indian Liberation League. It means we get extra rice rations. It's best to do that. My wife is locally born Jawi Peranakan, but she stopped wearing the kebaya and sarong and started wearing the sari because it confused them. It's best not to confuse them. That's what we were told. They know the sari is Indian and they don't bother you."

"Yes. I see. Very wise."

Martin handed his card to the man. "I want you to keep an eye on the house. If anyone comes back, you call me, you understand? And make sure no one goes in. Call me about that as well. I'll see you're rewarded."

"Oh yes, sir."

Eva Abraham had come to visit her sister and found her missing and in the hands of the Kempeitai. What had been her thought process from that moment? Sheer panic, and then she had remembered buried treasure. She must have decided that the only way to get Rose away from the military was with money. This made some sense but not a lot if she was implicated in some sort of plotting. She had asked Nomura to help, but he could not and so she had turned to Hong. It was a scheme born of absolute desperation.

He needed to find Hong. And he wanted very much to find Rose. For that, he needed the Japanese clout of the detective chief inspector.

When he got back to the office Sergeant Ibrahim stopped him instantly. "Hong's been found," he said. "Dead. Throat cut. Stinking."

Martin shook his head. "Damn. Damn. Where is he?"

"Morgue." Ibrahim continued. "The chief inspector has left. And you've been ordered to go to see Colonel Masuda at the Tokko tomorrow morning."

Martin felt an earthquake erupting in his guts.

CHAPTER EIGHTEEN

Insects battered against the window screen, drawn towards the low light bulb hanging from the ceiling over Ah Loy's kitchen table. This room was the only space in his cramped upstairs quarters that was free of boxes and crates.

"Ah Loy, you've barely room to live in here."

Ah Loy shrugged. "Yeah. Eh? I need to move this stuff out. If I'm raided there'll be trouble. It's booze. This Formosan I know is taking the lot. All happened in a bit of a hurry. Nature of the game. Yours will be kept here, though. That's stored out back. You owe me one hundred dollars."

"Tomorrow. It'll be banana money."

Ah Loy grinned. "Sure."

Martin put two necklaces and a pair of earrings on the table. Sapphires, rubies, and emeralds sparkled. "Take a look at these, please." It had occurred to Martin that if Eva needed money so badly, why hadn't she simply sold her jewelry?

Ah Loy gave the jewels a quick once-over. "Nice. Bit old-fashioned but nice."

"Okay. Want to know what they're worth."

"You selling? I'm buying."

"Just tell me, please."

Ah Loy took up a loop and got down to business. After a minute or two, he looked up at Martin. "Are you kidding?"

"What?"

"Paste. But really excellent paste. Worth a few hundred dollars, I suppose. Or you could try to pass them off as real. Japs would never know."

"They're fake?"

"Yes. Brilliant fakes. Only a couple of men in Singapore can make fakes as good as these. I can ask around."

So, Eva Abraham had taken the jewels that her old, doting husband had lavished on her and arranged to have copies made.

"Yes. Keep the sapphire necklace. It was Mrs. Abraham's. Give it back to me, Ah Loy. Not my property."

"Sure, sure." Ah Loy wrote in his spidery ledger and put the necklace into a drawer.

"I don't really care where the real ones are. Long gone. But dates. I'd like to know when Mrs. Abraham was doing this stuff and for how long."

Ah Loy nodded. "Right. Now. What's this about a birth certificate?"

Martin had no wish to tell Ah Loy about his sudden and embarrassing family situation. "Lost. Burnt in a raid. I need something to show the Tokko that I'm not a Englishman in disguise. And I need it by tomorrow morning."

"You might be in luck. I have some boxes of documents and papers from a bunch of government offices. They were looted top to bottom before the occupation, and I bought a bunch of stuff."

"You bought papers?"

"Yes, official forms, certificates. Pro forma papers, you know. I buy Japanese papers, too, smuggled out of the printing office. You'd be surprised how profitable papers can be. People who need a document or a pass or something will pay for them. Just like you. Though naturally this service is free for a friend. Help me move some of these boxes."

After some grunting and shuffling, Ah Loy and Martin created a corridor between the piles towards a second room. This room was also stuffed, but Ah Loy made a beeline for a cupboard and, after checking for a minute, turned, flourishing a paper in his hand.

"You have birth certificate forms?" Martin was incredulous.

"No. But I've got something that you can use."

Martin took the paper. It was a blank pro forma for the Municipal Health Office, marked "Midwife's Report." The British authorities required all births, live or dead, to be reported to the health officer. It carried blank spaces for date of birth, father and mother's names, location of the place of birth, et cetera.

"But why would I have this form? Wouldn't it be with the municipality? Why would I have it?"

"I dunno. I ain't got any birth certificates. This is the best I can do tonight. Talk about ungrateful."

Martin sat at the table under the naked lamp bulb and contemplated his future. He had to find something to give to Masuda.

"Tea?" Ah Loy said.

"Thanks."

Ah Loy filled the cheap tin kettle with water from the tap.

"You have water?" Martin said.

"Yeah. Came back on a few days ago. You?"

"Not yet."

Ah Loy lit the small kerosene burner and set the kettle to boil. The only sound in the room was the spatter of insects throwing themselves against the screen and the hiss of the flame on his burner. Right now, Martin felt like one of those insects.

"All right," Ah Loy said suddenly. "What about this? During a raid all your papers were burned, right? Eh? So, you needed to replace them and were told to go to the Health Office and get a copy of this report. Eh? What about that?"

"Would I be told that?"

"I dunno, do I? But neither do the Japs. Right? You had to have proof. The only other place you could get proof would be a church. Eh? Baptismal record. Were you baptized? You got one of those. That'd do."

"Hmm. I don't think I have a baptismal record. Not in Walter's papers anyway. I suppose I was baptized. My mother was..." Martin stopped. Maman wasn't religious. Who was he? Who was she?

Ah Loy interrupted these thoughts. "So, you take this and say that before you could get a new birth certificate, the British surrendered. And how glad you are about that. Long live Dai Nippon. Banzai. Something like that."

Martin nodded. "Yes, all right. Might work. Let's fill it out. I'm bloody tired."

CHAPTER NINETEEN

Paper in hand, Martin reported to the Tokko the next morning. The Tokko offices were on the same floor of the Municipal Building overlooking the Padang but on the opposite side. Whereas the CID occupied the offices of the old Improvement Trust, the Tokko's had been the Department of Sanitation and Sewage. The sign above the door had been cursorily painted over, but the dark lettering was still visible. It was childish, perhaps, but it gave him a secret pang of pleasure. Rain spattered the windows of the waiting room.

A Japanese guard gave him the eye. He waited. He knew how these things worked. He would be left waiting. It made suspects nervous. He kept his eyes down. The Japanese didn't like it if you looked them directly in the eye. He toyed with reading the copy of the *Syonan Times* on one of the chairs but decided against it. If you looked casual, the Japanese didn't like it either. But he'd seen the article about Eva's death. How she and her husband were great friends of Nippon and how the detectives were on the job bringing justice to the poor victims of the city. The commissioner and the mayor had given an interview and so had the newly arrived chief justice of Syonan. The civil courts, the newspaper informed the public, would reopen and the laws of Britain would apply. Martin held out no great hope that justice would actually be done. Justice in these times was not a collective matter. It lay in the heart of each individual.

An hour crawled by. The clerk glanced at him from time to time but presumably dared say nothing. The ceiling fan rattled and turned, barely moving the air. In the boredom, his thoughts ranged about and it occurred to him that someone had taken over all the files of the British CID offices on Robinson Road. Among them might be the file on Irene. He was tortured by the uncertainty that their affair had been detected by her husband, Paul Sheridan, Australian managing director of Malaya Rubber.

She was shot in the course of a robbery was how the coroner put it, by a person unknown. An open verdict. But Martin knew that Paul Sheridan, on the surface urbane and gentlemanly, was, behind closed doors, a violent man. What the CID had suspected or done about that he did not know. He had never been questioned in connection with Irene and was not privy to the case, which was investigated entirely by British detectives and headed up by DCI Newlands, a man currently locked up in Changi. Now, though, he might be able to get hold of the file.

A thin Chinese man approached him. A nest of ancient pockmarks lay on his cheeks and his shiny forehead. "Mr. Bach?" He pronounced it Batch. Martin didn't bother to correct him and stood up.

"Yes."

"I am Toh. The interpreter."

"I see. How do you do?"

Toh bowed. "Thank you. Please follow me."

To Martin's surprise, Toh left the office and went down the stairs. Round the back a car idled. "Where are we going?"

"To see Colonel Masuda."

Martin got in next to Toh and the car took off, heading towards Stamford Road. The journey was not long. Within a few minutes, the car stopped behind the YMCA, now the headquarters of the Kempeitai. Martin felt the cold hand of fear grip his stomach.

Instead of entering the YMCA, however, Toh headed towards a long flight of steps that led to the Wesley Methodist Church directly behind. It had been damaged by shells and looked deserted. As they approached, Martin heard the sounds of an organ. Toh opened the door of the church and they entered. It was dark, eerily so, light slanting through the stained-glass windows and the hole in the roof. It smelled of damp, mold, grease, and kerosene. The place was packed with boxes of ammunition. At the far end, under the high rose-shaped window, was the organ, upon which rested a large candelabra, its candles wavering. In the semidarkness they advanced and the music rose. It was, Martin recognized, Bach's Toccata and Fugue, a piece of music synonymous with the creepy Jekyll and Hyde film he had seen a few years ago.

The whole place had the air of a film set. At first, Martin thought that the figure at the organ must be Colonel Masuda. Toh put out his hand and they came to a stop. Martin realized he was mistaken. He recognized one of the organists who occasionally played at St. Joseph's, a Frenchman.

The Tokko's chief was seated in a pew listening, his attention fixed on the Frenchman. In the wavering candlelight, Martin's first impression was of shininess. His boot-black hair was slicked back. A neat, shiny mustache sat like a small black brick above his fleshy lips.

Martin caught a pungent whiff of sweat under the powerful scent of eau de cologne. It wasn't the first time he had encountered this particular mélange of odors. The problem was tweed. For reasons he could not fathom, Japanese officers' army uniforms were fashioned out of tweed, perhaps an excellent choice in the iciness of the northern Chinese winter but hopeless in the hot, damp tropics. Perhaps they had a surplus of tweed and were convinced that common sense and climate had no dominion over will. Whatever the reason, almost every Japanese officer he had so far met had desperately tried to mitigate tweed's inevitable assault on bodily functions in the tropics by every scent at his disposal. Masuda was no different. He had his vanity. A touch of vanity made the whole world kin. But only for a moment.

The Fugue ended. Masuda rose and waved his hand in dismissal. The Frenchman disappeared and Masuda turned to face the two men. Martin bowed, hands stuck to his sides, his trunk at a strict right angle to his legs. In the presence of a superior being, it was customary to keep the bow like a wooden marionette, rigid and unmoving, until you were acknowledged. Some seconds elapsed. Martin could feel Toh's nervousness, but any second-rate police constable knew that silence and disrespect were meant to intimidate. He waited.

Eventually Masuda spoke and Toh translated. "You are Martin Bach, second-in-command to Keibu Hayashi-san?"

Martin took up a standing position but gave another small bow. "Yes, sir."

"Are you related to Johann Sebastian Bach?"

Toe translated this with some tongue-twisted difficulty, but Martin, despite the unexpected nature of the question, understood. The Japanese thought that anyone named Bach was related to the most famous Bach. A Churchill might obviously also be related to Winston. It was a semantic and genealogical confusion. All this heavy music, gloom, and candlelight. The man was some kind of demented romantic reeking of eau de cologne.

"After more than three hundred years it isn't possible to say positively, as you can imagine, but I think that most German Bachs are related in some way to Johann Sebastian." God help me, thought Martin. But a small bit of him smiled.

"You are not pure German, are you?"

"My father was pure German. He married a French Indochinese woman."

Actually, right now Martin had no idea who he was, but for the colonel, and men like him, nuance was confusing and dangerous. You were this or that or the other, but they had to be clear. They needed to categorize you, stick you in an easily identified box. And if they couldn't, well, they shot you.

"Why did your father marry an Indochinese woman?

"He was far from his homeland, Colonel. A lonely life and no good German woman to be his companion."

Toh translated, his voice somewhat shrill. Masuda seemed to contemplate this. The candles wavered; the sun slanted into the dark and dusty air.

"Are you married?"

"Not married."

"I see." Masuda approached Martin on a waft of scent. "Do you attend Nippon-Go classes?"

The question seemed banal. But Martin knew it was not. They were obsessed with their language and culture. He'd dismissed the routine urgings of the mayor and the commissioner to get enrolled in one of those classes. Grace, to her credit, had warned him. She and Mary had both signed up. An evident, if hypocritical, willingness and a little knowledge of Japanese, she'd said, flattered them. He knew a couple of words gleaned from the daily newspaper lesson on the back page and decided to chuck them out now.

"Gomen nasai," he intoned, wondering if he'd gotten it right. It meant "sorry." What else did he know? He searched but found only air. "My apologies, Colonel. Naturally I shall do so right away."

"You are waiting for the British to come back. You all go to church and pray for this. You love the British. But there is not the slightest hope of them ever coming back. Do you love the British?

"Under the British, I would never have received promotion. Since the Japanese have come to Syonan, I have been made an inspector. I am very grateful."

"You keep a radio? You listen to the BBC?"

"We have a radio. It is soldered to Radio Syonan. We cannot listen to any other station. It is forbidden."

"But you would like to listen to the BBC."

"I don't care about the BBC. Why should I believe anything they tell us?"

This answer seemed to mollify Masuda. He clasped his hands behind his back and began to pace, like a professor in front of a pupil. He lowered his voice and spoke conversationally, as if he had invited Martin to tea. "What do you think of your Keibu-san?"

"He is my boss. He knows his job."

"I think he is not happy about the prosecution of the war."

"I don't know, Colonel. We do not talk of such things."

"Hayashi-san does not approve of the war. Has he not told you this?"

"No. We do not discuss the war."

"Come now. Who does not discuss the war?"

"I'm sorry. I don't know what to say. We don't discuss political things. We only discuss our cases."

Masuda approached. His breath smelled of mint and tobacco. "Mr. Bach. You should know about this man. I must warn you that he is not a man to be trusted. He thinks himself above others because he is kazoku."

Martin frowned. Toh had translated that sentence but stumbled on that word, which he had merely repeated. Kazoku. What did that mean?

"He does not approve of the war. If he talks to you about the war or is critical of other Japanese it would be wise to tell me about it. He will accuse you of anti-Japanese sentiment to cover his own remarks. And I shall regrettably be forced to arrest you."

He smiled and inclined his head towards Martin in a friendly manner. "He would not defend you, I assure you. Men like you are suspect in all these matters."

Martin hardly knew what to make of this speech, which Toh was struggling to translate.

Masuda suddenly grew tense. His face lost its hard, slick smoothness. A twitch developed in one eye. His face erupted in sweat. Martin recognized the incredibly sudden onset of the symptoms of malaria or possibly dengue. Colonel Masuda might have helped defeat the Allied forces on the Malayan peninsula, but the Malayan mosquito had gotten him. Masuda rose and moved into the half shadows.

"He is untrustworthy, a cheat and … "

Masuda sagged, his face now gray and slick, his body trembling. He waved his hand and growled at Toh, who bowed sharply.

"Come on. Hurry up. We go."

Martin bowed and followed Toh out. At the bottom of the long flight of stairs, they parted. Martin walked back to the office. His interrogation, he had realized, was not about his birth but about the bad blood between Masuda and Kano Hayashi. Everything here was not here. It was buried in the past.

CHAPTER TWENTY

Martin was glad of a walk, glad to shake off the tension of this meeting, but there was, naturally, a price to pay. He counted the number of bows between the steps of the church and his office. Forty-three. Forty-three times he had to stop and bend from the waist to every passing Japanese, sentries, soldiers, man, woman, child. He'd shown his identity card seven times, but on the plus side he hadn't been called stupid or spat on once. A no-spit day was a good day.

It was then he noticed the headlines on the discarded newspaper on the pavement. Wife of richest man in Asia murdered! And a picture of Eva's dead face. He knew where it had come from. It was from the morgue and bloody Mat had taken it. He picked it up and tucked it under his arm.

Hayashi had obviously been waiting for his return. He looked at his watch and then at Martin. "He kept you waiting."

"Yes. It's pretty usual. Make me jumpy. I think we both know that trick."

"What did he say?"

"Odd things about my name. Thought I might be related to Johann Sebastian Bach. Then suddenly he was ill. Malaria, I think."

Martin didn't mention Masuda's criticisms of Hayashi.

"Colonel Masuda is an old acquaintance. He has much…
well…" Hayashi glanced at Martin. "There is an expression in
Japanese: Akuji mi ni tomaru. Evil clings to the body."

Martin nodded. "Yes, sir. *Ab igne ignem.* We reap what we
sow." He was keen to change the subject and laid the newspaper
on the desk. "Sir, you'd better have a look at this."

Hayashi whisked. "Right. Sort that out and let's get everyone
together for a review."

Martin told Mary and Grace to join the meeting. They had
become a strange and unlikely unit, close and unified. It had a lot
to do with the chief inspector and Martin knew it. Hayashi sat to
one side and Martin stood in front of the incident board.

Martin pinned the front page of the newspaper to the
incident board next to the photos of the crime scene and the
morgue.

"As you can see, this picture was taken at the morgue. "Mary,
get Mat Ahmed in here after this meeting."

"Yes, sir."

"Right, let's review." Martin pinned up the picture of Eva and
Rose. "I'll go through what we know. If you have anything to say,
please speak up."

He looked around. Everyone gave a curt nod.

"Eva Abraham's maiden name was Shultz. The other woman
in this photograph is Rose Shultz, her sister. She was last seen
being picked up at the house where she was living at 24 Petain
Road about a month ago. Arrested by the Kempeitai, possibly
connected with anti-Japanese activities but that is speculation."

Santamaria raised his hand.

"Yes."

"Shultz. The Indian spice shop, the one next to where her
body was found, that used to be known as Shultz's Apothecary.
I grew up round there. Everybody used it. He was nice, the old
man."

"All right. Good. That might explain why she arranged to meet Hong there. Nostalgia. Familiarity. And it was deserted, of course."

"Hong met her, bashed her on the head, took her jewelry, shoes, and ran off?" This was Santamaria again. "Sold some on, hid stuff in Neo's cubicle. Case solved."

"Shoes," Seah said and looked at Martin. "He wouldn't take shoes."

"Yes," Martin said, "that's odd."

"Why?" Hayashi said. "Explain."

"Well," Martin said. "Certain objects are taboo for the Chinese. Clocks, scissors, pears, handkerchiefs, that sort of thing. And shoes."

"Oh," Kano said. "Honto?"

"Yes, sir. The word in Chinese sounds like evil or rough. Hong would be unlikely to take the shoes." He shook his head. "But then you never know. Maybe he wasn't the superstitious type and he thought he could sell them. So maybe he bashed her, took her stuff, and ran off. But why does he drag her to the censer and stuff her head into it? She died of suffocation. Why does he hang around to do that? Does it serve a purpose?"

"She could identify him," Seah said.

"Yes," Ibrahim said, "but would she? She was intending to invade a Japanese stronghold and commit a robbery. She was conspiring with criminal elements. Would she admit to that? Would Hong fear that?"

"The death feels personal," Hayashi said. "Not for gain. A shoe on the back of the head as she struggles. Would a man like Hong take the trouble to do that? I don't think so. Who else do we have?"

"Not too many prospects," Martin said.

"What about Miriam Abraham?" Hayashi said. "She didn't like Eva. Thought she was stopping her marriage."

"Right. But she's frail and handicapped. Could she have done it with a withered leg to drag around? And it was only a matter of time until the marriage took place."

Hayashi held up his whisk. "I seem to recall a Holmes story about a crippled man. What was it, now?"

Martin raised his eyes to the window. "Thank you, sir. She might, of course, have convinced Weber to do it. Worth a look. She and Weber have alibied each other. Can we shake that? Find someone who saw either of them outside when they claim to be sleeping?"

"I'll ask at Meyer Mansions and check around," Seah said, and Martin nodded.

"I'll get back to you on the Holmes story," Hayashi said.

"Yes, sir. Thank you."

Santamaria put up a finger. "I checked with Weber's friend about the ladder story. Turns out to be true. He fell off the ladder."

"You believe him?"

"The house was being repaired. He said Weber was giving him a hand. Hard to know."

"For now, we won't believe it. I want to know about David Weber. See what he was doing before the war and at the surrender. Says he worked for Solomon Abraham. Find out what he was doing for him. And, Seah, what did you find out about Mrs. Abraham before she married?"

"Nothing much. Warshowski's Secretarial School was rubble. The family apparently got out just before the surrender. No one admitted to knowing Eva or Rose Shultz, but there were a lot of people crammed into the buildings who didn't live there before the war. Nobody wanted to talk to me around the Gohs' guesthouse either."

Martin looked at Grace. "Grace, you go along with Constable Seah to Weber's place. Try to talk to the women in the building. They'll know more than the men. And might speak to you more freely. A light hand. Nothing official."

Grace smiled. "Actually, I know several people who live in that building." Seah made the face of a disgruntled gibbon but no comment.

"Eva Abraham owned a Rolex Princess watch," Martin said. "Here it is in the photograph. You can see that Rose Shultz had one too." Martin put the jewels he'd shown to Ah Loy on the incident table. "These jewels are paste."

Hayashi stood and took up a necklace.

"Sir, Mrs. Abraham was making fakes of her jewels and selling the real ones."

Hayashi considered this. He glanced at the photograph of the two sisters. "She needed the money. For her sister?"

"Could be. They were orphans. They were close and intensely loyal to each other. She almost certainly married Abraham for his money. She'd share it with her sister. She'd have to have a way of doing it which wouldn't be noticed."

"Yes." Hayashi frowned. "Jewels worth tens of thousands of dollars. Did Rose Shultz buy the Petain Road house with this money? Did she own it? A place for her to live, to be secure."

"And then," Martin said, "when Eva finds Rose gone, she's frantic and needs more money and comes up with this crazy scheme to dig up the garden and gets in contact with a man as dangerous as Hong. It makes some sort of sense."

"Yes, it does." Hayashi nodded. "If you're desperate. Constable Santamaria, search the house. See what you can find. If she owned the house, there will be a record. I will speak to Nomura-san. I'll get him to find out."

"Evidence," Martin continued. "The keys. One to the front door of her apartment, one to her room. The third is to the door of Petain Road." He detached the key and passed it to Santamaria. "Don't know what four and five fit yet. Small one might be a cupboard."

"Or a strongbox," Grace said. Eyes swiveled to her and she blushed and straightened her skirt.

"Yes," Martin said and smiled encouragement. "A strongbox. Look for one."

They split up. Mary picked up the telephone. Martin called Seah to one side.

"I don't want any nonsense about Grace. Just call her your assistant or something, I don't care. Let her do the female thing. Gossipy, you know. Women trust women. We need all hands to the pump at the moment. She's shrewd. Orders are to solve this case and quick. The mayor wants this to be the first case in front of the court. We only have a short time."

Seah left, mollified, Martin presumed. It didn't matter. Time was important now.

Hayashi replaced the telephone receiver as Martin joined him. "I am going to see Nomura. Will you walk with me?"

"Inspector," Mary called. "Mat will be here in two hours. He said he was busy."

"All right, thanks, Mary."

The two men left the office and strolled along the corridor.

"I have procured a house," Hayashi said. "I have been in a hotel, but it will be pleasant to have a house. It is one of those quite nice houses on Emerald Hill."

The stolen quite nice house of someone who had fled in terror, you mean? Or died. Again, it was extraordinary how easily the detective chief inspector chose to forget what had gone on here. But it had given him an idea. It was Nomura's business to discover the fate of houses and apartments. Perhaps he could find out about his mother's flat in Tiong Bahru.

"Sir, may I once again raise the question of a car?"

"It is out of the question for the moment."

Martin lapsed into a frosty silence. They walked on. Hayashi stopped abruptly and turned to him. "The young woman, May."

"The waitress?"

"Yes. I … Well, I … I dined at the restaurant the other night with … it doesn't matter. I … I … Well … I would like you to speak to her. I hardly dare ask myself. I think she might be frightened. I would like her to be my housekeeper."

You randy bugger, thought Martin. You'd like her to be more than your bloody housekeeper.

Hayashi went on, clearly uncomfortable. "I thought if you explained. It would be an entirely professional arrangement. She'd have comfortable accommodation. She would have a wage, of course, and my protection. And she would not be alone in the house. I have engaged a Malay servant boy and his mother, who cleans, and a Chinese cook."

"I see. I thought she wanted to work in the civil service. Probably wouldn't suit her at all."

"Yes. Yes." The softness disappeared.

"And think of what it looks like. A good woman like May living with a widower. A Japanese widower. What would the neighbors say? She'd be a target for all kinds of comments."

"Yes, well, all right."

"A girl has to be careful in dangerous times."

Martin was starting to enjoy himself. The detective chief inspector was so obviously uncomfortable with the conversation. It served him right. Squirm away. I want a car.

"I merely thought to improve her situation and obtain a pleasant and efficient housekeeper." Hayashi strode away.

Hayashi's interview with Nomura was quickly concluded. All the land registry documents had been captured from the British. Nomura was eager to help. Clearly, he had cared for Eva. He was surprised that she had a sister.

Now, as Hayashi made his way back to the office, he began to regret his quick temper and his tone. Why should Martin not wish a car? He really ought to help the man. As for May, he had lied horribly. He had the gentlest but, he recognized, romantic intentions towards her.

He had been a widower for several years. In that time, no woman had been of interest to him, though many had been presented as prospective brides. He knew himself. He wasn't a man to frequent brothels—dispiriting and barren places with not an ounce of true human contact, and sex interested him less and less anyway. His marriage had been for love, and he had enjoyed the quiet, homely pleasures that married life brought in a busy policeman's life. Yukiko's death had been long, slow, and inevitable, but it had been a shock. He had mourned her and Yoko, turning inward and away from all other connections but his children, who had needed him most.

And so it might have remained for the rest of his life. But the sudden move to this hot tropical island, at first resented, had been like an extraordinary rejuvenation, like a tired, cold plant suddenly finding fresh fecund earth in the sun. The new experiences in culture and food, the wonderful car, the prospect of comfort and enjoyment in a lovely, old, and interesting house. These were delightful in their luxurious originality. He had become a little drunk on Singapore.

He was eager to understand the Malays, Indians, and Chinese of these southern regions. Every day brought something new. Just today, he had discovered the beauty of a garden of red hibiscus and white frangipani and the tasty and unexpected pleasures of Indian food. May was, he knew, a prize he desired. She was a woman beyond his limited experience; the embodiment of the South Seas in all its exotic thrill resided in her smile. But she was not soft. She was tough. She'd had to make a life for herself, and her very independence drew him to her. He could not get her out of his mind. Though she barely seemed to need it, he longed to surround her with comfort and protection. Perhaps because she didn't need it. It wasn't clear in his own mind. But was it predatory? A sudden flush of shame consumed him. Of course it was. She would feel obliged to accept, wouldn't she? He wished he'd never spoken of it.

CHAPTER TWENTY-ONE

The Kublai Khan restaurant was open but it was early and no customers had yet arrived. Martin found May with a mop in the kitchen. The kid with one ear gave him the once-over then returned to cleaning the sink.

"Hello, Inspector," May said and rested on her mop a moment. Her arm was still bandaged.

"How's your arm?"

"Better. Aloe vera, that's the stuff. Good for wounds."

"Right. Can I have a word, please, May?"

She dropped the mop in the bucket, wiped her hands on her apron, and called to the kid. "Hey, kid, you take over mopping. Inspector, want some tea?"

"Thanks." Martin smiled and sat at one of the two kitchen tables. May went to the kettle on the smaller stove, which was glimmering with fire.

She brought the teapot and served up some fragrant jasmine tea. Martin decided to get straight to the point. "May, look, I've come for a couple of reasons. One is about my detective chief inspector."

"He comes here quite a lot."

"Right. Frankly, I think he's attracted to you."

"I think so too."

Martin laughed. "And how do you feel about that?"

"I don't mind."

"What if he wanted more than just a nice house and pleasant conversation?"

May sipped her tea. "What has he said?"

"He's said he'd like you to be his housekeeper in this new place he's moving into in Emerald Hill."

"Nice address. Housekeeper?"

"That's what he said. I think whatever happened after that would be up to you. It's better to be clear about it."

"I see." May studied her tea as if some kind of prophetic insight might be there.

"I think the detective chief inspector is lonely and a bit of a romantic, May. I think he wants a comfortable and pleasant home life with a nice, loyal, and loving woman. A woman he would protect and care for. What that might entail would be up to you, I imagine."

"I don't love him."

"No, of course not. Look, you'd better think about it."

They drank the tea now with a dash of awkwardness.

"May, did you know Eva Abraham's sister, Rose Shultz?"

"Rose? Yes, course. I went to secretarial school with Rose. Eva wasn't my friend. Rose was. I was upset about Eva for Rose's sake. She was devoted to her."

"What did Rose Shultz think about her sister's marriage?"

May shrugged. "I don't know. She didn't tell me. Probably delighted. It was quite a catch."

"Were you envious of that marriage, May?"

"We were all madly envious of that marriage, Inspector. A rich husband on death's door. What poor woman isn't looking for one of those?" May shook her head. "But Eva was a nice girl. And I was glad for Rose."

Martin looked at his watch and finished his tea. As he got to his feet, May put out her hand to his arm. "Tell your detective chief inspector to come and see me here. If he wants me to be his companion, he should come and tell me himself."

Martin nodded, glad to get out of this business as quickly as possible. He felt like a damn pimp. He wasn't far from Neil Street and decided to call in on Mrs. Goh, see how she was, and ask a few more questions about Eva and Rose Shultz.

The old woman was pale and seemed frailer than during his last visit. She'd had a shock. A young woman who had grown up under her care had been murdered. She was grieving.

"I'm sorry, Mrs. Goh, to have brought you such shocking news."

"The world is a horrible place, Inspector. A horrible and strange place. I don't understand anything. Where are the British? Who are these people? Heads. Heads. Cut heads on bridges. What kind of people are they to come from a land so far away and hate us all? What have we done to deserve this? Oh God, I don't want to live in this world anymore."

Tears fell on her cheeks. Martin waited for her to find some semblance of calm and then he said, "None of us, not one of us, can fully grasp what has befallen us. It is outside of our understanding, even our imagination. To go from unshakable belief to bloody and absolute disaster in the matter of a day must cause the deepest trembling of our soul. But it'll pass, Mrs. Goh, I'm certain of it, though it may take time. So, you must not succumb to misery. I beg of you to not succumb to misery. This is the situation, and one way to cope with it is to seek justice. I am trying to get some sort of justice for Mrs. Abraham—Eva—and I need your help."

She seemed to contemplate his words, then nodded and gazed at him out of watery, tired eyes.

"Who came to visit them?" Martin said. "Can you remember?"

"They had friends. Lots of them came to visit and sit in the parlor. Before the war, of course."

"Anyone special? A boyfriend perhaps? Did Rose have a boyfriend?"

"Men friends came by. She's a levelheaded sort of woman. I don't think she cared much for any of them. She worked and took care of Eva. Oh wait, she did have a special friend, Marion Brown. She worked with her at the Department of Fisheries. They saw a lot of each other."

Tears welled in her eyes suddenly. She put her handkerchief to her lips. "Inspector. Have you found Rose? Does she know about Eva? Oh dear, that poor girl. Will you tell her to come to me?"

"I haven't yet found Rose. I am looking. I will ask Marion Brown. And yes, I will tell her to come to you."

"Come back, Inspector. Tell me what happens, please."

At the office, Martin saw Ching, Miriam Abraham's maid, seated in reception.

"Been here an hour," Mary said.

Ching stood as he approached and passed him a letter. "Asked to wait for answer," she said.

Martin opened the letter. It was from Miriam Abraham. She was complaining about the key to Eva's room. She wanted it handed to Ching and Ching was to stay until this had happened. Martin spoke to her in Cantonese.

"It's evidence, Ching. I can't give her what she wants."

"I have to wait. She's upset."

"Yes, I understand. Death is difficult."

"Not just that. She's frail. Despite what you see, her life's been difficult. She's upset because of the marriage delay." Ching shrugged and shook her head. "Though she shouldn't be."

Martin raised an eyebrow. "Really. Sit down. Why don't you tell me about this?"

Ching's lips tightened. "I'll wait. Nothing else to say."

"Perhaps if you told me what is going on, the chief inspector will make an exception and give you the key. Then she would be less upset."

Ching seemed to reflect on this a moment. "I saw him at Sir Solomon's house. I saw them both."

"Who did you see, Ching?"

"Mr. Weber kissing Miss Eva. After she was married to Sir Solomon. I saw that."

"You saw David Weber kissing Mrs. Abraham, is that it?"

Ching nodded.

"Did you tell Miss Miriam?"

"No. It was a long time ago. Before the bombs. Before Miss Miriam came back from India. Before she wanted to marry Mr. Weber. Now Miss Eva's dead. What good to tell her?"

She looked up at Martin. "I'll wait for the key."

CHAPTER TWENTY-TWO

Martin sent Ching away with the promise to visit Miriam that afternoon and settle the key business.

Mat Ahmed sauntered in and gazed at Mary. Sergeant Ibrahim approached, grabbed Mat's sleeve, and dragged him towards Martin.

Martin put the newspaper in front of Mat. He lost a little of his swagger, but not as much as Martin would have liked.

"You did this?"

"Just a picture, Inspector. Gotta make a living."

"No, Mat. You've got to respect this office. If you can't do that, you will have to answer to the commissioner and be removed from this job in disgrace. How will your family like that? Upsetting the Japanese?"

A moment of defiance, then Mat seemed to deflate.

"Put a stop to it, Mat."

"Yes, Inspector." Mat threw a glance at Mary and reddened.

Martin wondered if he should have tackled the boy privately. Was it possible he had a crush on Mary? A Malay man with a Straits Chinese woman? It was an impossible idea. But, as Martin well knew, young men had impossible urges and ideas. He softened his tone.

"All right, Mat. Good man. Right, now get along with Sergeant Ibrahim to the morgue. I want a photo of Hong's body. One photo, Mat, and from now on all forensic negatives will come with the prints. All right?"

Mat didn't answer. He turned on his heel and left the room trailing resentment.

Hayashi came into the room and Martin relayed the information Ching had revealed.

"So, desu-ka? The victim and Mr. Weber were having an affair. All right. What is everyone doing at the moment?"

"Sergeant Ibrahim's at the morgue with Mat. DC Santamaria's at the Petain Road house, DC Seah and Miss Tobin are interrogating the neighbors of Miriam Abraham and David Weber."

"We need more people," Kano said and shook his head. "More than one case and we'd be swamped."

"Any likelihood of that?"

"Not yet. If we solve this. If we bring in a murderer and the marquis is pleased and the mayor gets some appreciation from Tokyo. Then, maybe."

Despite the news about Weber and Eva Abraham, Martin knew he had to deal with the business of May instantly.

"Sir, I've spoken to May."

If a man could be said to visibly squirm, Hayashi did so now. He reddened and twisted away from his desk, walking quickly to the window, his back to Martin, shoulders hunched.

"That was a mistake," he said. "I had no right to ask you. No right to press my attentions on a woman like that. It puts her in a terrible position."

"Well, yes. I suppose so. Still, I spoke to her and she wasn't shocked. I think if she wants to refuse, she will. She asked you to go along and speak to her yourself."

Martin wanted to rid himself of this burden. A knock and the door opened. Santamaria put his head round the door. "Found something in the Petain Road house. A tin box."

Hayashi glanced at Martin, then walked out, back straight. Clearly, he was as glad of the interruption as Martin.

The box was new and shiny. "Found it concealed under the floorboards of the bedroom upstairs," Santamaria said.

Martin took up the smallest key and inserted it into the lock. It turned and all the men smiled at one another, like a bunch of schoolboys who'd found hidden treasure. The box contained some photographs and two documents. The photographs were of Eva and Rose Shultz and their parents. There were others of the Shultz Apothecary shop, of them all in a car, at the beach. Memories of older, happier times, family times. As he looked through them, Hayashi opened up the documents and lay them on the table.

"Deed to the house," he said, scrutinizing it. "She owned it." He picked up the second document. "Last Will and Testament of Solomon Abraham." Hayashi read through it quickly. "This revokes all previous wills and legacies and leaves everything to Eva. What previous wills and legacies?"

"Exactly." Martin nodded. "I'll check with Weber."

Hayashi called Mary, scribbled a rapid note in Japanese, and handed it to her with the deed document. "Get this to Nomura." He turned to the others. "I've asked the office of the Custodian of Enemy Property to locate Rose Shultz for a signature or whatever it is they do to regularize the property situation. It's our best chance of finding out where she is without alerting the Kempeitai to our interest. And if she's in prison, of getting her out even temporarily."

He turned to Santamaria and passed him the will document. "This was drawn up by an Indian lawyer two weeks before Abraham Solomon died. Find him and find out everything you can about this business."

Hayashi picked up the remaining unidentified key. "This key, could it be for Weber's apartment? I think Mr. Weber needs to answer some questions."

"On my way." Martin pocketed the keys.

CHAPTER TWENTY-THREE

At Weber's apartment, Martin knocked, then, without waiting, put the key into the front door. It did not turn. He cursed quietly. He'd been convinced that this key was to this door. Before he could think further on this, the door opened and Weber stood before him. The scratch on his face had faded somewhat. Martin suddenly regretted that lack of a photo of that face and the man's hands. Well, if he arrested him that would be solved.

"Mr. Weber," Martin said. "May I come in? Some questions."

"Inspector, I've told you what I know."

"Now, Mr. Weber, that isn't quite true, is it? Let's go inside."

Weber stiffened but retreated into the apartment. In the living room, he turned and faced Martin.

"Sit down," Martin said, pointing to the overstuffed chairs that sat on either side of a large radio. Weber sat, his face set into a look of defiance.

"You were having an affair with Mrs. Abraham. You told us you hardly knew her, but we have a witness who saw you kissing her."

"Don't be ridiculous. Who?"

"Never mind who. A reliable witness who has no reason to lie. Was Eva pregnant with your child?"

Weber rose and went to the window. The sound of Japanese voices barking orders and the rumble of heavy vehicles drifted into the apartment.

"Mr. Weber. You were seen kissing Eva Abraham. You should tell me the truth."

Weber turned. "All right. I had a brief fling with Eva. It was nothing. It was all over and done with before Miriam came back from India in December. I suspect Eva became pregnant by her husband. It seems the most logical thing."

That could be true, Martin thought. If the pregnancy was fourteen to sixteen weeks, it would mean Eva had conceived in January. Her husband, Solomon, was, by then, ill. Too ill to have sex with his beautiful wife? But then, if she'd wanted to have a son and heir by Abraham? Cement the inheritance? He wasn't inclined to believe Weber, but he let it go for the moment.

"What was your business with Solomon Abraham?"

"I was drawing up a deed of trust. Solomon wanted his fortune kept in trust for Miriam."

"Did he?"

"Yes. He left the beach house at Katong and a settlement on Eva, but the bulk, including all his properties, was to be administered as a trust for his daughter."

"Where is this document now?"

"I have it. I took all the important papers from Solomon's house at the surrender and kept them. That was my duty as his lawyer."

"Get it and anything else you have of his."

Weber rose and left the room. Martin looked around. Not bad furniture. A man's apartment, but a certain elegance and there were some nice things. A Chinese vase and two Venetian mirrors. He wondered if Weber owned this flat, and it crossed his mind that if Weber were to swing for Eva Abraham's murder it would fall conveniently empty. It almost made his pulse race.

Weber returned with a metal box, opened it, and handed a document to Martin. "All quite legal. Witnessed and signed."

Martin looked at the date. January 1942. He quickly read the conditions of the trust.

"Kept in trust and administered by you until such time as Miriam married, after which, well, well ... "

Martin gazed at Weber. "After which the trust is dissolved and all rights revert to Miriam and her husband. How handy. Did you suggest that clause, Mr. Weber? Did you in fact suggest the entire idea of a trust? Especially after you met Miriam and realized that if you married her, you would get your hands on a massive fortune."

Weber shook his head. "No. It was Solomon's idea. He realized he hadn't long to live. There was some gossip about Miriam in India. She was young and easily influenced. Her mother's family are all society types. Smoking and drinking and carrying on. I think he wanted protection for his daughter."

Martin ignored him. "So, you transferred your affections from the rich future widow to the rich daughter."

"No. No. There were no affections with Eva. I told you. I love Miriam. I want to marry her."

Martin took a look inside the box. Weber owned the apartment. The deed was there. It had been sold to Weber's father and Weber had inherited it. Solomon's will was there, too, and simply backed up the trust arrangement, confirming what Weber had said. Other papers: birth certificates, marriage certificates, the papers of any normal family. Martin was certain that Weber knew nothing of the last will that Solomon had drawn up.

A ring at the bell. Martin left the living room and opened the front door to Seah and Grace.

"Inspector," Seah said. "We have a witness who says she saw David Weber leaving his apartment through the back door."

"Back door. Is there a back door?"

"Yes, they all have back stairways for the maids to come and go."

Martin fished the key out of his pocket and gave it to Grace. "Go and see if this fits the back door. Quietly. Don't show yourself to him, and come back here."

Grace darted into the apartment.

"Tell me," Martin said to Seah.

Seah adjusted his glasses and consulted his notebook. "Grace knows this Miss Woodford in apartment 15. She goes out into the courtyard in the early hours of the morning to check her rat traps."

"Rat traps? What do you mean?"

"She lives with her sister and her sister's husband, Mr. and Mrs. Barker. She has a little dog and can't get meat for it since rationing, so she traps rats and mice and boils them for the dog. She goes out early so no one will know."

"Grisly but righto."

"Says she saw Eva Abraham cross the courtyard. She knew it was Mrs. Abraham because she caught her red hair as she passed under the courtyard lamp. A few minutes later she recognized David Weber leave through the back stairs and cross the courtyard after her. Around five o'clock on the morning Mrs. Abraham was killed. Says she hid from them both. She's terrified someone will find her traps because apparently some old biddy in the Mansions has a couple of cats and ... "

"All right, Constable."

"Yes, sir."

Grace returned with a broad smile on her face. "Fits, sir."

"Right. Grace, go and get Miriam Abraham and bring her here. Seah, search this apartment. Anything connected to Mrs. Abraham. You know what to look for."

Martin went to the living room and put the key on the coffee table. "This key fits your back door, Weber. It was on Mrs. Abraham's key ring. Why would she have the key to your back door?"

"We used to meet here. Where else? I gave her a key. She must have kept it. She wasn't happy at me ending our ... arrangement."

"I see. And where were you going the morning of Mrs. Abraham's murder? We have a witness who saw you cross the courtyard at around five in the morning. Where were you going when you told us that you were sound asleep in Miss Abraham's apartment?"

Weber's countenance hardly changed, but Martin saw the nervous flexing of his fingers. Martin picked up the key and united it with the others on the key ring. "Shall we go and ask Miss Abraham?"

"Don't involve her."

"Then?"

"All right. I didn't stay in the apartment with Miriam, but she didn't know that. The bed in the maid's room is appalling. I left and came back here. But I couldn't sleep. It was hot, so I went out for some air. I got back after an hour or so and then came back to my apartment to get some sleep."

"You went out for some air, is that it? In a city crawling with Japanese patrols? Where did you go?"

"Towards the river."

"That isn't true, is it? The witness also saw Mrs. Abraham cross the courtyard. Then you, trotting behind. I think you followed her. But Mrs. Abraham wasn't in her apartment that day, was she? She'd had a row with Miss Abraham and took off somewhere. Was it here? Did she fall back into the arms of the man she loved?"

Weber's jaw clenched.

Miriam Abraham arrived, pale and leaning heavily on her cane. "What's happening, David?" she said, walking unsteadily to his side. "What's happening?"

"There, there, my dear. Calm yourself."

"Miss Abraham, you say that David spent the entire afternoon, evening, and night with you the day Mrs. Abraham was killed."

"Yes. Yes. I told you."

"However, that is unfortunately not true. Mr. Weber left your apartment after you went to sleep and we believe subsequently met Mrs. Abraham, perhaps here, and then, after she left through the back stairs, he followed her in the early hours of the morning she died. We have a witness to that effect."

Miriam flinched and stared at Weber. "What?"

"Mrs. Abraham possessed a key to the back door of this apartment. Mr. Weber has admitted that he and she were lovers."

"It was over long before I met you," Weber said, his voice as tight as a shamisen string, his eyes beseeching.

"What?"

"It was all over, my dear."

Miriam stood as if frozen. Seah appeared. In his hand was an ivory satin nightgown. "Fallen behind the bed," he said.

Miriam's eyes went to it. The blood drained from Weber's face and he stood up, his eyes bulging. "No. No. That's not possible."

Martin saw his chance. "I believe, Miss Abraham, that after you had a row with Mrs. Abraham, she came here, to Mr. Weber's apartment. This apartment. I believe the affair never ended. This nightgown is proof. She was pregnant with Mr. Weber's child. He was fooling you. He was marrying you for your money."

Miriam let out a strangulated cry. She turned wild eyes to Martin. "I don't ... He wasn't sleeping? Is that it?" Miriam's voice shook violently.

"No. He was out pursuing Eva."

"It's not like that," David cried. "Miriam, please."

Miriam stared at Weber as if she'd seen a ghoul.

"You cannot positively alibi Mr. Weber between the hours of midnight and five o'clock. Is that right, Miss Abraham?"

She shook her head. "I was asleep."

Martin had no idea if he had to use the usual arrest statement in this new Japanese world, but it was habit and so he did.

"David Weber, I'm arresting you on suspicion of the murder of Mrs. Solomon Abraham. You have the right to remain silent, but anything you do say will be used in evidence against you."

Miriam let out a sob and sank into an armchair.

CHAPTER TWENTY-FOUR

Martin joined David Weber in the interview room. Seah had found further evidence of Eva's stay in Weber's apartment. A lipstick and comb were found in a drawer in the second bedroom. As if the sight of these objects had cracked his resolve, Weber had abandoned pretense. He admitted that he and Eva had continued their affair until the surrender. Then the meetings had stopped. But after his engagement to Miriam, they'd rowed. Eva had come to his flat after the fight with Miriam. She'd spent the Sunday there sleeping while he was with Miriam. When Miriam had gone to sleep, he'd gone back to his apartment. That's when Eva told him he had to break off the engagement. It was in his best interests. That's what she'd said. Then she told him she was pregnant. The child was his.

"What did you do?"

"I was angry. Really. And felt trapped. We had a row. I told her I wanted to marry Miriam. She was almost crazy. She said she was leaving but the next day she'd tell Miriam and it would all be over. She left and I followed her."

"Where?"

"To the shop of her father. She loved that place. She told me about it many times. It was bomb damaged. I couldn't think what she was doing there. I caught up with her. I tried to explain that I truly loved Miriam and wanted to start a family with her. A Jewish family. She laughed."

He stared at his hands. "As if I was ridiculous. Jewish money, she said. That's what you want. But you won't get it. I've sorted that out. I didn't understand and, anyway, I was furious by then. I ripped the locket from her neck and flung it on the ground. She bent to pick it up and I found a rock and, God help me, I hit her."

He stopped speaking. Martin waited. Grace's busy fingers came to a halt.

Weber sighed, a great exhalation of breath. "I was terrified. I bent down to see if she was still alive. She was." He turned his eyes to Martin. "You have to believe me. I just struck her. Nothing more. Then I heard something. Someone walking through the rubble. I ran away."

Martin smiled. "Bit unlikely, isn't it? She's about to tell Miriam all about you. Money is flying off into the wild blue yonder. Your prospects are suddenly zero. And all because of this stupid cow that is threatening you. So, you finish her off."

"No. No. I heard someone and ran. That's the truth."

"The truth is you shoved her face into the pile of incense and suffocated her. Then you left her and went calmly back to your apartment and went to sleep."

"No. No. You have to believe me. I didn't kill her. There was someone else."

Martin reflected. It was madly annoying, but they knew about Hong. It was perfectly possible that the sounds Weber heard were of Hong arriving.

Nothing connecting Weber to the murder of Eva had turned up in his apartment. Her shoes and earrings connected to Hong directly. None of Weber's clothes had blood spatter or smelled of incense, none of his shoes carried any blood or ash. But did that matter? He could easily have disposed of them. And she might have been dead when Hong came upon her. That was the point. Suffocation, that was the issue. Suffocation was personal. And Weber had very pressing and personal reasons to get rid of her. There was no reason for Hong to kill her. He could have robbed her without resorting to murder. It hardly mattered whether or not he had taken the shoes. Except it did, but Martin couldn't make the connection. So, Weber had killed her. It was glaringly obvious.

"You will be charged with murder. I can assure you, you will be found guilty. The Japanese want this case solved. And right now, you are the only one who has opportunity and motive."

Martin ordered Weber taken away to the holding cells in the Supreme Court temporarily until a custody jail could be sorted out. It was late and he let all the others go.

Martin filled the detective chief inspector in. "You're sure he's the man," Hayashi said. Martin hesitated. Hayashi saw it. "You aren't sure?"

"What do you think?"

"I think he had motive and opportunity. We have witnesses and his own admission. Of course, he denies murder. He would."

"Just something about his denial. I don't know. It's late." Martin was tired and had a long journey home.

"I spoke to May," Hayashi said, and Martin sagged inwardly. Why did he have to be involved in this?

"She's happy to, well, to come and stay with me. I'll be helping her move her things to Emerald Hill in a few days."

"Happy that all worked out for you, Keibu-san."

"Staying at the hotel for the moment. I can walk to it so thought you might like to take the car home tonight."

He put the keys on the desk. For the first time today, Martin felt a small kind of joy.

CHAPTER TWENTY-FIVE

In the gloom of the next morning's darkness, Martin drove the Vauxhall back to the office. A gentle rain was falling and the windscreen wipers squeaked to and fro like a metronome, clicking in the silent, contained interior of the car. Martin slowed at a checkpoint. Ahead, he could see the shapes of the people waiting at the kumiai, a distribution center for rationed food. There were kumiais for rice, for soap, for wood, for salt, for oil, pork, fish, flour, and each one required a new queue and hours of waiting from before sunup, come rain or shine. Joan set her girls to queuing and they resented it. Noisy petty rows had sprung up. The house was tense and he'd been glad to get away this morning before anyone else was up.

The tension was not eased by, not only his, but Joan's anxiety about his paternity and the potential repercussions from the Japanese for them all. He'd told her about the conversation with Ah Loy about a baptismal certificate and Joan had agreed that it would be a good idea to seek out one of the priests at St. Andrew's Cathedral who had not been interned in Changi. If he had been baptized, it would have been there, she said. She had found a photo of Walter as a baby in a long gown in the arms of Marie, with Ernst by her side, outside the cathedral.

He crawled forward and came to a stop. The bedraggled sentry glanced at the Syonan Keisatsu flag on the bonnet of the car, took a cursory look at his ID card, and waved him through. He headed to Bishopsbourne, the priests' house, to see how it might be approached. The Japanese had allowed Bishop Wilson, James

Merril, and John Hammond to remain out of captivity and carry on the ministry. Why, he had no idea. The house, in the quiet, leafy backstreets of Bishopsgate, was guarded by a single sentry. It looked like he could approach them later and talk in safety.

DCI Hayashi was not at the office. Martin's first order of business was the will of Solomon Abraham.

"Made two weeks before the surrender, sir," Santamaria said. "The lawyer was summoned to Mount Sophia by Mrs. Abraham, and he says that Solomon Abraham was in his right mind and happy to sign the document."

Santamaria put a paper on the desk in front of Martin. "Signed statement. The lawyer said there seemed to be some dissatisfaction with Miriam's relationship with David Weber. He distrusted Weber's intentions."

Eva in his ear. How much had she hated the so-called romance between Miriam and David, all the time they were scurrying into bed together? She'd be the one to tell her ailing husband that Weber was a gold digger who'd be quick to squander his money.

"All right. Find Hong's girlfriend, Neo. I want another word with her."

The phone on Hayashi's desk rang. Where was he? Martin answered. It was Nomura.

"The Keibu-san is out. What is it? Can you tell me?"

Nomura's English was good. He had located Rose Shultz in Outram Road Prison. A request to bring her to Nomura's office to sign papers regarding the house had been granted. She would be there, this afternoon, at six o'clock.

"Thank you, Lieutenant. May I ask you a question?"

"Yes."

"I would like to find out what is happening with my mother's former apartment which we own in Tiong Bahru. Can you do that?"

"Do you have the deed to this apartment?"

"Yes."

"Then bring it to this office. Mrs. Pereira, my secretary, will have paperwork for you."

Martin thanked Nomura and hung up. He dreaded meeting Rose. The sisters adored each other, and what state would she be in to get this news? He needed the friend, Marion Brown. Rose would need a friendly face. He went to the secretarial offices. "Mary, I need you to locate a Marion Brown. She last worked at the Department of Fisheries."

Martin went to lunch. When he returned, Neo was brought in. She'd cleaned herself up, looked almost presentable. Perhaps Hong's death had released her from his vicious grip.

He kept her waiting while he read the autopsy report on Hong, which had landed on his desk while he'd been out. Hong's body had been found in a damaged storm drain by abandoned and bombed-out buildings off New Bridge Road covered in rubbish. He'd died where he fell. Cause of death was a slit in the carotid artery in his neck. He'd bled to death in a few minutes. The artery was pierced in a single stab, deadly accurate. By the angle of the stab, it seemed it was made from the side, low to high with a small, sharp knife, a common, often handmade weapon carried by every gang member on the island. The attacker, according to Harry Iyer, was very likely smaller than Hong, and the attack, given the disparity in height, might have taken him by surprise. There was no evidence on his clothes or his body of who the attacker might be. A gangland killing was Harry's opinion. Time of death difficult to ascertain, but best estimate was Monday night or early Tuesday morning. The picture of the dead Hong wasn't pretty, the body having been munched by whatever fancied a bite and lying rotting in the heat for several days.

Martin turned his attention to Neo. In the interview room, he offered a cigarette. "Tell me everything you know about Hong and Eva Abraham. Don't lie. Leave nothing out."

"Hong agreed to meet her at some place by the hill."

"So, you saw him on Monday?"

"No. I told you I ain't seen him since he agreed to meet that rich bitch. That's it. That's all." She puffed on her cigarette. "It's the truth, Inspector. I don't know nothing."

Martin reflected on this. If Hong was killed Monday night, he might not have seen Neo in the meantime. She admitted Hong's involvement. Now there was Weber saying he heard someone coming, presumably Hong. They were all such consummate liars he might as well stick with Weber. Hong was, after all, dead. And the shoes and earrings could have gotten into Neo's cubicle through Hong. Hidden there until he could sell them. But that thought didn't satisfy. Again, it was the shoes. The shoes were like a small red flag. The shoes made this whole story odd.

He let Neo go. He was not farther forward. Hong was dead and Weber was still Eva's likely killer. Now he had to turn to the dreaded business of telling Rose Shultz of her sister's death.

Hayashi arrived at last. "Went to look at the house," he said, his face beaming with satisfaction. Martin's face revealed nothing of the turmoil he felt underneath. This new house, the new life, the new love. All stolen. What a fucking joke. He suddenly disliked this man's seeming contemptuous disregard for what was going on around him, while all wrapped up in his personal pleasures. Was Masuda right? Was Hayashi a devious liar ready to sacrifice anyone to his own needs?

"Rose Shultz will be at Lieutenant Nomura's office at six."

Hayashi stopped smiling. "Oh. Very well."

Martin left. He couldn't speak to the man in this revolting mood. Mary approached him. "I found Marion Brown. She isn't with the Fisheries anymore but they knew her address."

CHAPTER TWENTY-SIX

Marion Brown lived on Queen Street in an apartment building close to the now locked-up Portuguese church. He tramped up the stairs. The building had that sour smell of drains. There was bomb and shell damage. He knocked on the door. It was opened by an attractive brown-eyed woman wearing a head scarf and an apron. She was pregnant. She eyed him warily.

"Marion Brown?"

"I was Marion Brown. Mrs. Marion Da Souza now."

"I see. I'm a policeman. Detective Inspector Bach, Mrs. Da Souza. Don't be alarmed. I'm not with the military. Can I ask you some questions?"

She looked barely reassured. He got it. Any knock on the door could be the Japanese coming to accuse you of something. She stepped away from the door and he went into her small apartment. She'd been cleaning. She took off the apron and offered him a seat on one of the hard wooden chairs.

"I looked for you at the Department of Fisheries. You haven't returned to work?"

"No. I resigned when I got pregnant. I have an aged father who was wounded in the war and a younger brother who is crippled. My mother died of TB years ago. I got permission to take care of them. My husband and his brother work at the docks. I queue. And that gets harder as this goes on." She patted her bulge.

"I understand."

She nodded. "Want some tea?" she said. "I have stocks of India tea."

"No, thanks. I've come to ask you some questions about Rose Shultz. Do you remember her?"

"Of course. Yes. Where is she? I lost contact with her after the surrender."

"I'm sorry to say that she is under arrest."

Marion sat down and put her hand to her mouth. Tears sprang to her eyes. Damn, thought Martin, all I do is bring horror to decent women.

"I'm very sorry," he said. "I have the chance to see her this afternoon. I would ask you to please be with me when we meet. She'll need a friendly face. You were friends?"

"Yes. Yes." She wiped the tears away quickly. "We knew each other at school. And then at the secretarial. We are friends. What is she accused of?"

"Sheltering communists. It's probably not true, but that doesn't matter much. Do you have any photographs of Miss Shultz?"

She went to a chest of drawers and took out a photographic album. She shuffled through it a moment, then removed a photograph, handing it to Martin. It was a group photograph of about twenty women taken in front of the secretarial school.

"It was Mrs. Warshowski's birthday. That's me." She put her finger on her small face. "That's Rose next to me."

"Her sister Mrs. Abraham's not in this photo?"

"No. Eva came to the school much later on. She's younger than Rose."

Her hand flew to her mouth. "Oh. What about Eva? Does she know about Rose?"

"Mrs. Da Souza, I'm sorry to say that Eva Abraham was killed. I'm investigating her murder."

"Oh God." She began to cry again. Martin handed her his handkerchief and waited while she sobbed quietly.

"I'm sorry. I bring nothing but bad news."

"There is nothing but bad news. This war is bad news. And this enemy city. I don't recognize my home. I can't get used to calling it Syonan." She glanced at him. "I shouldn't say that, should I? I could be arrested."

"You could. But not by me."

Marion wiped her eyes. "How can I help you?"

Martin peered at the photograph. "Can you name any other women?"

"Their names are on the back. I wrote them down when I got that."

He turned the photo and skimmed the names. A name popped out. "Which one is May Desker?"

Marion searched a moment, then put her finger on a barely distinguishable face caught half behind the portly Mrs. Warshowski.

"She was friends with Rose?"

"Yes. We all came together when the war started and we joined the Medical Auxiliary Service. My husband was an ARP warden. That's how we met. On a bomb site. Not very romantic." She smiled. "We got married just before the surrender."

"Do you ever meet up with the women in this photograph?"

"One or two. Some got out. Some were killed. Some injured. It was just luck if you lived or died."

"Mrs. Da Souza, I would like you to accompany me to meet Miss Shultz. I have to warn you I don't know what we might see. She has been in prison."

"Yes. Yes. I want to. I want to see her."

Martin looked at his watch. Rose Shultz was due to arrive at six o'clock. It was three thirty.

"Can you come to my office in the Municipal Building at half past five? The CID offices on the second floor."

"Yes. I will come."

"Might you have something to give Miss Shultz? Some old clothes, perhaps. I don't know what she might need. A towel perhaps and some soap, sanitary things. I don't think she had a chance to take anything with her."

"Yes. I will look for something. Oh, Inspector. I'm very afraid."

"I will be there. We will face this together. We will do what we can for her."

Martin left Marion. He walked back to the office, got the keys to the police van, and headed to Bishopsgate. He bowed to the sentry and showed his ID. The man waved him through.

He was greeted by John Hammond. Tall, erect, with a salt-and-pepper mustache. Martin knew him quite well. "How are you, John?"

"Martin. Nice to see you. We get along."

"You're still free?"

"For now. Thanks to Lieutenant Ogawa, director of religious affairs and a very devout Anglican. The Japanese have been more than reasonable with us. We can work."

"Who is in charge of St. Hilda's? My sister-in-law thinks that the school may be reopened."

"At the moment, its Reverend Yeh. We have no money to pay him but, good man, he continues anyway. Still, that can't last and we hope the authorities will authorize the opening so that he can be recognized as a teacher and get some wages and rations. But surely that is not what brings you here. You are back with the police?"

"Yes. Trying to bring some justice, even poorly."

"This is a bad situation. We must all do what we can. I am grateful we have been allowed to continue outside. We have no rations, you know, but the people are incredible. Never a day goes by when some food is not left for us. We have a garden. And some chickens and goats. We are allowed to hold services in

St. Andrew's, a privilege not given to the Catholics. The Japanese permit the bishop to visit the civilian prisoners. Small mercies."

Hammond gazed at Martin. "Martin, how did this happen? Were we all so unprepared?"

"Yes. Totally unprepared, yet so reassured that we were impregnable. I was with the volunteers. Had an ancient rifle, almost no training, and at the first artillery shell, we all got split up. Constantly fighting a rear-guard action. Must have been like that for the troops too. The Japs were just too fast and too fanatical. Always surrounding us."

Hammond nodded, contemplating his hands.

"The idea of a fortress was nonsense," Martin went on. "I was in the north. There were no proper northern defenses. The Japs just poured onto the island and no amount of courage could stop them. We'd expected myopic dwarves and we got well-armed, crack troops. It's as simple as that."

Hammond shook his head.

"We believed all the arrogant nonsense spouted by the government," Martin said. "Right to the very end."

"God help us all."

Martin was pretty sure God wasn't listening. But he wasn't here for that.

"John, I have to confide in you. It's something personal."

Hammond led him to a sitting room and ordered tea. "I have nothing much to offer you, but we do have tea. No milk, I'm afraid. Our goats' milk all goes to the children of the convent. So, Martin, what can I do for you?"

"I need to find out whether I was baptized."

"I see. Your mother and father were of the Anglican faith?"

"My Indochinese grandmother became a Christian, Catholic probably, when she married my French grandfather. My mother was indifferent to all religion, but obviously my German father was a Protestant. I know that my elder brother, Walter, was baptized in St. Andrew's. Do you still have the parish register?"

"We do, of course. Our records have fortunately been preserved. The cathedral was spared the worst of the battle. What is your date of birth?"

"Twelfth of November 1912. But, John, it may be that I was not baptized under the name of Bach."

Hammond raised his eyebrows but said nothing.

"Thank you for your discretion. My father was not Ernst Bach. My mother, Marie, you see, had a liaison with someone. Her maiden name was Colbert. Shall I write it down?"

"I will remember. Marie Colbert. You think she might have baptized you under that name?"

"No. I just mention it as a possibility. I'm merely presuming she had me baptized since Ernst was apparently aware that I was not his child. As far as I knew, until a few days ago, I was Martin Bach and my father was a German. Now I've no clue."

Hammond nodded. "Confusing and upsetting. Let me look into it. You know you can always come and talk, Martin. And I urge you to attend Sunday services. They can be a comfort."

Martin smiled. "Thanks, John, but not sure I'm ready for that just yet. Don't see a lot of God's good work around me."

"It's there. I see it every day in the goodness of the people. It's in these terrible times that we see his hand most clearly."

A strange God, then, and even stranger his priests. Martin didn't get blind faith. But then he reckoned that few homicide detectives did. He thanked Hammond and left. His watch told him he had to get back to a meeting he was dreading.

CHAPTER TWENTY-SEVEN

Marion was waiting at reception in the CID. A bundle sat on her lap. "I've brought some things for Rose, Inspector."

Hayashi emerged into the reception room. Martin introduced Marion, who had a look of constrained terror on her face. She relaxed slightly as he spoke to her in English, bowed low, and glanced at Martin.

"Mrs. Da Souza," Hayashi said, "we have an unfortunate meeting. The inspector is right to bring you with us. We do not know what to expect."

Hayashi set off to the opposite side of the building. Marion and Martin trailed behind. Nomura greeted them and ushered them into his office. Documents lay on his desk.

"I expect Miss Shultz at any time," he said. They sat. Martin wanted to take Marion's hand but she kept them grasped and in her lap, to herself inviolate, untrusting, contained. Her way of dealing with the fear of being surrounded by the Japanese. Her way of dealing with the terrible unknown of what might come through the door. She did it for love of her friend. Nomura had insisted on opening the bundle. A blouse and skirt, some underwear, two towels, a washcloth and a bar of soap, a bottle of aspirin, three boiled eggs. Pathetic but precious items that Marion had given up for Rose.

A knock came at the door and Marion practically jumped out of her skin. She shot up and Martin rose with her. Nomura and Hayashi also rose. The tension was palpable, even for the Japanese men. A soldier entered first and stood aside. Another soldier held Rose Shultz by her arm and firmly moved her into the room. She was, to Martin's horror, in a bad way. A very bad way.

A great bruise spread down one side of her face, which was badly contused. Martin was sure she had other bruises. She sagged and staggered into the room. Hayashi and Nomura, Martin could see, were horrified. Marion broke out into a great cry and rushed towards Rose. The soldier holding Rose barked, but Hayashi spoke rapidly in Japanese. Both soldiers bowed deeply, turned, and left the room.

Marion helped Rose to a chair. Her hair was filthy, her clothes ragged and stained. She smelled of filth and shit. Hayashi turned to Nomura.

"Where is the bathroom? She needs to be cleaned up."

Nomura picked up the phone and Mrs. Pereira came into the office.

"Please take these women to the bathroom. Go the other way. Avoid the soldiers. Get her some food and drink."

The women left. Hayashi slumped into a chair. "This is a filthy business," he said in Japanese to Nomura.

Nomura nodded, silent. He went to the long windows of his office, which gave out onto the Padang, and opened them fully. Rose's stench dissipated and a breeze swept in from the sea. He stood a moment staring out, then turned. "I have drawn up the paperwork in Japanese and English. I cannot see any way we can help her. Can you, Keibu-san?"

Hayashi shook his head. He turned to Martin. "The Kempei want her back. Before you tell her about Eva, you do the questioning. Find out what we can."

Martin wondered what Hayashi and Nomura thought about their people, these barbarians who visited horror on simple people.

When Rose returned, it was a transformation. Marion and Mrs. Pereira had helped shower Rose and put her in the clothes

Marion had brought. Martin was glad he'd suggested this. She now smelled of soap. The open wounds had been cleaned and dressed.

"She's had some food and water," Mrs. Pereira said.

"Arigato," Nomura said, and Mrs. Pereira, with a sorrowful glance at Rose, left the room. Marion sat at Rose's side, holding her hand.

"Rose," Martin said, "we have brought you here today to sign some papers. You own the house in Petain Road?"

Rose nodded. "Yes, thank you for bringing me. Thank you." She spoke quietly but with a certain tight dignity. "Thank you for letting me get clean. It is the worst part. Being so filthy."

"Tell me what happened."

"During the war, I sheltered some families. Refugees from Malaya with nowhere to stay. One of the men was a communist. I didn't know. I've told him that. I don't know anything about communists. He just won't believe me."

"Who won't believe you, Rose?" Hayashi said. "Who did this to you?"

"Lieutenant Yamada. There is a sergeant too, but the worst is Lieutenant Yamada. He interrogates me and beats me, but how can I tell him anything when there is nothing to tell?"

Rose's eyes strayed to the open window. "I am alone. I see no one and never leave the cell. A bucket's the toilet. I never wash. It is so hot. I am always thirsty. The guard comes at any time, day or night. Yamada never stops questioning. And beating."

Marion started to cry. Rose took her hand. "Marion, what about Eva? Where is she?"

Hayashi exchanged a glance with Martin. Martin shook his head at Marion.

"Miss Shultz," Hayashi said. "Lieutenant Nomura has some papers for you to sign. It puts your house into the care of the Custodian of Enemy Property, who will be responsible for it. Do you understand?"

"Yes. Is that why I'm here? About the house?"

"Yes. And to answer some questions."

Nomura handed a pen to Rose and she signed the papers. "Does it mean I have lost the house?"

"No," Nomura said. "Oh no, miss. If not rented, you may return there. I will arrange it."

"I see." Rose almost smiled. "Not sure I'll get out of prison, though. Not alive at any rate. I should make a will. Can I do that with you?" She looked at Nomura. "I want my sister to have it. Can you arrange that, please?"

"I understand your wishes," he said. "I will add it to this document."

Rose smiled. "Thank you. May I go to the window, please, and look out? I should like to stand in the sunshine for a moment."

"In a moment," Hayashi said. "You bought the house. How did you pay for it?"

"Eva. She sold all her jewelry and we bought the house together. My name is on the deed, but Eva bought it for me. Kind, sweet Eva. My darling sister. Where is she?"

"Miss Shultz, do you have any next of kin other than Eva?"

"No. We just have each other. May I go to the window?"

Hayashi nodded and Marion led Rose to the window. She stared out into the sky and turned her face to the sun. Marion shot a desperate glance at Martin.

"Miss Shultz, I have some bad news for you," Martin said.

Rose did not move, basking in the sunlight, eyes closed. Marion held her arm.

"Your sister Eva has been killed. I am seeking her murderer. That is why we want to ask you questions. I'm sorry."

A silence fell. Martin wondered if Rose had heard him.

"Eva … Eva is dead?" she said quietly. She did not turn.

"Yes," Martin said. "She was killed a week ago. I'm sorry."

"A week ago. Really. A week ago. You're sure it was Eva. There is no mistake."

"No. Her stepdaughter and her stepdaughter's fiancé have both identified her."

"Are you lying?"

From the file Martin took Eva's picture taken at the morgue.

"I have a picture. Please identify her for us to be absolutely sure. We need you to be absolutely sure."

Martin moved forward and handed her the picture then stepped back, giving her room to take in this dreadful fact. Marion gasped and put her arm around Rose's shoulders. Rose gazed at the picture, perfectly still, then a violent sob shook her body. She threw off Marion's arm, climbed onto the parapet of the window, and threw herself out.

Marion screamed. The men rushed forward.

"Damn, damn," Hayashi said. They stared down. Rose lay sprawled, broken, in a pool of blood. Marion screamed and screamed. Mrs. Pereira came in and dragged Marion from the office. The three men rushed downstairs.

"I should've held on to her," Martin said. "Goddammit. God damn it."

Nomura called for a doctor. The Health Department was a few offices away.

Martin went to her. She was still alive, barely. A young Indian doctor rushed out. Nomura, Kano, and Martin stood to one side as the doctor gathered his people around and an ambulance clanged up. A stretcher arrived and Rose was loaded into the ambulance. The doctor climbed in, and it raced off. Her blood pooled on the pavement. Passersby hurried on. Nomura called to the soldiers on duty to clean it up.

Marion rushed out with Mrs. Pereira. "Is she dead?"

"No," Martin said. "She's gone to hospital. Kandang Kerbau. Go home, Marion. I'm sorry for what you had to deal with today. I will let you know what happens."

Marion turned and walked quickly away.

Nomura shook his head. He bowed to Hayashi and Martin and departed in a hurry. Mrs. Pereira followed.

"Come on," Hayashi said. "We both need a brandy. And I need to try to make sense of… "

He didn't finish the sentence. His life, his people, this brutality, what they were doing here? It might be all of those things. If it wasn't, it damn well should be.

CHAPTER TWENTY-EIGHT

"She's got until tonight, perhaps tomorrow morning." One of the emergency doctors was taking her pulse. "The top surgeons are in Changi," he said, "but that's not the problem. We can manage ourselves, but there's no anesthetic for non-Japanese cases. And she wouldn't survive anyway."

"Will she wake up?"

"I hope not. She's on morphine. We have stocks of that. We've set up an opium extraction laboratory here in the hospital for our needs. Fortunately, opium stocks are plentiful for the moment and morphine extraction isn't difficult."

Martin watched the doctor depart. The local doctors had picked up all the scattered pieces of the surrender and, in an instant, adjusted to the disappearance of the British as if they'd never been there.

Hayashi had insisted on a private room for Rose. A small but kind gesture that only a Japanese official could have made. Marion Da Souza entered. Another woman was by her side, fraught, frail. As she saw the bandaged body in the bed, she let out a small sob and clutched a handkerchief to her mouth.

"Hello, Inspector. What did the doctor say?" Marion's voice was firm. No tears. That shock was for yesterday. She had come to say goodbye.

"No hope. She probably won't wake."

"I hope she doesn't. She knew what she was doing. Eva dead and her future in that prison to be tortured and beaten to death."

"Yes."

Marion turned to the other woman. "This is Betty Yeo. We were all at secretarial school with Rose." The two women moved around the bed to be at their friend's side.

Martin's thoughts went to May Desker. She'd been Rose's friend too. "Do you think, Mrs. Da Souza, that I should ask May to come? May Desker. I know where she is."

Marion exchanged a glance with Betty Yeo. "May? What do you mean?"

"Well, she was at school with you all."

"May's dead, Inspector," Marion said, and Betty nodded. "She was killed in an attack on the Singapore General Hospital a week before the surrender."

Martin stared at the two women. "You're sure?"

"Of course. Betty and I were in the same MAS group. We joined up together and trained with May and Ingrid. Betty and I were stationed at a school which had been turned into a hospital for soldiers. May and Ingrid went to Alexandra Hospital. Once the Japs began pushing us all into central Singapore, we were ordered to Singapore General. We had to move the wounded away from the front line. May was killed by an artillery shell. Ingrid was injured too. Remember, Betty?"

"Yes," Betty said. "She got shrapnel in her hip. May and Ingrid had also been ordered to SGH when the British nurses were evacuated. Every MAS nurse came in because the area was being overrun by the Japs."

Martin's mind was churning. May Desker was dead. A woman called Ingrid got a shrapnel wound to her hip. The woman he knew as May had a limp.

"We carried May to the mass grave which was dug in the grounds," Marion said. "There was no way to bury anyone any other way. Bombs and shells raining down on us nonstop. The dead were lucky, because we couldn't do much for the wounded. No water. No medicine. Nothing. Hundreds of kids without anyone. It was hell."

Betty nodded. "The smell was horrific. Bodies piling up in the corridors. There was no water. That was the worst part. No water and the heat was awful."

Martin frowned. He remembered watching a fellow volunteer's head explode and his encounter with an ape and a ditch full of decomposing human corpses. Marion's lips pressed tightly together. Betty took her hand as they gazed at the broken body of their friend.

"Ingrid," Martin said. "What was her last name? What happened to her?"

"Olsen. Ingrid Olsen," said Betty. "The surgeon fixed her up. I nursed her for a while. When we heard of the surrender, I chucked off my MAS armband and went home. The British matron and all the English and Australian nurses had already left anyway. No one was in charge."

"I stayed," Marion said, "until the Japs ordered us out. They took over Singapore General for themselves. We took all the patients to the Woodbridge Mental Hospital. It's called Miyako now. The Japs told the English doctors to go with us. Dr. Williams was in charge. She told me to go home."

Marion looked at Betty. "Ingrid left," she said. "She told me she'd tell May's family. See they got the news. They'd been friends. She was terribly upset at May's death."

Martin digested this news. Was the woman at the restaurant actually Ingrid Olsen? But why? And what was he to tell DCI Hayashi?

From her handbag, Marion took out the group photo of the secretarial college and handed it to Betty.

"That's May," Betty said. "There behind Mrs. Warshowski. Poor thing. She was a lovely woman. Everyone liked May." Betty peered at the photo. "There's Rose. God, poor Rose."

Martin looked at the photo too. Marion, May, Rose, Betty. Where did Ingrid Olsen fit? Maybe she didn't.

"Did Rose or Eva know Ingrid Olsen?"

"Don't think so. She wasn't at the secretarial school with us, was she, Betty?"

"No. No idea what Ingrid did before the war. She didn't talk much."

Martin left Marion and Betty with Rose. He knew they would stay with her until the end. MAS nurses, ordinary women who'd had to be extraordinary. They'd seen every kind of gore and horror and brought comfort and some kind of succor to hundreds of the dying. Why did men talk of women as weak? When they were released from these prejudices and thrown onto their own devices, they were profoundly strong, clever, admirable. Just like Joan. And Grace. Rose was in the company of women. They would be at her side.

He found Seah in the corridor talking with Harry Iyer.

"Bad business, Martin," Harry said.

"All a damn bad business. You still got Mrs. Abraham?"

"Yes. Waiting for you lot to tell me what to do."

"Her sister is dying up there on the second floor. When she does, can you keep them together in the morgue? They'd want to be buried together."

Martin felt a sob in his throat and turned away. He took a deep breath. "Get the van, Constable."

Seah left and Martin turned to Harry. "Sorry. It's not fair. They remind me of Irene."

Harry knew all about Martin's torrid affair with Irene. In the course of it, he'd warned Martin time and again to give it up. He hadn't, of course. Someone else had done that by shooting her. "You need to solve that murder too," Harry said. "You'll never get over it until you do."

CHAPTER TWENTY-NINE

M artin got Seah to drop him in Chinatown. "Go back to the office, Seah. I've got something to do here."

What he had to do was get a look inside May's cubicle. If he was going to tell Hayashi that the woman he was infatuated with was an imposter, then he wanted to know as much about her as possible.

The house smelled as bad as he remembered it. Sour, dirty, rat-ridden. The lock on May's door was a good one but didn't take long to pick. He'd learned that trick years ago. He was surprised one of the other residents of this den hadn't done it already.

He opened the door. The first impression was of order. The second was the odor. The room was extremely neat. No easy feat when the walls were crumbling and full of crevices allowing dust and insects to penetrate. The sills of the window were riddled with white ants. She'd blocked the holes with newspaper to keep the dust at bay, but it was an impossible task. The place was a slum. The window shutters stood ajar, allowing air into the room so it was fresher than the corridor, but there was something else. Incense. He found the burner immediately. She probably burned incense to mask the smell of the house. A suitcase lay on the bed. She'd begun to pack up her belongings for the move. Clean, simple underwear, a cotton nightdress. Two blouses and three skirts. A dress hung from a hanger on the wall. A pair of plain black shoes stood neatly underneath next to some straw sandals. A large tin washbowl on a small bedside table, next to a paraffin lamp. Inside it was a bag with a washcloth and soap. This room told him a lot about the woman who was calling herself May Desker. She craved order.

He opened the drawer of the bedside table. Some makeup. An odd collection of talismans. A wooden crucifix, a small, seated Buddha, a string of Indian prayer beads, one of the star gods, and a money frog. Was she superstitious? If so, she'd covered all the bases. No personal photographs or mementoes of any kind. A life stripped bare. What could you make of that? People had lost everything in the firestorm of the final battle.

Before he went any further, he had to speak to May. He relocked the door and set out for the Kublai Khan.

The detective inspector's car was parked in the street. A couple of hawker stalls were selling coffee. He grabbed a stool at the first one and drank, watching the door of the restaurant and furiously mulling over what to do. Other patrons left. It was Japanese day so he couldn't go inside.

Finally, Hayashi appeared in the company of May. He smiled at her and she bowed. Hayashi was clearly smitten with this woman. Martin couldn't put it off. When May disappeared into the restaurant, Martin went forward.

"Chief Inspector."

Hayashi turned and greeted Martin with a look of surprise.

"Martin. Some developments in the case? Rose Shultz?"

"She won't live beyond tonight."

"I am sorry. Very sorry. We must do justice for her and her sister, Martin. It's important. We must be sure that David Weber did this. Ideally, I'd like a confession, but I think we have enough for a prosecution."

Justice for Eva, perhaps, Martin thought, for there would not be justice for Rose.

"Sir, I need to speak to you about something else."

"All right. I'll drive us back to the office. Get in."

"Sir, I need to tell you now. It's about May."

Martin told Hayashi what he knew.

"There must be a mistake," Hayashi said. His body had grown rigid, as if every fiber of his being had suddenly and violently clenched. "We shall sort this out now." He turned on his heel. "Come," he ordered. It was a bark.

May was clearing tables. The restaurant was empty.

"May," Hayashi called gently. She turned and smiled. "Please join us. Sit down."

May wiped her hands on her apron and sat.

As Martin relayed what he had found out, May's hands clutched the apron. She sat, head bowed, never looking up. Tears slid down her cheeks and gathered around her lips. Hayashi sat, rigid.

"What do you have to say?" Martin said. "Are you Ingrid Olsen?"

Her voice was tiny. "Yes," she said and wiped the tears from her lips.

Hayashi put out his hand to hers. "Calm yourself. Don't be afraid."

She clutched at his hand and looked up at him. "I want to tell you. I would have, perhaps. Later. When we knew each other better."

Hayashi's faced showed nothing, but he released Ingrid's hand. "Inspector, leave us. Not CID business. Go back to the office."

Martin rose. He had to obey, however reluctantly. What story would Ingrid tell? Whatever it was, DCI Hayashi wasn't the man to judge it.

CHAPTER THIRTY

Martin watched Mary tagging the evidence for trial. She'd typed up the charge sheet and the witness reports for the public prosecutor. Weber was still in the holding cells. The civil courts would reopen in just over a fortnight. Until then, Weber would remain in custody. Where they would move him to until then had yet to be decided. He continued to stick to his story. Eva Abraham had been alive when he left her.

Martin approached the table. The red nail was a reproach, the manifestation of the victim's struggle to the death. He looked at it and knew it was important but not how. Eva's locket, the keys, the rose-embroidered handkerchief, the shoes, the jade earrings: these had been accounted for. All the other fake jewelry was there. A telephone call from Ah Loy had told him that he hadn't been able to find anything about the fakes. The jeweler had fled the island during the bombing. Eva had spared nothing, not even her wedding ring, in her anxiety to turn everything to cash. But the Rolex Princess watch was still missing. He ran his eyes over Mat's photographs. The body, the broken shards, the beads. One of the photographs of the ground farther away from the body where it had not been scuffed showed a print in the dry earth. He picked it up. One of the POWs had mentioned paw prints. A dog had passed by and left its mark. It had done little damage but perhaps it had been disturbed. It was slim pickings for dogs and cats in this new world and they were currently fair game themselves for the cooking pot.

He put down the photo and took up the box from Rose's bedroom. The deeds, the will, they all painted a picture of absolute devotion. Everything Eva had done, the marriage to the old man, everything had been to ensure the financial security of their future. Then the terrible moment when Eva had found Rose had been arrested and the need for money to buy her freedom. What anguish and terror and hopelessness had enveloped her? And then the man she loved had dumped her. He was going to get hitched to the rich heiress. And then the announcement, the fatal moment when Eva had told David she was pregnant and Miriam would know all. So, he had killed her. And now Rose would die of horror, desperation, and a broken heart. He blamed the Japanese for Rose's torture but wasn't about to shed tears for David Weber.

His eyes stopped on the still dusty shrine. The two star gods, *Lu xing*, the god of prosperity and *Shou xing*, the god of longevity, were cracked and broken. The missing one was *Fu xing*, the god of happiness and good fortune. He checked the photograph. It hadn't been looted on some previous occasion, nor lost and broken in the bombing. No evidence of that existed, and the hurly-burly was long since done here at least. No, the little god had been taken that night, the night Eva was killed. He'd forgotten that. The dustless space told him so. And now he knew who had taken it.

CHAPTER THIRTY-ONE

Mat checked his camera, glanced coldly at Martin, and took up position at the door of the tenement building. Seah and Martin made their way to the first floor.

"Shall I check on Neo, Inspector?" Seah said.

"No. I'm done with her for the moment."

As he turned onto the landing, Martin saw that May's cubicle door was ajar. Damn. He was too late. If she was here and packing up, the evidence could have been destroyed. He cursed himself for not seeing all this sooner. In this case, as in his own life, nothing and no one was what or who they seemed.

He signaled to Seah to wait and pushed open the door to the sight of the detective chief inspector, standing over the open suitcase, one of Ingrid's black shoes held to his cheek. What was this? Was he befuddled with love? Or a shoe fetishist? He'd run into all kinds of fetishes working in the vice squad, but never actually met one who was sexually aroused by shoes. But who knew what the Japanese found erotic? How was he going to get through to the man? Clearly, he was packing her things.

Martin took a step forward as Hayashi turned. "Sir, a word?"

Hayashi dropped his hand abruptly, his eyes narrowing. "What do you want?"

"Sir, some new evidence." Martin darted a glance beyond Hayashi and into the room. He couldn't see what else had been moved.

Hayashi placed the shoe on the bed next to the suitcase. He frowned, obviously suddenly realizing how odd it was for

Martin to have turned up here. "It will wait. This is not the time or place."

"It is the place, sir. The evidence is here."

Hayashi stood stock-still, his eyes never leaving Martin's face. "What evidence?"

Martin hesitated. The evidence of the statuette was slim. But it was in his gut. He needed to follow where it led. Martin didn't know Hayashi. The man talked of morality, the high road, and the search for good karma, but when it came to his personal happiness, Martin had no way of knowing what he would do.

The minutes ticked by. Eruptions of noise from time to time in the house, children cried, men yelled, women screamed. The two men stood like statues. Finally, Martin had to speak. "She's involved in some way. There are too many connections. I'm sorry."

Like a good Japanese, Martin observed, Hayashi had mastered his facial emotions. But the veins in his neck seemed to throb and his hands clenched. For a second, Martin thought the detective chief inspector might do the unthinkable and punch him.

"She has explained the change of identity." Hayashi's gaze was steely. "War obliges strange choices. It has nothing to do with you or this case."

What yarn had she spun the man, with tears in her eyes? What bloody sob story? He wanted to scream at Hayashi and shake some sense into him, but he drew all the wobbly threads of those feelings inside and said calmly, "Sir, I think it does. I can only tell you what I've found. You are my superior officer. The rest is up to you."

Hayashi abruptly stepped away from the bed. "Show me your evidence, Inspector."

Martin went to the drawer and opened it. To his relief, nothing had been moved. He put the photograph of the shrine and its shattered gods and dusty spaces on the top of the drawer. With a handkerchief he took out *Fu xing* and placed the little god next to the photograph. The statuettes were identical.

"I think this statuette was removed from the crime scene. The space where it stood is clear of dust. It meant a recent removal."

Hayashi looked at the photograph, then gave a small, tight shake of his head. "Anyone could have this kind of statue. Hong could have taken it."

Martin frowned. What kind of skewed logic was this? "Sir, why would Hong take it? A cheap statuette. And why, then, is it here?"

The detective chief inspector remained mute.

"Ingrid Olsen has a connection with Eva Abraham," Martin said. "It's not conclusive, but it deserves a closer look. I need to search the room."

Hayashi frowned at the floor. The voices of the house had stilled and only the noises of the street penetrated, shrill calls to patrons to consume wares, caged birds squawking, the bell of the candy man. They were getting nowhere. It was like pulling a cow up a tree, as his old amah used to say.

"Sir, we need to search this room."

Hayashi remained unmoving. It suddenly occurred to Martin that he might refuse. Could he? There was easily enough evidence to convict David Weber for this murder. If Hayashi could settle his conscience, then he could have happiness. Nothing absolutely connected Ingrid to the crime; it was circumstantial. But if she was there, what was she doing? He knew, as sure as joss was joss, that Hayashi was thinking this too. Doubt, as insidious as ash itself, must be creeping through his mind.

Martin went to the door. "Do you want me to leave, Detective Chief Inspector?" His implication was clear. Leave you to destroy evidence. Leave you to save your girlfriend.

Hayashi's eyes met Martin's. "Yes. Go back to the office."

Martin wanted to strike the man. All that talk of bloody moral certainty, justice, and karma. Through clenched teeth he managed to hiss. "You want me to leave?"

"Yes. Go." Hayashi pointed to the door.

It was now or never. He knew that Ingrid Olsen was dirty. He couldn't work for this man if all that talk was a bunch of lies. If Ingrid had killed poor little loyal Eva Abraham, he wanted her brought to justice.

"Sir, he said, "you said you wanted justice for the Shultz sisters. What were all those fine words about good karma for your sons?"

Hayashi's face gathered into itself, closing tight. Martin didn't wait for fury. "If you don't investigate this, then I regret that I shall have to offer my resignation."

The words hung there, like the bad smell of the ratty corridor. Actually, Martin wasn't in the least sure he could actually resign. He could be shot, probably, but not resign. Still, it was too late. "I'll ask for a bloody transfer" hardly had the same ring of defiance. He knew Hayashi understood.

Hayashi turned abruptly, went to the window, and threw back the shutters like a man starved of air. A hot breeze wafted through the cubicle carrying odors of frying food, garlic, and hot chili. A minute ticked by. Martin could only imagine what moral maze Hayashi was embarked on but he knew it was a test: the first real test of his integrity and their working relationship.

Finally, he turned to face Martin. There was no visible emotion but his voice held an edge of sadness. "You do me a disservice, Inspector. I was going to search the room myself. Because, you see—"

"Sir, with respect, we should do that together."

Hayashi held up his hand. "Yes. Yes. All right. There is something." He picked up the small incense burner. "The perfume of the incense. It's sandalwood."

Martin shook his head, uncomprehending.

"Sandalwood. Not aloeswood. Not the incense in which Eva Abraham was suffocated."

"I don't understand."

"But the shoe ... " He spoke almost to himself. Martin had to strain to hear him.

"I thought I smelled ... " Hayashi pointed to the shoe. "There is joss ash in her shoe. It is not sandalwood. It is aloeswood."

Martin turned his gaze to the shoe. Now he understood. "Aloeswood? You recognize it? She was there?"

"She was somewhere where she got aloeswood ash in her shoes. They've been dusted off, but it's impossible to remove every bit of the ash or its scent without washing so well you ruin the shoe."

Martin saw that Hayashi had recovered his composure. "I think you should search the room. I would, however, ask that when dealing with Ingrid you continue to act and speak as if she was May Desker. Whatever you may find."

Martin frowned. "Is that necessary? Should not her lies be known?"

"She had her reasons, Inspector. However, if this information becomes known to the Tokko or the Kempeitai, she will be tortured and shot. That is how they deal with anyone who misleads them about their identity. There is no argument. No appeal."

"Yes, I see. And if she did it? If she murdered Eva?"

"Then it won't matter, will it?"

Martin nodded and Hayashi bowed. He strode to the door and disappeared into the darkness of the hall. Martin went to the window. He watched Hayashi thread his way through the crowds, get into his car, and drive away, not in the direction of the restaurant but towards the Padang. He was not warning Ingrid. Seah was standing below with Mat. He had clearly retreated when Martin had discovered the detective chief inspector's presence. He whistled down to them.

Martin carefully wrapped the shoes and placed them in the suitcase. He and Seah began a systematic search, each starting on either side of the room. "What are we looking for, Inspector?" Seah asked, pushing his glasses up his nose.

"Anything connecting May Desker to the crime scene. Jewelry, watch, handbag, anything."

Seah began taking apart the bed, checking and folding the sheets, removing the cover from the pillow, feeling the hard yellowing mattress.

Mat went to the window. He stood a moment, then turned to Martin. "Inspector, I'd like to shoot some street scenes. My first job is for the magazine, after all." Martin heard the resentment in Mat's voice. He'd made a bit of an enemy of this young man and though his reprimand had been warranted, he didn't want to prolong bad feeling.

"Go ahead. Whatever you need to do." Martin gave his attention to the drawer.

Mat perched on the ledge, which, with a crack, broke. He tumbled to the floor, holding his camera up, and let out a yelp.

Martin turned. The sill of the window had given way. Crumpled paper, some bundled cloth, and half the wall littered the floor around Mat. Cockroaches scrambled back into the safety of dark holes.

"Sorry," Mat said as he started to get to his feet.

Martin held up his hand. "Don't move." He bent down. Something had fallen from the crumpled paper. Martin smiled. "Constable Seah, do you see what I see?"

Seah stepped next to Martin. "Yes, sir. I do."

With the end of Ingrid's toothbrush, Seah picked up the object. "A Rolex Princess watch," he said and smiled.

CHAPTER THIRTY-TWO

Ingrid sat in the interview room, composed and quiet, her hands in her lap. The fan churned the turgid air and whatever passing breeze managed to squeeze in. Grace sat behind her stenography machine. Martin had explained to Ingrid that she was, for now, to be officially considered as May Desker and told her the reasons. She made no acknowledgment. He wondered if she understood how fortunate she was to have the detective chief inspector's favor.

The first thing he'd done when Ingrid got to the office was to have her fingerprints taken and then remove the bandage from her arm. The burns were suppurating. It must have been painful, but Ingrid sat unflinching. He could see no indication of anything other than the burn. One area was particularly bad, with a large blister. If Eva had scratched Ingrid, could she really have scalded herself to cover it up? Grace had washed the bandage and applied some coconut oil before putting it back on and giving her some aspirin.

Ingrid's statement lay on the table in front of him. It was marked for his eyes only and written in Hayashi's sloping legible hand.

Ingrid Olsen had been raised in a brothel in Bugis, the fatherless daughter of a Danish prostitute who had died when she was thirteen. She had received some formal education but had soon taken to petty thieving, though she adamantly denied ever being a prostitute. She'd been arrested several times. She'd become the girlfriend of a minor gangster who was killed during the first wave of bombings. She joined the Medical Auxiliary Service and met May Desker. That meeting, she said, that call to service when the country was in danger, that friendship, had changed her life. She had seen a higher mission, a better way. She was injured when May was killed. May's death had been devastating and she had mourned her friend, mourned her even now. After the surrender, she told May's family that she had died but kept May's identity papers and a burning desire to be a different person. The Desker family had moved to upcountry Malaya immediately after the surrender. So, she'd taken on May's identity to get as far away as possible from the old life and her police record. She got her ration card and the residence certificate in May's name, found the job in the restaurant, and began to learn Japanese.

"No complaints at the Japanese taking over, eh?" Martin said. "You fell on your feet."

Ingrid smiled. "No complaints. I like the Japanese. I've no special liking for the *ang mo*."

"It was all going so well. New job. New name. Perks. So why kill Eva Abraham?"

"I didn't kill Eva. She was dead. I robbed her, sure. But I didn't kill her."

"All right. Tell me your version."

"Met her in the restaurant with her little Japanese lapdog. I knew who she was. Her picture had been in the paper. Married that millionaire. I knew she was Rose's sister because Rose talked about her during MAS training. I didn't tell her my name in case she rushed off and told Rose. Just said I'd known Rose in the MAS and asked where she was."

"You found out? You went to Petain Road?"

"Sure. Went to take a look."

"Never know, do you? A little larceny. They've come into money so why not you? Eh?"

Her face hardened. "Got a cigarette?"

Martin passed the 555s. "What about Petain Road?"

"She wasn't there. All empty and abandoned."

"Right. Looted too. By you?"

"No."

"Hmm. So?"

"I asked around. Turned out she'd been arrested not long before I got there. Some sort of communist stuff."

"Then what?"

"I'd gotten to know Eva a bit. Figured there might be some money in it down the line. Little snobby bitch. She looked down on me, I know that. No better than me but she'd married the rich Jew."

"And?"

"Not long after that she's all upset. Tells me Rose has disappeared. Course I knew that. Cries on my shoulder. Asks if I know any villain who can do a job for her. She needed money in a hurry."

She lit the cigarette and blew smoke. Her lips turned down into a grimace. "Naturally, she figured I'd know men like that. Gave me some money. I put her on to Neo and Hong."

She looked at Martin. "She was rich. Why'd she need money? Didn't make sense."

"Never mind that. Go on."

"Neo's a blabbermouth and an addict. Found out about this meeting and where it was."

"You went there?"

"Yes. I don't care about the Japs. I know the back alleys. And that place is deserted at night. Backs onto the hill. Spooky. People stay away. When I got there, she was already dead."

"Really?"

"Yes. It took me longer than I thought. Getting across the river can be difficult. Have to avoid bridges because of the guards. Had to find a sampan. When I got there, I thought I was too late.

No sound, no one around. But when I went into the shop, I saw her. She was already dead."

"You robbed her?"

"Sure. Why not? Hong had got what he wanted and just killed her. I took her watch, the earrings, and the shoes. Then I heard the watchman whistling. They always whistle loud. They don't want to catch anyone. I took off. That's it."

She blew more smoke and watched Martin.

"You put the earrings and shoes in Neo's cubicle?" The business with the shoes suddenly made sense. May wouldn't necessarily know or care about Chinese superstitions.

"The shoes were a holy mess and the earrings were fake. I know fakes when I see them. When you came looking I stuck them in Neo's cubicle. To implicate Hong. He killed her, didn't he? Who else?"

"You told me the wrong cubicle. The man who ran away wasn't Hong, was it? He was already dead. Did you know that?"

She crushed the cigarette into the ashtray, ignoring the question. "How'd you get on to me, Inspector? That was a surprise, I must admit."

"You took the statuette. I found it. Why'd you do that?"

She laughed. "The little god. Dunno. Just saw it there, standing untouched in all that mess, and it seemed like an omen of good luck. Picked it up."

"Not so lucky."

She shrugged.

"How was Mrs. Abraham when you saw her dead? Describe it."

"She was lying facedown with her head in the incense burner."

Martin sat back. Gone were the tears; gone was the persona of the sweet little waitress just trying to get by. The true woman sat before him. The thieving child of the whorehouse. The shoes, the joss ash, the watch. She was there. All the rest of this little story could easily be a pack of lies. She could have stuffed Eva's face into the incense. Out of spite. Out of jealousy. Taken her stuff and got out. Or it could have been Hong. And, of course, it could be Weber.

CHAPTER THIRTY-THREE

All the effects from Ingrid's cubicle had been brought to the evidence room. Grace was recording each item, occasionally touching her fingers to her temple to smooth her hair. Why did she do that? There was never a hair out of place. Martin stood for a moment, smoking and watching her. Smart, fast, shrewd, and thorough. She looked over to him. "She denies the murder?"

"Yes. Weber, Hong, or Ingrid. Take your pick."

Grace continued recording the meager contents of Ingrid's life. Martin blew smoke and watched the rings evaporate into the air.

"Sir, I went to the morgue and took the fingerprints of Hong. Dr. Iyer had just received half a dozen microscopes from the Health Department. He gave me two. My brother has been able to use them to construct a comparison microscope. It involves connecting them by an optical bridge. I can now compare fingerprints."

Martin moved towards Grace and sat down. "All right."

"I have compared the fingerprints on the keys to those of Eva Abraham and found a match. Smudges on the earrings. Nothing there. So far that is all I can say."

"Well, at least we now have some science. It is going to come down to that because I can't tell which of them did it."

"Shall I continue to examine fingerprints?"

"More than that. Fingerprints, of course, but everything else. Grace, you must be the forensic eyes and ears of this department. We have no one else. I want you to concentrate on that. I'll ask to get a new secretary for the other work including the stenography. Perhaps you know someone."

Grace gave a small, dimpled smile.

Hayashi was at his desk when Martin got back to his office. "Well?"

"Admits she was there. Admits the robbery. Says Mrs. Abraham was dead when she arrived."

"Perhaps she's telling the truth."

Martin pursed his lips. DCI Hayashi hadn't seen the hard little nut lying inside the sweet woman he thought he saw. Perhaps he should. "Perhaps you should interrogate her yourself."

"No. But I would like you to be quite sure."

He glanced towards Martin. Dammit, the man was annoying with his bloody romantic crush.

"I want to be sure," Martin said, "but if everyone lies, it may be difficult."

The day had grown dark. Rain began to beat down, lashing the windows.

"I know you have to keep her here," Hayashi said, "but can she be made comfortable?"

"I can arrange for a cot in the interview room. Other than the holding cells in the court, it is the only place we can keep her for the moment. If you'd like, I will stay here tonight. Let the others go. It will take me hours to get home in any case. I'll see she is all right."

Hayashi rose. "Thank you. I am obliged."

He gave a small stiff bow and left the room. It had taken a lot to ask this favor, but Martin recalled his kindness in seeking a private room for Rose Shultz. He rang the hospital and spoke to Marion. Rose was not expected to live through the night.

Santamaria found a cot. A meal was brought from the canteen. Grace accompanied Ingrid to the bathroom. Ingrid said nothing, mechanically going through these motions of living, and when Martin locked the door of the interview room, he relinquished the case for the evening. Mary caught up with Joseph Santamaria and fluttered her eyelashes as they departed. Grace hesitated, a small glance in Martin's direction indicating a certain concern.

"Don't worry. I'll sleep on the sofa."

That wasn't what concerned her, he quickly realized. "Sir, I don't like this. She should be behind bars like David Weber. There's a second holding cell in the court building."

"Yes, I know. But I promised the detective chief inspector. It's just for tonight. Sergeant Ibrahim has made arrangements with the Beach Road station."

"Inspector, just be careful. She's clever. More than you think. She asked what would happen if she needed the bathroom in the night. Seemed like she thought she could have someone open the door. So, I told her that she'd just have to make do. I've left her a jug of water and a chamber pot. If she asks for water or to go to the bathroom, remind her of that. I wouldn't open the door to her while you're here alone."

Martin smiled. "Well, I'm sure I can manage, Grace, but thanks. We'll sort it all out tomorrow."

"Sir, I ... Well, I'd rather there was a bolt on the outside of the door if it's to be used as a holding cell. I'll see to it tomorrow first thing. In the meantime, I've hung a small bell on the door handle. It will jangle if she tampers with the door."

"Worrying about nothing Grace, but fine. Good night."

"Good night."

Noises of departure rang over the cavernous interior of the building. The clack of receding footsteps, the faint clang of a door. He went to the main door of the CID and locked it.

The meal of chicken rice was cold, but he ate it slowly, reading the newspaper. He noted that democracy was dead in the US and Bernard Shaw was predicting the collapse of the British Empire. In other news, two journalist lovers of Nippon in Berlin and Tokyo were married over international radio, car accidents in Syonan had plummeted since the Nippon takeover, and Tiger beer had gone up five cents. He turned on the radio and began to model a page with General Tojo's photograph into a boat. The brassy sounds of the "Song of the Bivouac" poured out of the radio. It was one of the endless martial ditties that occupied the airwaves during the evening. He switched it off.

He walked lightly down to the bathroom, passing the door of the interview room. He listened a moment. The little bell was on the handle and he smiled at Grace's nervousness. There was no sound from inside the room.

He watched the sun descend over the Padang, put Hayashi's brandy to good use, and followed the wave of cigarette smoke fluttering into the breeze. The heavy rain had washed away the heat and the air was fresh.

He lay on the sofa as the afternoon faded. His mind went to Irene. He'd turned up at her bungalow just over two years ago. The morning of January 12, 1940, to be exact, his car curling up round the drive between the spreading travelers palms. There'd been a break-in.

She'd come to the door to greet the police, a white cotton dress, no makeup, glossy blond hair pulled into a loose ponytail, filled with youth and an easy Australian, informal manner. He'd hardly been able to take down the statement for looking at her. She'd seen it and smiled. His constable had ribbed him about it on the drive back to the station.

The culprit, it turned out, was a young Indian boy who worked in the garden. He'd nicked some silverware and broken a window to make it look like a break-in. It all got sorted out pretty quickly and they'd met again at the magistrate's court. She'd asked the judge for leniency for the boy and he'd liked her for that. They'd got talking afterwards. Her husband, Paul, older than her by ten years, was away a lot on business, on hunting trips, climbing small mountains, God knows what, the pursuits of the colonial bachelor, unused to a marriage he'd apparently contracted on the spur of the moment. They'd started to see each other. A breezy lunch at a small place he knew out of the way where Europeans never went. Walks along a deserted beach. Innocent. That's what he told himself. Of course, it wasn't. Within a month they were that cliché, furtive lovers.

He tossed onto his side, wanting to fall asleep, wanting to dream of those days, but remembering now, with the temperance of time, the misery of it all. Remembering, too, the bruises on her from Paul, who didn't much care for a wife, at least not one who asked him for anything like affection. She hated the life here, the life of the colonial wife, tea parties and gossip. She hated sleeping with Paul. He hated it too.

Martin had actually contemplated killing Paul. He knew the underworld, the triad gangs who'd do anything for a few dollars. Certainly arrange an accident in a car. But it had never happened. A pregnancy ended their liaison. He never asked, but half suspected the child was his. When she got dengue, she miscarried. Paul, the stupid arrogant oaf, hadn't been able to see her deep sadness, so she'd come back to him. He had no idea if she loved him, but it made no difference. He'd been sleepwalking through the whole thing. He couldn't have ended it. Murder had done that. The last time he'd seen her she was on a slab in the morgue and only then because he'd paid the Malay guard to let him in during the night and say the briefest, impossible goodbye with a kiss on her cold, dead lips.

He got up, nerves jangling, flicked on the light, and lit a cigarette. In the bay, the fire from the oil depots began to cast a rosy glow into the darkening sky. The heavy rumble of military vehicles came from the seafront. He watched a hundred young Japanese soldiers at bayonet practice on gunnysack dummies on the Padang, their attacking war cries echoing in the dusk.

CHAPTER THIRTY-FOUR

Hayashi turned the key and went inside his new house. The Straits houses were not grand like the great mansions that the powerful military men coveted. These houses were smaller, compact; they exuded a restrained beauty but yet had flourishes of exuberance.

Furniture had been left in every room, a mixture of English, Chinese, and Malay. The number of statues, objects, vases, and paintings taken from the government buildings, galleries, and private homes of Singapore was staggering. They had been separated into different categories and kept in the classrooms of a school on the flanks of Fort Canning Hill. Japanese officers were invited to select whatever they wanted to adorn the walls, shelves, and cabinets of their new mansions. It was rumored that Yamashita had taken a small bust of Queen Victoria on which he hung his helmet each night.

Hayashi had studied fine art in London at Slade. It hadn't taken him long to discover he would not be a great artist, but it didn't matter. London's museums and galleries, its libraries, its streets, were available to him. In that heady time before the war, London had been a magical place to be young. Young, privileged, and monied, of course. He knew that now.

For this house, Hayashi had chosen a copy of a painting of Emma Hamilton by George Romney. The mistress of Nelson reminded him of another Emma, the daughter of one of his professors. It recalled to him the rush of passion, the enormity of first love. He and Emma had walked and talked, accompanied everywhere by a chaperone, for a public outing with any man, much less a Japanese man, was forbidden.

She had been married off to a man she had been betrothed to as a young girl. And he had left England because his studies had ended and, in any case, he couldn't bear to stay. Now looking back down the tunnel of the years with clearer eyes, he wondered if he had made it, for too long, everything in his young life, and she hadn't even noticed. It hardly mattered. He preferred his illusions, and it was, after all, his romance.

He wandered from room to room. A dark thought came to him. Who had lived here? Did he dare even ask? Open up that viper's nest and look into the darkness of what was happening here?

He locked the door and drove back to his hotel. This house was ready for him, but he wasn't ready for it.

The package Hayashi had asked Santamaria to fetch was on his bed at the hotel. He took out the shallow, three-legged tekoro and filled it with some of the white ash. Then he opened the six packets of koboku wood chips, the precious fragrance of Southeast Asia. He lit the small cube of charcoal and waited for it to turn grayish white, then with the metal tweezers he held the small mica stone over the heat. In his youth, he had joined his father and his friends in the art of monko, listening to incense, passing the tekoro around from nose to nose. An incense guessing game that had its origins in the court of Kyoto centuries before.

He took up first the kyara wood and placed it on the mica stone. A gentle scent with a touch of bitterness. He felt the bitterness that lay at its heart. Next, he took the sasora. It resembled kyara, especially at the beginning, but developed into a scent that was cooler. Kyara was like an aristocrat, his father had told him, sasora like a monk. He had never forgotten and could easily tell them apart.

He waited a time, replacing the small mica plate, waiting for his palate to clear. Next, he took sumontara. Like kyara but with something ill-bred about it, like a peasant disguised as a noble. He could hear his father's words. He did not find it so ill-bred. His opinion had changed over time, and now he found manaban to be more peasant-like, sweet and sticky, coarse and unrefined. He held the managa in his hand. Then placed it on the new mica plate. There was no mistake. He had known there was no mistake. The fragrance of aloeswood, light, enticing. He put it away and quickly replaced it with rikoku, the sharp pungency driving the managa from his head. Rikoku was the fragrance of the warrior.

He packed them away. He felt restless and knew sleep would not come. There was a shop just off the Padang that had stocks of English confectionary. Bassett's Liquorice Allsorts were a favorite from his time in England and rediscovered here.

He set off, enjoying the cool evening air, purchased the sweets, then sat for a moment at the edge of the sea. He looked up to the CID offices. The light was on. Martin was still awake, perhaps unable to sleep in the stuffy interior. Perhaps Ingrid, too, was not sleeping. He pocketed the licorice and headed towards the office.

As soon as he opened the door, he heard Ingrid's voice. But what was she doing talking, and to whom? He moved forward silently, sensing something was quite wrong. From the darkness of the outer offices, he could see Ingrid standing by Martin's desk, lit by the low light of a lamp. She was holding a knife. His senses on high alert, he moved forward and saw Martin in his chair. From the way he was sitting, he knew rather than saw that Martin's hands were tied behind him. His head hung forward, his white shirt collar was bloody, but he was not unconscious, far from it. He was gazing at Ingrid from beneath his lids, listening. Martin did not seem in imminent danger. Ingrid was not standing near him. Hayashi felt in his pocket for the thin roll of jute rope he always carried on him.

"You must have money here. I didn't kill Eva. She was dead already. I robbed her, but I didn't kill her."

"Where you going to go, Ingrid? If you didn't do it, then help me prove it. You can't go anywhere, you know that."

"I ... I won't lose my head for this. Where's the money in this place?"

The knife wavered as if exhaustion had suddenly hit her or she had relaxed her guard. Hayashi moved forward and pulled Ingrid's hands behind her back. She dropped the knife and let out a loud scream. He looped the rope around her neck, across her back, around her arms and wrists, finishing with a flourish of knots. Martin watched, mouth agape with shock. It was a performance of magic. Within five seconds, she was tied up like a package, pinned in the embrace of the rope. Ingrid's screams turned to sobs of fright.

"Shh, shh," Hayashi murmured, pulling her into his arms. "It's all right. We will discover who did it, once and for all. If it is you, I will know. If it is not, I will know. Do not struggle now. I will be just. There will be justice. If you are innocent, you must trust me."

She collapsed into a chair, head bowed. Hayashi released Martin, then led Ingrid to the sofa in the reception room. "Go to sleep. Tomorrow this will be over one way or another." Ingrid, trussed and exhausted now, obeyed. Within a few moments, she was asleep.

"Come, Martin," Hayashi said and headed towards the interview room. Martin followed, silently astounded at the chief inspector's sudden undreamt-of abilities. Ingrid had picked the lock. The bell stood neatly by the door. Martin cursed himself silently. He, of all people, knew how easy it was to pick a simple lock. Two hairpins was all it took, and Ingrid must have made sure she had some on her somewhere. A sorry case of underestimating the enemy. Grace had warned him and he'd arrogantly ignored her. The whole bloody British establishment had underestimated the Japanese. You'd think he'd have learned something.

"Sorry, sir," he said. "My fault. I was warned."

Hayashi nodded curtly. "I, too, did not think her capable of this."

"Why did you come back?"

"To offer you some English sweets, but under the circumstances I think you probably need some sleep." Hayashi pointed to the cot. "You can sleep there. I will stay with Ingrid. Good night."

Martin watched the chief inspector depart. He lay down. Hayashi was a man to be reckoned with. More than he had even imagined. He felt black fatigue overtake him.

CHAPTER THIRTY-FIVE

Martin woke with a headache and recalled the night. She had taken him entirely by surprise, brought the metal water jug down on his head, then trussed him up with the telephone wire. Then Hayashi had turned up and performed some kind of magic trick with a rope. He got up, groggy, and went to the bathroom and cleaned up the wound.

Ingrid was still asleep, curled up on the sofa. She had been released from her restrictive bonds, but her hands were tied and the rope attached to the leg of the sofa in a series of such intricate knots that Martin had no idea how to undo them. He saw Sergeant Ibrahim and glanced at the clock. It was ten.

"Morning, Inspector," Ibrahim said. "Some shenanigans last night."

Martin had no wish to discuss it and went into the small kitchenette and made coffee. A dollop of palm sugar sweetened the brew and with the addition of two aspirin he felt almost human again.

Hayashi arrived. "Sergeant," Hayashi said, "take Miss Desker to the holding cells in the court. See she is comfortable." He did not look at Ingrid as she was led away but went to the evidence table. "We have no time left, Martin," he said. "The mayor wants a decision by the end of the week. He wants an announcement of an arrest by Friday afternoon for the Saturday edition of the paper." He ran his hand over the table. "This is what we have. Martin, and you, too, Miss Tobin, look at this table, go over the evidence, and tell us the story."

Martin stepped to the table. "When she goes out, Eva Abraham is wearing a dress and matching shoes, her locket, and her fake jade earrings. She does not take her handbag. Instead, she puts the keys in the handkerchief and into her pocket. She tells David Weber she's pregnant, that when she returns everything must be sorted out between them. Doubtless she underestimates the depth of Weber's feelings. He follows her. A witness sees them both leaving the building at the break of curfew at five o'clock. However, it is, in reality, three thirty and dark. Sunrise isn't for another two and a half hours. I will double-check with the witness that she is sure of her facts."

Martin nodded to Grace.

"He confronts her in the shop," Grace continued. "He has no idea why she is there, but an argument begins. It's lonely, deserted. He rips the locket from Eva's neck and as she stoops to pick it up, he picks up a rock and brings it down on her head. If nothing else, he could easily have killed her with that."

"Yes," Martin said. "Knocks her out and puts her head into the incense ash and suffocates her. Gets out as quick as he can. Then Hong turns up and finds her dead?"

"Or Hong turns up and finds her injured," Grace said. "If David Weber is telling the truth." Grace touched the shoes. "Why would Hong kill her? He didn't steal the shoes and earrings. Ingrid did."

"Yes," Martin said. "Why would Hong kill her? He doesn't rob her, we know that. Ingrid does. Surely, he finds her dead and gets out." Martin glanced at Hayashi. "Ingrid knows Hong was there to meet Eva. She doesn't know about Weber, does she? So, she presumes Hong has killed Eva. She takes the shoes and earrings and then the little god as a lucky charm. Get something for her trouble."

Martin looked at Grace. "And when I come sniffing around, she puts the stuff in Neo's cubicle to implicate Hong. She believes Hong killed Eva."

"Or," Grace said, "she finds Eva alive but groggy and kills her, robs her, and leaves. Then implicates Hong to cover her actions."

"I can see no reason for Ingrid to kill Eva," Hayashi said. "She could have robbed her without resorting to murder. Eva must have been dead when Ingrid arrived. It's the only thing that makes sense."

There was to be no convincing Hayashi of Ingrid's guilt, Martin thought. The man was a stubborn fool.

Hayashi took the sweets from his pocket and proffered them. "Okashi?"

CHAPTER THIRTY-SIX

There was one coffin near the open grave, bedecked with local flowers fashioned by women's hands; frail woven wreaths of ixora, frangipani, and orchids. Rose and Eva had been laid to rest in each other's embrace. Martin and Harry had got Old Zhao to do the undertaking, and Nomura had allocated funds from the Abraham estate, over which he now had jurisdiction.

Tatiana Goh, her daughter, and several of her family stood nearby. Marion and many of Rose's and Eva's friends had come. John Hammond, the Anglican priest, began the funeral oration. "Ashes to ashes, dust to dust..."

Martin saw Hayashi standing under a tree and walked to join him.

"I did not want to intrude," he said.

The coffin was lowered into the grave.

"I asked Nomura what would happen to all the money," Hayashi said. "Solomon left everything to Eva, who left everything to Rose, but Rose left no will. Miriam Abraham has written to me to ask about all this, but, so far, I have not responded. She does not know about the changed will. Nomura has frozen all the assets of the Abraham estate in Syonan and Malai for the present."

"What about Rose's house?"

"That's frozen too. Nomura was very upset, you know. I think he is a decent man. He could not come here today but I know he wanted to."

The gravediggers did their work. Hammond had moved to one side and was reading. The words came faintly on the breeze. "I am the Resurrection and the Life." The late afternoon sun pierced through the clouds and illuminated the gravesites, a sight, if one were of a religious bent, that stiffened faith.

The graves were filled, the final clods put in place. Soon, Martin mused, the lush green grass would grow over them and they would be as forgotten as all the other souls who lay around them, including Irene and his mother, both of whom lay in different parts of this cemetery. It was as if Hayashi had read his mind.

"Grasses sway over men's dreams," Hayashi said.

Martin caught the moment. He had begun to understand something of this man. A poem, another half-forgotten legacy of Mr. Stevens, came to mind. "And all that beauty, all that wealth e'er gave, awaits alike the inevitable hour."

Hayashi moved away. "I will wait for you."

"Thank you."

The mourners moved towards the gate and Hammond joined him. The Japanese sentries slouched under a tree, ignoring them, half-asleep in the lazy heat of the afternoon.

"We can only do our best," Hammond said, "but it feels poor. Sometimes, at night, I fight despair and wonder where it will all end."

"That is exactly what we all feel, John. You're not alone."

"No, I suppose not. Above all it behooves us, the men of the church, to keep up the spirits of the people."

The cemetery was somewhat removed from the town. Transport was a big problem in Syonan, which made their presence all the more remarkable. But somehow, collectively, they had found transport. They waited silently by the truck for the priest.

Hayashi's car approached. Hammond turned to Martin. "I can't speak to you now, but please come to me tonight. I have some news about your request."

At the office, Martin found Ching, the *majie* of Miriam Abraham, waiting, two heavy bags at her feet.

Ching stood as he approached and threw him a withering look. "You said you would open the door for Miss Miriam."

"Well, Ching. I was a bit busy arresting her boyfriend."

"She has sent me again to ask for the key. If you don't give it, she'll find the lock man."

Martin sighed. Perhaps he'd better ask Hayashi. "Wait here." Ching sat.

Hayashi waved his hand dismissively. "She will have to be told about the will eventually. The least we can do I suppose is open the door for her. Get Seah to do it."

Martin smiled. "I'll do it. I'll take the car? The *majie* has some heavy bags by the look of it. I will help her and then go on to Meyer Mansions."

Hayashi nodded, distracted. Martin removed the key from the chain and joined Ching, picking up the bags. She protested but he shook his head.

"Heavy. What's in here?"

"Wood. For the kitchen. My turn."

"Right. Well, I'll run you back to your house and we can drop off these bags."

"Thank you. Thank you."

The car loaded, Martin headed to Victoria Street. The house had been, before the war, a *chai tong*, a sort of religious retirement home for older single Buddhist women. Now it appeared to have taken the role of a *coolie fong*, a series of rooms where the *majie* sisters lived. He mentioned this to Ching.

"During the war," she said, "at the end, when the British were all leaving, many of the *majie* decided to move here. It was safer to be together. The house was spared during the battle. We are lucky to have this house. I could not live with Miss Miriam so I am lucky to be here with my sisters."

Martin carried the heavy bags and followed Ching down a corridor to the kitchen. The house was spotlessly clean and the kitchen was well equipped and, it appeared, well stocked. Ching noticed his eyes on the shelves.

"Many of the sisters took what was left in the British houses. They were empty in any case."

An old, stooped woman entered the kitchen.

"This is Yang. She is seventy. She has been a *majie* since she was eleven years old. She does the cooking for us and we support her. Yang saved my life when I was very ill."

Yang gave Martin a toothless grin. "Put the wood there, please," she said waving her hand at the wood piled under a long low table. Something flashed, ruby red. A memory penetrated. Martin deposited the wood and turned back to Yang. He pointed to her wrist.

"Your bracelet. Very pretty. May I see it?"

Yang, with a look of suspicious wariness, put out her arm. On her skinny wrist was a bracelet of red glass beads. Martin had seen these beads before on the evidence table at the CID.

"Where did you get the bracelet?"

Yang stared at him.

"Please, there is no trouble. I just want to know where you got the bracelet."

Ching stepped forward and took Yang's arm. Yang whispered to Ching. "She says it is a gift from another *majie*."

"Who?"

Yang whispered again.

"Ah Mai. She is the *majie* to another lady in Meyer Mansions. I know her."

"Does she live here?"

"No. In another *coolie fong*. In Chinatown."

"She works for a lady in Meyer Mansions. Who?"

Another whispered consultation.

"Mrs. Barker."

That name rang a bell. Why?

CHAPTER THIRTY-SEVEN

Martin took the keys to a nearby locksmith, passed a copy of Eva's room key to Ching, and parked near Meyer Mansions. A telephone call to Grace had given him the information he needed. Mrs. Barker was one of the tenants of the Mansions, and she had a sister, Miss Woodford, who caught rats for her dog and had seen both Miriam and Weber leave the premises in the early hours of the morning Eva had been killed. Miss Woodford opened the door to him. The dog, a silky terrier, tail wagging, sat by her feet. Considering he had a diet of rats, he looked healthy. Maybe rat wasn't too bad, all things considered. Perhaps they'd all be eating rats soon enough.

"We can't take him out of the courtyard, you know," Miss Woodford said. "He has to get all his exercise on a lead in the evening. Otherwise, he'll be eaten. That's how things are now. Terrible."

"Yes indeed. Miss Woodford, you have a maid called Ah Mai?"

"Yes. Why?"

"I'd like to speak to her, please."

Miss Woodford summoned the maid and stood to one side, listening intently.

The maid's story was short and to the point. She had found a scarf with the beads attached in the communal bin in the courtyard on Monday morning when she was taking out the rubbish. Cloth was valuable. It was a waste. So, she had taken it and removed the beads to make a bracelet.

"Where is the scarf now?" Martin asked.

"In my room."

"Fetch it, please," Martin said, relieved.

Martin examined the scarf quickly. It had no smell of incense and was pressed and neatly folded. "Have you washed the scarf?"

"Of course. It was dusty and dirty."

Martin shook his head. "All right. Ah Mai, do you have any idea who might have put it in the bin?"

Ah Mai shook her head.

"Can you show me where you found it?"

Miss Woodford stepped forward. "I can show you, Inspector. Ah Mai, you can get back to work."

Miss Woodford led Martin down the back staircase to the inner courtyard and indicated the bins, which were lined up along a wall by the side entrance.

He went to the bins. Why was the scarf thrown away? Who was wearing it and what were they doing at the crime scene? He was certain it wasn't Ingrid's. She didn't wear this sort of thing. If Eva was wearing it, how did it find its way into this bin? Why would Weber bring it back? Unless there was someone else.

"Inspector," Miss Woodford said, "do you think the police can do anything about the veranda?"

"Sorry. Veranda?"

"Yes, it's terribly inconvenient, you see. We actually have stocks of tinned food and that sort of thing in the stores in the veranda."

"Miss Woodford, I have no idea what you mean."

"Oh, sorry. You see, the Japanese have piled crates in front of our storerooms in the veranda. Each apartment has one. We can't get at them."

She indicated the long veranda on the entire side of the courtyard opposite the back stairs, piled with crates from floor to ceiling. A Japanese sentry eyed them both.

"We've been told to stay away from them, but it's terribly unfair. Why couldn't we just clean them out and then, you see, the Japanese could use them. I've tried talking to the concierge, but he just ignores me. It's most annoying."

"Yes, I see that. Perhaps I can have a word with my detective chief inspector."

"Oh, thank you. You know poor Miss Abraham was reprimanded publicly by the garrison commander for going near them and made to stand for two hours in the sun in the courtyard as punishment. We were all made to watch. It was simply disgraceful. But you know she's terribly strong, despite her handicap. Terribly strong."

"Is she?" Martin said.

Miriam opened the door to her apartment. She leaned heavily on her cane. He saw little evidence of the strength Miss Woodford had described.

"Inspector Bach," Miriam said and smiled. "Thank you for letting me have the key. Have you come about David? Is he all right? Do you still think he did this?"

"Yes. Why? You don't?"

Miriam looked down at her fingers. She wore fingerless gloves and now Martin wanted to see what lay under those gloves.

"Miss Abraham. Might I ask you to remove your gloves?"

"What?"

"Remove the gloves. I would like to see your hands."

She stared at him.

"Perhaps you would just do as I say."

He could see she was scandalized. But it was just her hands. He'd hardly asked anything disgraceful.

"Ching," Miriam called. "I'd rather Ching were here," she said with a hard little look at Martin.

"By all means."

Ching arrived and stood by her mistress. Miriam removed the gloves and held out her hands. To his disappointment, he could see nothing. Not a scratch. Her hands were white and smooth.

"Thank you."

Miriam replaced the gloves. Martin brought out the scarf. "Do either of you recognize this scarf?"

"No," Miriam said. Ching shook her head.

"Do you do the laundry, Ching?"

It was Miriam who answered. "Ching doesn't do laundry. She is my amah. She takes care of the house and me. All our laundry goes to the dhobi."

"Including Mrs. Abraham's?"

"Yes. Eva dealt with her own laundry. Ching wasn't her maid, to do her bidding. That was agreed. Eva was planning to move out anyway."

"What would you say, Miss Abraham, if I told you that this scarf was at the crime scene?"

She frowned. "Nothing. Perhaps it was Eva's."

"Do you know if it was hers?"

"No. I merely offer it as a possibility since you say it was there."

"Are you sure you haven't seen this scarf before, Ching?"

Ching shook her head. Both women gazed it him.

If it was Eva's, then she might have been wearing it that night. Perhaps it fell off when she was knocked down. But then it had to be Weber who picked it up and put it in the bin. But why?

Martin returned to the office. A Chinese boy of fifteen years or so, strongly built, hair like a dirty porcupine and missing most of his left ear, sat in the reception. Martin recognized the scruffy dishwasher from the Kublai Khan restaurant.

"Inspector," Ibrahim said, rising from his chair. "This is Charlie Chan."

Martin stared at the boy. "Really?"

"Yes, sir."

The boy rose and stuck out his hand. "How ya doin'," he said in what Martin recognized, with surprise, as an American accent.

Martin looked at the hand and ignored it. The kid needed a good wash. Not in the least bothered, Charlie grinned. "I hear you guys need some help," he said.

"Don't be cheeky," Ibrahim growled.

Charlie shrugged, sat down, and pulled out a cigarette from his grimy shirt. He looked at the sergeant. "Got a light?"

Ibrahim's face took on a thunderous demeanor.

"Right," Martin said. He found Seah. "Get this round to Weber and show him. Ask him who it belonged to. Then show it to Ingrid as well. Don't say anything else. Don't tell them where it was found. See what they say and come back here."

He returned to reception. "Ibrahim," he said to the sergeant. "Where's the detective chief inspector?"

"Went out. No idea where."

"All right. I'm going out for an hour. If he returns, tell him what we've found."

He looked at Charlie. "You want a job?"

"Yeah."

"Right, let's see how well you do. Find out who killed a man called Hong in Chinatown. Sergeant, fill him in and give him some money." Martin sniffed and made a face. "And next time I see you, Charlie Chan, you'd better be cleaned up. This is a police headquarters, not a Tong hideout."

Martin left the office and drove to Bishopsgate. Along the way, gangs of Australian and British POWs were clearing rubble, carting goods, and turning earth. They were a common sight all over the city, a constant reminder of their plight, their deteriorating physical state, and their punishment—what the Gunseikanbu, the military administration, wanted everyone to see.

If the Japs hoped the civilians would gain pleasure from it, they were sorely mistaken. The more the POWs were paraded around, the more everyone felt sorry for them. He'd seen women giving them food when the Japs weren't looking, though the punishment for such actions was severe, even death. He'd heard from John Hammond that extra food was getting into Changi from local people through the English doctors who were allowed to practice outside; that Hammond and the Swiss Red Cross man were organizing credit on the never-never for the prisoners to pay for goods inside.

It was Hammond who met him at the door and ushered him into the sitting room. "I have some news for you."

Hammond laid out a paper on the table. "This is a copy of your baptismal certificate. As you can see your mother is marked as Marie Bach and your father as Ernst."

Martin took up the paper. "She lied, then?"

"If your information is correct, it would appear so. Nothing terribly unusual in that. She would doubtless have claimed Ernst as the father on the birth certificate too, no matter what Ernst thought. She could have made those declarations without Ernst being present. Perhaps he even agreed to avoid scandal."

Hammond sat forward. "You are quite sure that this information about your parentage is true. It is entirely reliable?"

"I think so. I don't know. My aunt Helga, Ernst's sister, says he knew that I was not his child. Why would he say that?"

"All right, then let us presume it is true. Look here." Hammond pointed to Martin's name. "Can you see you have a middle name?"

"A middle name. Do I?"

"See here. Martin Neville. Did you know your middle name was Neville?"

"No. First I've heard of it. How strange."

"Yes. Perhaps not so strange."

"What do you mean?"

"It isn't marked here on the certificate, but on the official church register the name of a godfather appears."

"I've got a godfather?"

"Yes. His name is Martin Neville."

Hammond sat back and waited. Martin stared at the paper in front of him. "Do you mean that...?" Martin looked up at Hammond. "This godfather was my father? Is that what you think?"

"I think it is possible that Martin Neville wanted an official, written connection to you and that your mother wanted it, too. Your father—pardon, Ernst—would never have seen the register; he wouldn't have known. It would've been a secret between your mother and the man, hidden in the registry and in their own hearts."

The room had suddenly become hushed. All the noises from outside ceased. Martin looked around and realized the hush was inside his head and he was unable to think, as if the confusion of this news had blanked out his brain.

"Martin, are you all right?" Hammond's voice intruded.

"Yes. Yes. Sorry. Who is Martin Neville?"

"I have no idea. Thirty years ago. That's a long time. I wasn't here, nor was the bishop."

"How can we find him?"

"I can check the registers of the church. If he or anyone by that name was baptized, married, or buried in the sacraments of the church, we would have those records."

"Is he in Changi?"

"Martin, really, that is most unlikely, don't you think? The man must be well over fifty if he is alive at all. This all happened thirty years ago."

"Can you find out? Can you see if there is a man named Neville in Changi?"

Hammond nodded. "I will find out what I can." He stood and handed Martin the baptismal certificate. "Take this with you. It's proof for the Japanese if you need it. God bless you. I will be in touch."

CHAPTER THIRTY-EIGHT

The two Japanese guards pulled smartly to attention and saluted as Hayashi got out of his car at the entrance to Outram Road Prison. The deference was not for him, of course, but for the armband of military rank pinned to his jacket. Today it would come in more than usually useful.

"I've come to see Captain Sato," he said, and one of the guards bowed and turned into the entrance. A moment later, a sergeant appeared, saluted, and ask him to follow. They passed through the shadow of the corridor and out into glaring sunshine. Above him, to one side, he could see one of the many three-story prison blocks that occupied the site. The sergeant led him through a maze of buildings and into an office marked "Warden" in English. Apparently, no one could be bothered to replace it with Japanese.

Captain Sato appeared. The left side of his face was deeply disfigured. He was missing an ear and most of his left cheek and wore an eye patch. Two fingers on his left hand were stumps and his left arm hung limply at his side. He was a mess. He bowed.

"Major, welcome. May I offer you some tea."

"Thank you, Captain. You have suffered in the war?"

"Ah yes. Caught in a mortar attack around Maur."

"Honorable scars, Captain. You survived."

"Many did not."

"Yes. Indeed."

Fragrant green tea was brought, and the two men sat for a moment, as was the custom, inhaling its aroma before sipping appreciatively. Captain Sato, Hayashi learned, was a career soldier. He'd served in Chosen, in Manchukuo, and in Yamashita's Twenty-Fifth Army. Once his injuries had ceased to be life-threatening, he had been seconded to this job to continue his recovery. A fact that, Hayashi saw, hadn't pleased him.

"You miss active duty, Captain?"

"Naturally. But I fear my injuries mean active duty may be some way off."

The man was dreaming. Half a hand and face and a useless arm pretty much excluded him from future service. He must be forty-five at least. The man should be retired. But then perhaps he was. Retired to prison service. Not, perhaps, what he had hoped for. Hayashi felt the full force of the man's courage.

"You must give yourself time for a full recovery, Captain. The war is going well."

The fact hardly seemed to appeal to the captain. Obviously, he was annoyed that it was going well without him. "Yes. The British have withdrawn from Burma. We knock on the door of India and Australia. It is a remarkable achievement in so short a time."

"It is indeed. You may count yourself among the heroes of Japan and one of His Majesty's greatest servants."

Hayashi meant it. Those words were easy to say, but they were true. He had not tramped through mud and filth as bodies piled up on every side. He had never seen war, had never held a bloody dying friend in his arms, not known terror, nor died a thousand times, never lost half his face. What these men did, what they endured, was beyond anything he had ever experienced. He bowed to the captain, keen to show the man the respect he held for him. Captain Sato, perhaps, caught the feeling, for he bowed too.

"Thank you, Major," Captain Sato said. Having felt good, this made Hayashi feel ashamed once again. His military title was meaningless. But the captain had moved on. He sipped his tea. "There is a new campaign. In the north. A new attack on America. A great prize. I am hardened to northern campaigns. I hope once I am fully recovered to get my chance there, in Alaska. I don't much care for the heat of these regions."

"No, I agree. Oppressive. I did not realize we were attacking in the north."

"No, of course, it is not common knowledge, naturally."

"It is to your honor, Captain. What soldier does not wish to give everything for the emperor? My only regret is that I am too old for active combat. I would be more of a hindrance than a help."

"Sir, you serve His Majesty here."

"Thank you. His Majesty is very keen to see that his new dominions are justly administered. We are fortunate, are we not, to have such a beneficent ruler."

"Yes. Yes. Indeed. Indeed. Yes. So, Major, you wish to visit the facilities."

It was clear Captain Sato had no idea what this clunky old man was doing in his office. Hayashi inclined his head. "Thank you, yes. The courts are reopening, and we will have civilian prisoners to send here, for incarceration and possibly for execution."

"Naturally. Allow me to show you."

As they walked, the captain talked. "This prison is used for all enemies of the empire—Europeans, Asians, POWs who try to escape, even Japanese who have committed grave offenses. We take women and men. Mostly Chinese, I must say."

"It is a military prison, Captain, run by the Kempeitai?"

"Yes," Sato said. "I'm under the command of Lieutenant Colonel Yamamoto, the head of prisons, commanding the civilian wing." The captain showed Hayashi a cell. It was a tiny concrete thing with two boards for a bed, barely long enough for a man to stretch. A toilet bucket was the only other object. It was filthy and stank of dirt, dust, sweat, and excrement. The policy was to keep the prisoners in solitary confinement and to never clean the cells, the captain said when Hayashi remarked on it. Also, to only give starvation rations. Water was restricted and bathing was once a week and that only to avoid the spread of disease to the guards. It was forbidden for the prisoners to drink the bath water.

Hayashi caught the cadence of the captain's voice. He did not say so, but it was quite clear that he thought these conditions were bestial and wished devoutly he was somewhere else. And here, in such a cell, Rose had existed, to be removed and beaten at any time of the day or night, only to be thrown back, thirsty, starving, broken. Hayashi said nothing and followed the captain to the place of execution, a dusty yard surrounded by high walls.

"This was the prison where the British incarcerated their Asian criminals. Now some of them are here inside. Ironic justice, I suppose."

It was a timely reminder. The British had built this place and thrown their Asian subjects inside with the same spirit of humanity as the Japanese. Who was worse? He'd seen enough.

"Captain, thank you. One of your prisoners, a Miss Rose Shultz, committed suicide while in my charge. It is entirely my fault. I would like to apologize to Lieutenant Yamada, who, much like you, I believe served General Yamashita."

"Lieutenant Yamada? Ah yes. He was in the field artillery before the surrender."

By the tone of his voice, Kano sensed that Captain Sato did not like Yamada.

"I see. But he is now a kempei officer?"

Sato looked away and Hayashi thought his body tensed. A kempei officer was a thing to be feared. They had absolute powers over even superior officers in all branches of the military. He did not imagine Sato feared Yamada. More that he despised him.

"Yes. He sustained some minor injuries and requested to transfer to the military police. There is surely no need to apologize, Major. I will tell him and convey your regrets."

"That's very kind, but I feel I would like to speak to him personally."

"I see." Sato turned away. "I shall ask him to come. Then, if you don't mind, I have work to do."

"Naturally. I will wait here. Thank you, Captain."

It was clear to Hayashi that Captain Sato wanted nothing to do with Yamada. He waited. Eventually Yamada arrived alone. He was thin and wiry, with a whiskered chin and upper lip, something of the weasel about him. He saluted and bowed.

"Major, you wished to speak to me?"

"Yes, thank you, Lieutenant. I have to tell you that one of your prisoners, Miss Shultz, committed suicide while in the charge of the police on a routine matter. It was most regrettable and entirely the fault of my police officers. She is dead. A report will be sent through official channels."

Yamada's face remained impassive. Hayashi was sure he didn't even know who Rose was. Just another tortured body among the many that passed through his hands.

"I see. Thank you."

"You see, I understand she was a communist? Doubtless you might have managed to obtain a lot of information from her. Information useful to our war effort."

Yamada's stiff posture relaxed. "Please, do not apologize, sir. I remember this prisoner now. She was not a communist. Actually, she knew nothing. She was stubborn and obstructive. She was wrong thinking. It is no loss, I assure you."

"I see. You could not beat it out of her."

Yamada grinned. "I tried, Major. I must say that I tried. Ultimately, she didn't know anything so it was a waste of my time."

"Yes, I see. Still, it must be enjoyable to have the power to deal with recalcitrant types."

Yamada nodded. "I enjoy my work."

"Very good."

Kano took his handkerchief and mopped his brow. The day had grown stifling but Yamada didn't seem to mind. "You seem to bear the climate very well, Lieutenant."

"Ah. Yes. I spent a great deal of my life in Formosa. It is the cold I don't like. I was briefly in Chosen. Freezing."

"Ah, I see. Well, thank you. Goodbye, Lieutenant."

"Sir, news." Martin said as Hayashi arrived in the CID office.

Hayashi positioned himself in front of the fan and listened. "You suspect Miriam Abraham on the basis of what evidence?"

"The scarf. I believe it belonged to Miriam Abraham and was recovered from the crime scene. It's missing its red beads, half of which were scattered at the crime scene and the other half removed to make a bracelet by Miss Woodford's maid, who discovered it in the bin in the courtyard of Meyer Mansions. Unfortunately, she washed and ironed it. However, it is nothing like the sort of thing Eva would have worn. Weber denies all knowledge of the scarf and is uncooperative. Ingrid says she has never seen it. Yet it was found at Meyer Mansions. Someone removed it from the crime scene and deposited it there. I believe that person is Miriam Abraham."

Martin paused. "Also despite her appearance when we see her, it seems that Miriam was not as she appears, as frail, but physically strong. She was able to withstand the torture of standing for two hours in the sun, a punishment for some infraction at her building."

"Ah. Tell me about this. Punishment?"

"Yes. The garrison next door to the Mansions had, without warning, stored crates of ammunition and supplies under the veranda in the courtyard of the Mansions. These crates fully blocked the storerooms of the apartments, which are located under the verandas. There was some fuss made and Miss

Abraham was, on several occasions, despite warnings not to approach them, found near the crates. The garrison commander used her as an example. It was harsh but she endured it. Speaks to a certain physical and mental fortitude."

"Ah," Hayashi said. "I looked up that Holmes story I mentioned before. It's called 'The Man with the Twisted Lip,' Martin. Do you know it?"

Martin sighed. "No, I haven't read any of those stories, sir."

"An error. Holmes is full of pith and wisdom."

What was it about the word "pith" the man liked so much? What actually was "pith"?

"Sir, you know that Holmes wasn't a real detective."

Hayashi flipped his whisk in a dismissive manner. "He makes a point in 'The Man with the Twisted Lip' when describing a crippled fellow. He says, and I believe it to be so, that weakness in one limb is often compensated for by exceptional strength in the others. Miss Abraham's condition may have given her exceptional strength in her other leg, her hips and torso, as well as her upper body. And think how often she had to find ways of coping with things we simply take for granted. How agile it might also have made her mind."

"Yes. All right. I see. Anyway, I believe she could have followed Weber with far fewer problems than we first imagined."

"But did she know Weber was following Eva?"

"That is yet to be discovered."

"We have to prove absolutely that she was at the crime scene. The scarf offers no evidence to that effect. She denies it. The maid says she doesn't recognize it. It was washed and ironed, you say? Really anyone could have put it in the bin. And was Miss Abraham injured, scratched? Have you seen evidence of that?"

"No."

Hayashi was silent. Martin waited. "It's flimsy. The Supreme Court and civil courts will soon open. A prosecutor has been appointed. The mayor wants a charge laid at someone's door so that the courts will have a sensational case to prosecute. If no one else can be charged, then Weber will be the one. If you think it is Miriam Abraham, then prove it. We have only a few days."

Martin felt tiredness sweep over him. His mind was filled with this name. Martin Neville. The clock ticked to five on Tokyo time. Dark clouds had gathered and rain began sudden and hard. He went to the door of Hayashi's office. The chief inspector was watching the rain pounding down on the Padang. Perhaps the man was lonely and disappointed. Perhaps he should offer to drink a glass of brandy with him. He was about to speak when Hayashi turned.

"Ah, Inspector." Hayashi picked up an envelope and held it towards Martin. "This is from Nomura for you. He has found out about your mother's apartment. Do you know about that?"

"Yes, thank you." Martin took the envelope.

Hayashi pointed to the car keys on his desk. "It's raining. I will spend the evening in my hotel. Take the car. Good night, Martin."

"Good night, sir. And thank you."

When Hayashi had left, Martin opened the envelope and read quickly. The apartment had been located, was undamaged and occupied by two Indian families who had been asked to regularize the situation by registering as tenants and paying rent. They'd promptly decamped and, Nomura wrote, consequently the apartment had been vacated. The locks had been changed and the new key was inside the envelope. If he wanted to take possession, there was paperwork to be filled out.

He didn't want to take possession. The idea of living in the place where his mother had died was abhorrent, but he wanted to take a look inside. He put the envelope in his pocket and picked up the car keys.

CHAPTER THIRTY-NINE

In the maze of streets of the Tiong Bahru housing estate the street vendors were setting out their wares in the cool of the evening. The rain had stopped as abruptly as it had started and charcoal burners flickered into light. Local people left their hot, stuffy flats and gathered, sitting on their heels or on stools, to chat, smoke, and eat and drink whatever the hawkers carried on their shoulders. Children ran about the alleyways, and it felt for all the world as if the war had never been.

Except for the Japanese patrols and the sentry boxes. But this evening, even the sentries seemed hospitable and relaxed. Japanese soldiers tinged the bell and lit incense for Buddha at the local temple, bought food from the hawkers, and walked peaceably about the streets. Perhaps this pretty, quiet estate reminded them of their villages back home.

Martin, not without trepidation, turned the key and went inside the corner apartment on the third floor of one of the older buildings. Built in the thirties, they had the charm of their art deco architecture, all feminine and soft, with rounded walls and decorative flourishes.

He was shocked at the state of it. It was filthy and smelled of curry and sprouting earthy things. The walls were painted in smoke and grease. What it had been before the war Martin could not even imagine. It was empty of every stick of furniture. The kitchen was stripped; not one thing remained. Even the light fixtures had been removed.

He stood in the middle of this devastation and tried to imagine Maman living here. It was impossible. He moved to the metal and glass doors of the living room and opened them onto a wide curved terrace, which hugged the corner of the building and gave onto the street. Here it was much easier to see her. The black-and-white tiles were visible through the dirt, and two teakwood chairs had been forgotten or abandoned. There was a rusty ceiling fan that did not turn. He sat and looked out onto the vista of the sky, listening to the low hum of the street. Perhaps this was what she had loved. Privacy, peace, and serenity in the midst of community.

He had learned to love her in the early years of his life when she had been at home with him and Michael. Looking back now, both he and his brother must have sensed her sadness. But what do children know of such things? She was there in the morning and at night when she read French to them. They couldn't understand it but it didn't matter. When she moved out, it was so painful and incomprehensible that both he and Michael had become numb. Michael started to wet his bed, and the amahs, both his and Michael's, went everywhere with them and slept by their beds for more than a year.

Though she had died here, there was no feeling of it. Perhaps the fact of the stripping of the whole place had cleansed it of death as well. He had expected to hate it, but he did not. He realized that to know her he might have to be here, for here was where she was most herself. He wished with all his heart that she had brought her children here. But then, of course, perhaps, it wouldn't have been the same. It was her sanctuary.

And then there were her neighbors. This estate had been spared the bombing. The solidity of the apartment blocks of concrete and brick meant they offered protection rather than instant death. People did not flee. And if they did not flee, they stayed, and if they stayed they might very well have known his mother. And human nature being what it was, they would have paid attention.

Could he live here? The thought shot into his mind. He went to the ledge and looked down. The red awning of the Monkey God Temple on the far corner caught his eye. He shook his head. Walter would hate him for it and that gave him pause. Only Walter had ever set foot inside, and that was to gather together his dead mother's effects. Not her body. It had been removed and Walter had identified their mother at the morgue. What had he seen when he opened the door that day? He could not put himself in Walter's shoes. Walter had borne the burden of it all. But he knew he had to find the courage to confront Walter, if not as a brother, then as a policeman.

Joan had rounded on him one day. "Stop being frightened of him. He's a mass of problems himself, and a lot of it comes from your mother's life and death. He puts his head in the sand but he needs to look up."

He'd seen tears in Joan's eyes. "You have to help him, Martin. He has to let it go."

Martin walked through each room, lingering in what must have been her bedroom. Had she died in here? He felt a shiver run down his back. Not of fear or horror. Rather of … what? He couldn't put his finger on it. *Genius loci*, a spirit of place, perhaps. No, that was too strong. There was no sense of substance, not fairies or ghosts. More an energy, like feng shui, running in lines, crisscrossing the room.

He shook his head. Don't be an arse, Martin, he said to himself. Next, you'll be shaking out fortune sticks or chucking moon blocks.

He locked the door and went down the stairs to the street. Two young Japanese sentries eyed him. He stopped, rigid, and bowed, joining the twenty or so others, men, women, and children, who, putting aside their bowls and conversations, rose also to bow. Any old itch for singularity had been beaten out of them. The soldiers passed on, indifferent now that the rule had been obeyed. For this moment, for perhaps a short interval of half an hour, no one had been slapped, no bones broken, no blatant humiliation administered, no one lay dead or hauled off into darkness. It was the collective understanding of what was required. That was how low they had been brought, and they all knew it. They picked up their bowls and resumed their lives.

He approached the temple. The Japanese might light incense to Buddha, a habit ingrained over a thousand years, but they worshipped above all one god, and he sat on a golden throne in Tokyo. It paid never to forget it. Martin moved on. It was a long way home from here.

CHAPTER FORTY

The next morning Hayashi ordered Seah to bring Miriam Abraham into the CID on suspicion.

"I have reflected on this matter all night," Hayashi said to Martin. "The evidence of the scarf seems flimsy but is still unavoidable. Dozens of beads identical to the scarf's beads were at the crime scene. It belonged to someone, and unless we imagine that yet another woman from Meyer Mansions was there that morning, it must have been hers. I don't imagine it was the woman with the rat traps, do you? The one whose maid found the scarf. Are we opening that area of investigation?"

"No."

"So, it was either Weber or Miss Abraham. If it was him, why did he bring back the scarf and put it in the courtyard bin? It's not logical. I think he suspects Miriam and feels guilty about the whole thing with Eva Abraham and apparently thinks, for the moment, that he is prepared to go to the grave with it."

"You've decided that Ingrid is innocent?" Martin said.

Hayashi leveled his gaze at Martin. "For the moment, I am inclined to believe her. Based on what she said to you when you were tied up. At that moment, she had no need to lie and could, if she were capable of it, have killed you and made her escape. An event, by the way, that could have been catastrophic for this department and for her, never mind you."

Martin grudgingly agreed, but he wasn't going to say that to the detective chief inspector. He merely nodded.

"Very well," Hayashi said. "In that case, we have to prove Miriam Abraham was there. There's no other way. It's up to you to get a confession out of her."

Martin went to the interview room and closed the door behind him. Grace, behind her stenograph, waited. Miriam sat, prim, her hands in her lap. The fan rattled.

"Miss Abraham, you have to know that we suspect you of being involved in this murder, either with David Weber as an accomplice or on your own. If he did not kill Mrs. Abraham, then your silence will get his head removed from his shoulders."

"I have nothing to do with this. It's ridiculous. I need to go to the toilet."

She rose with some difficulty and made to take up her cane. It slid out of her grasp and fell on the floor at Grace's feet. Grace picked it up.

"I'll help Miss Abraham," Grace said and handed Miriam her stick.

What a little actress Miriam Abraham was, Martin thought. When the two women returned, Martin left Miriam in the interview room to stew and called Seah and Grace together. "Get over to her apartment. I want every piece of clothing, bags, hats, umbrellas, scarves, shoes, furniture, knickknacks, everything, examined. Grace, ask Ching about clothes. Did everything go to the dhobi? Think like a woman."

Grace smiled. "Yes, sir. I'll try."

When Grace and Seah got back to the office, Grace came up to him, somewhat breathlessly. She glanced at Seah, who looked as pleased as a man with a full rice bowl.

"Sir, we've found something," she said.

He followed them into the evidence room. Grace picked up a stout cane with a lion's head.

"The maid wasn't there. We went through Miss Abraham's clothes and we found some incredible things. A huge surprise, wasn't it, Felix, er, Constable?"

Seah nodded. "Yes, she has this one wardrobe crammed with expensive clothes. Nothing like she's wearing today, sir. We remembered to smell them too."

Grace nodded. "Then, while we were going through them we saw a walking stick in one corner of the wardrobe. It was odd, because all the other walking sticks were in the hall. I took it out and saw the lion's head. And look, sir, look at the bottom of the stick."

Grace swung the stick upside down and Martin saw what she had seen. The foot was a thick lion's paw. Grace picked up a photograph of the scene.

"There, see that? The paw marks are almost certainly this, sir. There was no animal. And, sir," she said and smiled. Seah grinned. "I've examined the paw. It was wiped down but there is blood and incense dust in the crevices of the carving. And these marks match the marks on Eva Abraham's dress. She was there, sir."

Martin grinned. "Well done, you two. Get Mat in here to photograph that. The blood's not much use to us, but the detective inspector will be able to check the incense ash. Brush it off and preserve it.'

"Inspector," Grace said, "why didn't she wash it off?"

"I don't think Miriam Abraham has washed anything in her life."

Martin made a coffee and waited for Grace to collect the evidence and return with the cane.

"Sir," she said, "when you talk to Miss Abraham, ask her about menstrual buckets."

Martin almost choked on his coffee. "What?"

"Menstrual buckets. She'll know, I'm certain of it."

Martin and Grace went into the interview room. Grace took up her place behind her stenograph machine. Martin put the photograph of the paw marks of the scene and on Eva's dress on his desk and lay the cane alongside them.

Miriam made no reaction.

"You were there. This proves it."

She looked at Martin. Not afraid. Defiant. He hadn't expected that.

"Aren't you clever? Well, David did it. I was there but David killed her. I watched him. He killed her and ran away. I didn't stop him. I was terrified in that moment. Perhaps I should have, but I didn't. I was afraid of him, what he would do if he knew I was there. I went to her to check she was dead. I should have told you, perhaps, but I didn't want David to know. I didn't want to be involved in any way. I didn't do anything."

"Really. Perhaps you'll tell me all about it. Why did you follow him? How did you know to follow him? Enlighten us."

"I'd like a cigarette, Inspector. Do you mind? David hates it if I smoke, but who cares now, eh?" The change in her demeanor and attitude was spectacular.

Martin handed her a cigarette and lit it. She took a deep breath and exhaled. "What a lot you all expect, don't you? You men. First, Daddy. Then, David. Do this, do that. Don't do this and that. What a lot of rules you make for women which you hardly bother with yourselves."

"I thought you loved your father. Loved David."

"Oh, Daddy. Well, can't love someone you hardly know, can you? Never had much to do with him, just his damn rules. And what an old-fashioned bore he was. In India, you know, I was with my mother's family. My aunts thought me dreadfully biblical."

She wrinkled her nose. "They're all wealthy socialites who have balls and dances and hobnob with the British. They're terribly up to the minute. I loved it. They bought me new clothes and taught me how to smoke. But then I got back here and it was all like a dream."

She blew a smoke ring. It was rather good and Martin could see her in his mind's eye practicing in her fashionable dress on the terrace of her Indian aunt's lavish mansion amid the laughter and gaiety of the Indian social elite.

"Thankfully, David was gorgeous, and he treated me like gold dust and I adored being courted and thought it might be fun to be married. But, of course, then he told me to give up cigarettes and pretty clothes and be the good Jewish girl. He's rather Old Testament, you know."

She watched the smoke from the cigarette make swirls in the heavy air before being whisked away by the fan. "That was when I started to have misgivings about marriage to him, or anyone really. Then the war came and Daddy died and, you know, I didn't quite know what to do. And David said I needed marriage to get my inheritance. It was all organized in this trust they'd drawn up which I knew nothing about. I felt a bit stuck and really fed up. But then I discovered about the pregnancy."

Grace's fingers stopped moving as Miriam blew smoke.

"Tell me about the pregnancy?"

"Yes, well. It was Ching who found out, of course, because I don't have anything to do with the menstrual buckets."

Martin shot a look at Grace, whose lips twitched.

"It was Ching who noticed that Eva's was empty for two months."

Martin felt bewildered and uncertain what to ask. He glanced at Grace.

"Sir," Grace said. "I have five sisters. We each have a bucket where we put soiled period towels to soak before washing. Quite normal, sir."

Miriam laughed. "Oh, he doesn't know. Not married, Inspector?"

Martin actually felt himself blush.

Miriam rested her gaze on Martin. "Prepare yourself, Inspector." She smiled. "So, no menstrual towels, no periods. Ching didn't do laundry, but she did do my menstrual towels, always had done. Heavens, I learned about periods from Ching. Can't send those to the laundry. Eva did her own. Said she was used to it. Quite practical that way. Ching told me and we both thought Eva must be pregnant. It's quite simple, Inspector. Can I have a drink?"

Martin waited a moment, trying to recover from this factual and entirely unimagined onslaught. Were men all so utterly ignorant of the practical life of the other sex? He had a horrible feeling they were.

"Of course. In a moment. You knew she was pregnant but not by whom."

"Oh, that didn't take long. Ching asked about in the Mansions. All the *majie* know each other's business, and there was one young maid who cleaned for David part-time. Ching said it might be David. He always tells me to go to bed. I hate it, really. Like I'm a child. Telling me to go to sleep so he could run to a woman who wore bloodred lipstick and nail polish, high heels and dyed hair. Then tell me to not drink or smoke or wear a pretty dress. What hypocrisy."

Miriam's lips had formed a hard line. The thought came to Martin in that moment that Miriam might have set David up. He recalled David's amazement at the appearance of the satin nightgown and the other objects. Miriam might well have placed them in David's apartment to frame him. Was it possible that she was that devious?

"Well I must have dozed off but when I woke up, I checked the bed in Ching's room and he wasn't there so I went to the back door of his flat and heard them arguing. I hadn't decided whether to bang on the door and surprise them, when she came out. I hid and followed them both. By then it was pretty intriguing. If I caught them in some kind of act, I could break off my engagement to David without any boring denials. It was a bit of a relief, I can tell you."

She stubbed out her cigarette. "But then it turned nasty. They argued, all hissing and whispers. I couldn't quite make it out. David ripped Eva's necklace and chucked it in the dirt and she bent down to get it and he bashed her. I didn't dare move. I thought he'd go away, but he didn't. He put his foot on the back of her head. It was over in a second. I need some water."

Grace poured a glass of water. Miriam drank it down in one long gulp.

"I was so shaken I shrank into the rubble of the building and my damn scarf caught on something and half fell off. When David went off, I came out and checked on Eva and the scarf dropped off. I stood on it in trying to get it up in the dark. I'm not too stable on my legs, as you know. It must have lost some beads. When I got back to the Mansions, I put it in the rubbish bin. Thank goodness, David didn't come back to the flat then. I reckon he must have been changing his clothes. There must have been blood on them. I was exhausted and went to sleep."

Marion sat back, took a fan from her bag, and fanned herself.

"That's your story. David did it."

"David did it."

"And you decided not to tell me the next morning? You decided to lie?"

"I wanted nothing to do with any of it or with you. You work for the Japanese. Why should I help you?"

"Obstructing justice is an offense, Miss Abraham."

"Is it? You don't say. Justice. Don't be ridiculous. This isn't Singapore anymore. It's Syonan-to. You found him anyway, didn't you? I'll answer to not wanting to tell you anything out of fear."

Martin rose. "Your statement will be typed up for signature. You will wait here."

Martin signaled to Grace and they left the room.

Martin filled Hayashi in.

"You believe her."

"No. But right now, with this evidence, and her statement, Weber will be convicted whether he now chooses to deny it or not. We will have a guilty verdict and the mayor will be happy."

Martin looked at Hayashi and knew what they were both thinking. The mayor might be happy but neither he nor the chief inspector shared the joy.

"Sir, we need to visit Miriam's apartment together. You need to bring fresh eyes. I'm worried that all the rest of us have missed something."

CHAPTER FORTY-ONE

Hayashi, Martin, and Ching stood in the small hall of Miriam Abraham's apartment. Ching, eyes wary, stood very still, tense and anxious in the presence of the Japanese man.

"It's all right," Martin said to Ching in Cantonese. "The detective chief inspector is here only to get to the truth. If he asks you something, answer honestly. That's all you have to do."

Martin had asked Ching to show him the buckets and confirm Miriam's story. She did, every word.

"All right," Hayashi said to Martin. "Tell me everything you remember of the morning of the death of Mrs. Abraham. The afternoon you came here for the first time."

"Miriam answered the door. Ching let me in."

"Miss Yip," Hayashi said to Ching, and she clutched her hands. Martin translated. "The inspector knocked, and Miss Abraham answered the door. Where were you?"

"In the kitchen, making coffee."

"For Miss Abraham?"

"Yes, she woke up late and wanted coffee."

"What time did you get here? Tell me about that morning."

"I got here at eight o'clock. Miss Miriam was asleep. She woke up at twelve thirty and asked for coffee."

"Does she usually get up so late?"

"No. Always late, but not so late."

"The inspector arrived at ... " Kano looked at Martin.

"One o'clock," Martin said.

"One o'clock?"

"Yes, near that time," Ching said, bobbing her head.

"You didn't hear the door?"

"No. Miss Miriam called me to help her dress."

"That's right," Martin said. "She was probably not in outdoor dress when she answered the door. I only saw her headscarf."

"You helped her dress, Miss Yip, and then?"

"Then she told me to open the door and I saw the inspector."

Hayashi looked around the hall. "Martin, describe what you saw in the hall."

Martin looked around. Everything seemed exactly as he remembered it. "Mirror, hat rack, the stand with walking sticks and umbrellas, the wooden console table. There's nothing on the table now, but there was. Some shawls I think."

"And the doll," Ching said.

Martin looked at Ching. "Yes. Right. Shawls and a doll." He reflected a moment and addressed Ching. "You said something about them."

Ching glanced at Hayashi. "They were out of place. I asked Miss Miriam why they were there and if I should move them."

"And she said yes." Hayashi put his hand to his lips. Martin and Ching fell silent. "They were out of place. They hadn't been there the night before, is that right, Ching?"

She nodded and her eyes grew wary.

"But they were at midday the next day. Shawls and a doll."

"Yes. Bad joss, that doll."

"Why?"

"It was the doll of a nice little girl who came to play. Miss Miriam couldn't run and play like the other girls and she hated it. This girl in particular she disliked because she could skip very well. She took the girl's doll and never gave it back. I know she did. She hid it and said it was lost. But I knew she had it somewhere. I found it years later."

"Where is it now?" Martin said.

"In her bedroom. Bad joss."

"Yes," Hayashi said. "More important is where was it the night before. Where was the doll before it was on the console?"

"In the suitcase. She wouldn't leave it behind when we were kicked out of the house. She made me pack it with her shawls."

"What suitcase?"

"The suitcase in the storeroom."

"What storeroom, Ching?"

"In the courtyard. Every apartment has a separate locked storeroom for bags and cases."

Martin drew in a sharp breath. "Under the veranda, Chief Inspector."

Hayashi nodded at Martin but addressed Ching. "Please show me, Miss Yip."

Ching led the way through the kitchen to the back staircase and pointed down to the courtyard. "Behind all those boxes. The Japanese soldiers have blocked them all off. They didn't even warn anyone or care about—"

She glanced at Hayashi and closed her lips.

"When did they start unloading the boxes?"

"They were doing it when I arrived on Monday lunchtime," Martin said.

"And is the suitcase in this apartment now, Ching?"

She frowned. "No."

Hayashi looked down into the courtyard. "Thank you. Come with me, Miss Yip."

Martin and Ching followed Hayashi to Miriam's bedroom. The doll sat on a chair in the corner of the room. Hayashi picked it up and inspected it.

"Ching," he said. "Examine everything in this room. Tell me what is missing among Miss Abraham's effects. Anything. Take your time."

The room had a set of deep drawers and two separate wardrobes. Ching opened the drawers to reveal underwear and night-dresses. She went through them carefully. Then she opened the first wardrobe. Inside, neatly arranged, were Miriam Abraham's colorless and plain outdoor dresses. Ching looked through them, then turned to the second wardrobe.

This was entirely different. Dresses, coats, hats, and scarves of every hue crammed the racks and shelves: Elegant sequined gowns, cashmere sweaters, and jeweled scarves rubbed shoulders with silk saris and glittering shawls. Martin recalled Grace and Seah speaking of it but had not imagined such a sight.

"Ching," Martin said in Cantonese. "What is this?"

"Miss Miriam always liked pretty things. Some she brought from India, some she bought here. Her father forbade her to wear them, but she kept them. Her secret place. Poor Miss Miriam. She was a crippled girl and these things made her happy. Inside this apartment she would dress up. I would help her. *Yeh Hsien*, you know? That's what I called her. This was her world of make-believe."

Martin translated for Hayashi, then added, "*Yeh Hsien* is the Chinese Cinderella, Chief Inspector."

"I see. Miss Yip, please look carefully at everything and see if anything is missing in your view."

Ching removed every dress from this crammed wardrobe and laid them out carefully on Miriam's bed. In the bottom of the wardrobe now revealed by the removal of the clothing were three sets of elegant matching shoes, a pair, with a brace attached to one for Miriam's crippled leg. Ching brought them out and placed them on the floor. One solitary shoe of quite drab gray remained in the corner. She brought it out.

"This shoe," she said. "There should be a match."

"Ah," said Hayashi. "Yes. There should be a match with a brace attached."

"Yes," Ching said. "It's not there."

"No, it's not there. Thank you, Ching. You can go home now. You won't be needed here tonight or tomorrow. Give me your keys. You will be told when to come back."

Ching threw a glance of alarm at Hayashi but said nothing and passed him her key. Martin picked up the gray shoe and sniffed. It smelled of incense. He looked at Hayashi, who pocketed the keys. They heard the front door clack.

"You think the gray shoe with the brace is in the suitcase?" Martin said.

Hayashi smiled. "And it is in the store behind all those crates. She could not get inside to either clean it or dispose of it. Why she left this one I don't know. Arrogance probably. Fate intervened in the shape of the Japanese military. The little girl's hurt and sorrow attached it to Miriam Abraham's body through the doll. If she'd left the doll, she might have avoided this fate. Though not necessarily. Akuji mi ni tomaru."

CHAPTER FORTY-TWO

Martin watched the ceremony from the gallery of the Syonan Supreme Court. He didn't understand a word. The official opening of the Court and Japan's judicial enterprise was unsurprisingly carried out in Japanese. The mayor was there alongside Colonel Watanabe, the man he most despised. Commissioner Honda sat alongside the Kempei chief, Lieutenant General Oishi; Colonel Masuda, head of the Tokko, and Lieutenant Colonel Yamamoto, the head of prisons.

The new head of the Department of Public Prosecutions, Arthur Mendez, and the various local judges and lawyers clearly didn't understand a word either. They sat, as expressionless as him. Martin knew most of them. Like him, they had no choice but to throw in their lot with the Japanese. Chief Justice, Judge Nogi, stood and faced towards Tokyo. The entire room joined him, including Martin.

"Kimigayo" was sung, for some reason, twice. It was a short, truly uninspiring sort of tune, and the lyrics contained words like "stones," "boulders," and "moss." Obviously, it meant something to the Japanese, of course. Perhaps it was to ram home the fact of this new world of judicial and civil authority. You see, it seemed to say, in its double iteration, there is no going back. The civil and military are in perfect harmony to drive the mission of the Greater East Asia Co-Prosperity Sphere. As the ceremony of oath taking went on, Martin read the press briefing. It used words like "peace", "order," "respect," "justice," "impartiality."

The *Syonan Times* was already out, and he picked one up as he left the court. Underneath the article about the opening ceremony was Hayashi's picture alongside Honda and the mayor, highlighting the first murder case of the new court—the death of Mrs. Solomon Abraham, wife of a highly respected and wealthy family loyal to the empire and with connections to the Japanese emperor himself.

Martin was glad he was certain of her guilt. He knew now that neither he nor Kano Hayashi would ever bring a prosecution unless that guilt was irrefutable, for the courts could not be relied upon. A word from a Japanese officer in the ear of Mendez would be all it would take. And it wouldn't even be Mendez's fault.

But the suitcase was redolent of aloeswood and of guilt. The brace attached to the gray shoe had ash, blood, slivers of skin, and the second red-painted broken nail caught in its mechanism. The sole of the shoe had matched the mark on Eva's scalp and indicated the strength of Miriam's resolve. She had seen a way to rid herself of her stepmother and Weber at the same time.

"Eva fought," Hayashi said. "She knew her murderer. She knew the brace. Did she break off her nails into it to leave a message behind?"

"Yes, she knew," Martin said. "She must have desperately tried to pull Miriam's foot off her head and tumble Miriam to the ground. If she had managed to topple her, she would have lived. Miriam would not have been able to get up. It turned on a second."

"She tried to live; she knew what she had to do," Hayashi said. "Ganbarimashita. Brave girl."

He looked at Martin, who nodded. His mother. Irene. Had they fought for their lives? He didn't fully know why, but he knew that this mattered to the detective chief inspector and realized it mattered to him too.

CHAPTER FORTY-THREE

J oan glanced at Martin and placed the tray of coffee on the table. Walter was flicking through a Japanese pictorial magazine. The clock on the sideboard ticked. Water and electricity had been fully restored to the house. The ceiling fan groaned at each turn, moving the sluggish air. Joan picked up a record. A recent series of house sweeps seeking English books, records, or artifacts had turned up nothing of interest in the Bach household. The girls' comics were buried under some wood in the garden. Martin and Walter's family had arrived with virtually no possessions, and Michael didn't read much. His copy of *The Count of Monte Cristo* was by a Frenchman. It was left on the shelf. Most of the items in the house had been their parents' or rather Ernst's. And he had liked German classical music. Axis music. Joan put Brahms on the record player.

"Dear," Joan said. "Martin and I would like to speak to you about something."

Walter peered over the magazine.

"Don't look like that, dear," Joan said, "like a tank coming over a hill. There are matters which this family has to discuss."

Walter lowered the magazine. "I know nothing of this business of Martin's paternity, for pity's sake. I was a boy and at boarding school."

"Yes, Walter. I know. But there are certain things you do know. Things which Martin and I should know too."

Martin finished his coffee and put the cup on the saucer. "Not about my paternity. But about Mother's death. I want to investigate her death."

"Yes, dear," Joan interjected quickly. "Martin wants to find out why your mother died. The circumstances."

"I want to know how she lived, too. Don't you want to know that, Walter? Our mother lived a strange and separate existence from all of us and met an untimely end. I want to know about her." Martin met Walter's gaze. "And I think you do too."

"Walter," Joan said. "Dear, you told me you were six years old when she just disappeared one day. And that not long after that you were put into the Raffles boarding school."

Brahms, the ceiling fan, and the clock played a terzetto. Walter might simply get up and go out. That was Walter's way. Never a raised voice, never a storm, just the quiet crackle of ice. But he did not. He put the magazine on the coffee table and sat back.

CHAPTER FORTY-FOUR

The CID offices were quiet. Martin, seated in an armchair in Hayashi's office, picked up the newspaper. The headline and main story were the trial, conviction, and execution of Miriam Abraham. This case had pushed battle news to the bottom of the page. In this instance, the news of a Japanese invasion of the Aleutian Islands in Alaska.

Weakness of U.S. Defense Exposed, he read. *Our sensational assault on the Aleutian Islands has struck a demoralizing blow to the United States' outer ring of far-flung defense outposts. Psychologically, the Nippon assault on the Aleutians coupled with the raid on Midway Islands has struck terror into American hearts for its sheer boldness, which exposes the vulnerability of American naval defense—a fact which the American naval and government leaders have been seeking to shield from the American public.*

Whatever the truth of this report was, it was easy to forget that outside this little prison island, war was raging for the fate of the world.

"A letter from the mayor," Hayashi said. "His Majesty's household and General Tojo have conveyed congratulations. It is a great honor."

"Certainly. Your friend Mr. Asanari has made you famous. His article called you Baron Hayashi."

Hayashi shook his head. "It's nothing. A title acquired through default."

"But Colonel Masuda said you were kazoku. Aristocracy. I've been learning Japanese."

"So desu-ka? Subarashi!"

"Well, steady on, Chief Inspector. Or should I call you something else now?"

"No. By the way, the mayor tells us that more funds have been allocated."

"Ah. A car might be available, do you think?"

Hayashi ignored this. "The mayor also asks if there is any favorable thing he might do for you and myself." He looked pointedly at Martin. "Of a nonpecuniary kind."

"Oh. What did you ask for?"

"My request has already been made and answered," Hayashi said.

Martin thought that was devious, but what could he do about it? "I'd like to find a file. There was an Australian woman. Irene Sheridan. The British didn't want her death investigated. She was shot and nothing was done."

"A British miscarriage of justice. The mayor will be thrilled. Anything that makes the British look corrupt and vile."

"I think they were corrupt and vile."

"Yes." Hayashi nodded slowly. "I'm sorry. Yes, of course. I shall ask for that file to be located. However, it will coincidentally please the mayor and the Department of Justice, which means the search will be more zealous."

Martin had considered asking for the file on his mother, but he knew he couldn't do it now. Walter had agreed to revisit those events, but he was fragile. Slowly but surely, careful of Walter's feelings, they would piece her life and death together. For his own peace of mind, though, he needed to find out about Irene first, and this extraordinary favor might not come again.

"Keibu-san, what will become of Weber?"

"He will be sentenced to four years in Outram Prison. This is not a good outcome for him, but he did bash Mrs. Abraham and did nothing to help her after the fact. It shows a cold heart. And he began this train of events by his violence. He could not have known whether she would survive when he left her in the ruins of those buildings."

"And Ingrid Olsen?" Sergeant Ibrahim had given Martin a folder with the results of Charlie Chan's investigation. The word on the street was that Hong had been killed by a woman. That had sped round Chinatown like cholera. Hong was hated and feared, a known murderer, blackmailer, extortionist: ruthless and quick with a knife, especially on women. The idea that he had died at the hand of a woman was met with a general satisfaction, even amusement. And it was even better that the woman was injured. Perhaps by Hong, was the speculation. She had a limp. A revenge killing was the consensus. No positive identification.

Martin had given the complicated sequence of events of that night a lot of thought. It occurred to him that Hong might have arrived on the scene after the death of Eva. He might have seen neither Miriam nor Weber. All Hong might have seen was Ingrid over the body of Eva. Had he then threatened to blackmail Ingrid? He might have seen a likely source of income there. But he'd picked the wrong woman. Martin painfully remembered the evening she had trussed him so easily like a chicken. She could have killed him in an instant. She hadn't. But she was capable of it. He could ask her, of course, but there was little point. She would never implicate herself in Hong's murder.

"And Ingrid?" Martin said again.

Hayashi glanced at Martin. "I have asked for confinement in a prison factory. The conditions are less severe, less lonely. It will be up to the judge, of course. She remains known as May Desker, Martin. Perhaps we should refer to her as such."

Silence fell. Hayashi swished imaginary flies. The fan rattled to and fro. Martin's thoughts went to Martin Neville. John Hammond had told him that there were four Nevilles, three men and a woman, none named Martin, listed among the civilian POWs in Changi. Written contact was forbidden and it was not easy to make verbal contact with the prisoners as all the actions by Hammond and the Anglican bishop were watched obsessively by the guards, but he would try to find out more. In the meantime, he was searching church records.

Martin took a photo from his pocket. It was an image discovered by Joan in the bundle of his mother's possessions removed by Walter from her Tiong Bharu apartment. It showed a dinner in the Seaview Hotel in 1911. The photographic studio had recorded the date and place on the front of the photograph, and the decoration of the dining room included a banner in celebration of the coronation of King George V and Queen Mary. He recognized his mother and Ernst among the twelve faces, five couples and two single men, all smiling into the camera. On the back of the photograph, she had written the names of her companions randomly, including the name Martin N., but which man's face it belonged to wasn't clear. Three possibilities were the right age, all handsome and groomed in their dinner jackets and Brylcreemed hair. He and Joan had searched them for a resemblance but found none. It would be a process of elimination and it would take time. But, he thought, what else did they all have but time and no time zones. He put it back in his pocket.

He idly leafed through the newspaper and his eye stopped with no little surprise on an article at the bottom of page two. Indah, a female orangutan who'd escaped from a private zoo at Kranji after an air raid, had been spotted wearing an Imperial Japanese Army tropical-issue pith helmet but was still at large. He felt a sudden rush of joy, a soaring uplift so great he had to repress the urge to express it out loud.

Hayashi took up a different letter. This one was from Lieutenant Colonel Yamamoto, the head of prisons, addressed to him as Baron Hayashi. Clearly the news of this title had been passed around, doubtless by Honda, who made more of it than it was. But perhaps this fatuous title had been, and might in future be, of service, because Yamamoto's letter was somewhat gushing and praised him for his selfless gesture in thinking of the common soldier in a time of such a triumph for the civil jurisdiction of the empire.

His request to grant Lieutenant Yamada the honor of returning to the army and active service in the recent campaign in the Aleutians had been agreed by General Yamashita's chief-of-staff. Yamada was on his way to the island of Attu as part of the glorious and victorious invasion of American territory, where the garrison would be involved in building an airbase and extensive fortifications.

Hayashi rose and took down a British atlas from his shelf of books. He opened it to North America and then to Alaska. Attu seemed to be rocky and inhospitable, the outermost island of the long Aleutian chain, which curved into the Bering Sea. Imperial Forces had recently captured the islands of both Attu and Kiska to prevent American air attack on Japan. That was all he knew about it, but he noted that the temperature was often below zero. He shut the atlas. His eyes fell on the scrawled graffiti and the long-nosed figure peeping over a wall.

WOT, no planes? WOT, no ships? WOT, no idea! Mr. Chad.

"Martin, the writing here. What does it mean?"

Martin joined Hayashi and read. He laughed.

"It is funny," Hayashi said. "Why?"

"Not funny ha ha, but amusing in a wry sort of way. Commentary. The fellow is expressing the general dissatisfaction with the way the war was going in Singapore. A lack of everything, you see. Including the faintest idea what to do."

Hayashi frowned. "I do not see. Who is Mr. Chad?"

"Well, he's Everyman, I suppose."

"Everyman?" Kano shook his head. "Is it clever?"

"In a way. It's commentary. A sort of despair, but with a sense of humor. I think whoever wrote it was just fed up."

"Ah, and for this he defaced the wall?" Hayashi said shaking his head.

"It is ... pithy, Keibu-san."

"Is it? Ah."

A knock at the door and Santamaria entered. "A note from Commissioner Honda, sir." He handed the note to Martin. It was in Japanese.

Martin passed it to Hayashi.

"The body of a Chinese civilian has been found in hell," Hayashi said.

Martin raised an eyebrow but was not entirely surprised anymore at the manner in which his boss made pronouncements. "Hell? Are you sure, sir?"

"Jigoku. That means hell. It says there is a body of a Chinese man found in hell." Hayashi peered at the paper. "In a villa of some kind. It's called Haw Par Villa. Why does it say hell?"

"Ah, I see. Haw Par Villa is a kind of park with statues and scenes of Chinese mythology. It's like … " Martin momentarily couldn't think of a comparison. Perhaps there wasn't one. "Well, probably better if we go and see."

"Ah. Very good," Hayashi said and smiled at Martin. "This is the best part, don't you think? The opening act of the crime. The suspense, the unexpected. The time when two and two could make four or twenty-two."

That was quite good. "Two and two, twenty-two. Very pithy, sir."

Hayashi took up his fly whisk and waggled it. "Ikuzo! Time, Martin, is of the essence."

Martin looked at his watch. It had stopped. For an instant he felt the old irritation, the psychic disturbance of living on the clock-whim of a bunch of mad hatters. Then he shrugged and plucked the panama hat from the stand. A peculiar and unexpected future rolled out ahead in which sometimes two and two might make four and sometimes twenty-two. But the unforgiving minute was still sixty seconds' worth of distance run. Even on Tokyo time.

ABOUT THE AUTHOR

Aussie Dawn Farnham now lives on Noongar land in Perth, Western Australia but for most of her life lived in Europe, East Asia and Singapore. She is the author of six historical novels and has a Creative Writing PhD researching and writing women's experiences of the Japanese Occupation of Singapore. *Tokyo Time* is her first foray into the historical crime genre.

www.dawnfarnham.com
FB: farnham/author
Instagram: @farnhamauthor

Made in United States
Orlando, FL
10 December 2023